THE LEGACY OF OLD GRAN PARKS

ISOBEL BLACKTHORN

This book is dedicated to a small group of family violence survivors whom I had the privilege of teaching creative writing one year.

ACKNOWLEDGMENTS

This book could not have been written without the active involvement of my mother Margaret Rodgers. Her involvement from the early stages of plotting and characterization, through to her criticism and suggested changes to the final draft proved invaluable. A warm thank you, too, for choosing, when I was a kid, to buy a rundown roadhouse in South Australia. I had the time of my life!

PREFACE

It was three-deep at the bar. Friday, a scorcher of a day and the loggers were in town slaking their thirst. The generator out the back was taking the strain but what with having to open the fridges every few seconds, Gloria wondered if it would cope.

The teachers from the local primary school were in, as was the Postmaster. The farmers had come into town for the chook raffle, and while the men got pissed, their wives were seated in the lounge drinking lemon squash.

Gloria looked around for her husband. He was off shift and should have been helping her behind the bar, but he was nowhere to be found. She had young Jim from the general store in, re-filling the fridge and pulling beers, and Beryl, a farmer's wife and as hardworking as they come, in the kitchen, cooking the meals.

Gloria had never known it so busy.

They'd taken over the hotel twenty years before in 1931, after the first owner dropped down dead of a heart attack while he was pulling a dark ale. Back then, Gloria's husband, Frank, had been young and fit, and Gloria able, and they'd bought the pub with the proceeds from the sale of her recently deceased father's farm.

The day they moved in the trouble started. Gloria never could figure out why. First it was the put downs, then came the ridicule. It wasn't long before he was knocking her about. He seemed to think she was his to do with whatever he liked. Being a mean-spirited, woman-hating man, that translated into the sorts of acts a man would have done jail time for if he'd done it to someone other than his wife.

The night before had been the worst she'd ever known. Her body was bruised head to toe. It hurt to inhale, and she was sure he'd cracked a rib. She had to stand behind the bar serving her beery eyed regulars as she explained away her fat lip and the cut above her eye.

Gloria was no mouse. She was a big-boned bushie's daughter, as deft with a chain saw as she was with an iron or a whisk. It wasn't fear that brewed in her. It was anger.

With every full glass she passed across the bar, that anger deepened.

Six o'clock shaded into seven and then eight. By nine the meals were over, Beryl had gone home, and the clientele had thinned. At ten she had the lounge all wiped down and straightened out, and the last of the drinkers had staggered outside.

She paid Jim out of the till and let him go, closing the saloon door behind him on the best night's trade she'd ever known. She went behind the bar to clean up, thinking the night's takings would cover the doctor's bill and then some.

She was drying a tray of pots when Frank appeared. From his swagger, she could tell he'd been drinking somewhere else.

'Get me a beer,' he snarled.

She didn't answer.

Instead, she walked away.

He growled at her. She felt his growl as though it were a goblin clinging to her back.

She kept walking, rage pulsating in every cell of her. She went into the lounge and on through to the kitchen. Frank was close behind her. She turned.

There was nothing in his eyes but hate.

He took a step forward and she took a step back, sidling by the long kitchen table.

There was no escaping what he was about to do to her. Soon, he'd have her cornered.

Seeing no way out of the kitchen, she let him approach.

Three more paces and behind her was the stove. Beside the stove was a drawer. In the drawer, were the knives.

There was no time to open that drawer. He'd be on her in an instant.

Panic stirred, familiar, like toast.

Then in her side vision she saw Beryl hadn't finished clearing up. The cleaver was still on the bench.

Gloria glanced out the window.

Frank followed her gaze.

Her hand gripped the cleaver.

She brought the weapon down on his head, right between the eyes. She heard a crack.

The flesh burst open; blood sprayed in her face.

She flinched, disgusted.

He reeled and fell back hard against the table.

In an upsurge of power, she brought the cleaver down again, her aim sharp, her motion fierce.

Beryl had sharpened the blade.

It took two more blows to kill him. Another twenty to hack him in half.

CHAPTER ONE

MIRIAM

I didn't see it at first. The intersection was staggered so the two arms, north-south and east-west, didn't quite align. Not that I was thinking in symbols back then. That came later. It came with an awareness that crossroads are meeting places, drawing in forces from all four directions, for better, for worse. Although, that particular intersection didn't seem to want to be a crossroads. Then again, maybe it did. Best not to overthink things. I do know crossroads are places where decisions are made for you and crossroads are not places to get stuck in. My stay in Cann River taught me that.

My car rolled into town about six. At that time of year—it was autumn—the light of the day had begun to give way to the darkness. I'd been driving all afternoon, and I was on a downhill stretch of road coming in from the west. Didn't notice the lack of power until I'd reached the bridge and saw the scattered buildings of the town up ahead. It was then, as the road flattened out, that I realised something was wrong. I depressed the clutch and changed down, touched the accelerator and nothing happened.

I felt that rippling in my belly, a sensation I refused to give in to. I had to be practical, rational, calm. Things worked out better when people stayed calm.

It felt like good luck when I saw the roadhouse coming into view on my right, lit up in anticipation of the night. I depressed the clutch again and coasted towards it. Hoping to park out of the way, I jerked the steering wheel as the tyres hit the concrete driveway, coming to a full stop on the forecourt a bit shy of the bowsers.

I pulled the keys from the ignition, thinking with relief I'd been saved. As if some guardian angel up there in the heavens was looking down on me, kindly. In the moment, it was a reasonable thing to think. Had my car packed up a mile back, I'd have been forced to spend the night at the roadside on one of the loneliest stretches of uninhabited forest that corner of the world had to offer. Not a nice place for a single woman to find herself. People have been murdered out there. Bushwhacked, disappearing without a trace. Besides, my belly was empty, and I had no food in the car. My mouth was dry, and I nursed one mother of a headache too, after my send off the night before.

All the way from Cockatoo, that send-off had felt like punishment. I convinced myself my workmates had bought the cheapest grog known to woman or beast, and that it just about summed up their view of me. A sort of alcoholic good riddance.

Or maybe they were jealous.

After all, I was relocating up the coast. Set to take possession of a neat cottage in open country after taking early retirement from a position in local government. I'd had enough of the office lifestyle and thought to try my hand at something else. Besides, my house had burned down in the catastrophic wild fires of February 1983—Ash Wednesday, as they were calling the conflagration and, unlike some, I wasn't going to rebuild.

That was all behind me and I was looking ahead to the east in anticipation of a fresh start. Sun rising over sapphire waters. Rolling green country and cows. The village fair. I thought maybe I'd join the historical society. They were bound to have one. I was brimming with speculation and optimism. I couldn't get there soon enough.

Cann River was halfway from where I'd come to where I was heading. Halfway to paradise. The horror firmly behind me.

Even as I entered the roadhouse, taking in at a glance the young man seated by a window to my left, his multicoloured beanie failing to obscure his scarred brow, I had a sinking sense that my optimism was premature. On the jukebox, Joan Baez was busy lamenting poor old Dixie. Misgivings reared, and it was as though the carnage back in Cockatoo had followed me all the way along the highway, trailing behind me like a wraith.

I shook away my thoughts and approached the counter. The woman cleaning the pie warmer looked personable enough. Although she had her back to me, I thought she might have been a kindred soul. She seemed about my age and same in height and build. I thought it funny how women over fifty all ended up looking the same. Well, maybe on the surface. She wore her hair scooped up high on her head and as she turned, I saw the fingers of grey pinned back from her face. She'd painted her eyebrows—they were overly arched—and caked on the makeup, yet her cheeks still creased when she offered me a smile, waiting, hands on hips.

'What you want?'

'My car has died on me,' I said by way of explanation.

She eyed me with cool hostility. Any hope I had of conviviality withered. 'My car has died on me,' I repeated, deciding, despite my rumbling belly, that if she expected me to order, she had another think coming.

'That it, there.' She indicated with a tilt of her head and I followed her gaze back to my steel-grey hatchback, angled awkwardly, its rear jutting out, obstructing the exit.

'It isn't in the way, I hope.'

'I get Con to shift it.'

Her accent was thick. I couldn't place it. Italian? I detected a twang. Eastern Europe, maybe. Somewhere like Romania.

She held out her hand. I gave her my keys and she disappeared.

I shifted round a fraction and surveyed the roadhouse interior, avoiding looking in the direction of the scar-faced man. Set alongside the long run of casement windows were tables of lurid orange Formica with matching chairs. The sort of colour that showed every blemish. The floor was covered in cheap grey patterned linoleum, worn and chipped about the entrance.

The counter, with its display cabinets and vintage till, protruded into the space. In one cabinet were the remains after the day's trade: two sandwiches—egg mayo, and ham and salad —and an otherwise lonely Kitchener bun. I hadn't seen one of those since the weekend I spent in Adelaide several years back. It looked odd and out of place and homemade.

On a menu board, propped on a high shelf behind the counter, were listed hamburgers with the lot and chips, written in neat lettering. Beneath, written in large, clumsy letters by someone who couldn't spell, was a small range of gourmet pies: Venisen, Hunta and Stake. I thought maybe there was a good cook in residence, for those pies were obviously not bought in. Besides, almost no one deviated from the traditional meat pie, not even in the city. Meat slurry they were normally, with tomato sauce squirted in the crust vent.

The woman reappeared behind the counter.

'He's moving it into the garage.'

I looked around to see a burly-looking man heading past the

bowsers to my car. He had on the navy-blue overalls of a mechanic. I noticed a slight limp in his gait. He opened the driver's side door and reached in to release the handbrake and disengage the gears. Then he went around and leaned back against the rear bumper. Once the car was moving, he hurried back and took hold of the steering wheel. There was a brief pause in which I admired his strength.

'You want to order something?'

'I'll have a steak pie, please.'

'With chips?'

'Go on, then.'

'Fresh out of steak,' the woman said without turning. 'Only got the hunter.'

'What's in it?'

'This and that. Could be chicken.' She didn't sound that sure. 'He changes it,' she added as an afterthought.

'The baker?'

'Con.'

She gestured behind me. She didn't mean scar face. She was referring to the mechanic. It was a confronting revelation, that the man who fixes cars also bakes the pies. I chose not to make too much of it.

'Sauce?' she said, raising her eyebrows to her hairline.

'No, thank you.'

'Better with sauce,' she mumbled grumpily.

'If you say so.'

The woman flounced away, her piled-high coiffure bobbing behind her. I leaned against the counter and waited. My sense that I'd offended her was confirmed when she reappeared, grabbed the tongs from the bench and extracted the only pie in the warmer, plonking it on a plate and squirting on the side the sauce I expressly didn't want, and setting the whole affair down on the counter in front of me along with some cutlery.

'You have it here,' she said, nudging the plate in my direction.

'My chips?'

'Sit. I bring them across.'

'Can I get a drink?'

'Help yourself.' She pointed to the fridge beside the door to the kitchen. I went over and grabbed an orange squash.

Loaded up with my dinner, I made my way to a table far from the guy with the scar who sat there motionless, staring into space, ignoring his surroundings or oblivious to them.

I leaned back in my seat and waited for the chips. A few minutes later the sour woman came and plonked down a bowl. The chips were heavily salted.

Avoiding the sauce on my plate, which had taken on the colour of congealed blood, I proceeded to cut into my pie. Flakes of pale meat smothered in gravy oozed out. Looked like chicken. He must have used the thigh. I detected the flavour of fresh thyme beneath a liberal dousing of pepper and a hint of something unfamiliar. Aniseed perhaps.

Midway through my repast the mechanic, Con, wandered in, trailing a smell of diesel behind him which spread and infused the room. He put my keys on the counter, turned and scanned around as though observing a crowd, taking in each of the two of us in turn. I reciprocated, taking him in, and not with a sympathetic eye. He was broad shouldered, long in the body and he had a bit of a belly on him. His left foot kicked out sideways. He had fuzzy, brown hair, a cleft chin and his eyes were set too close together. His brow was arranged in a permanent frown, and his lips were the same as his mother's, thin and tight, curved down at the edges. I placed him around thirty.

Our eyes met and he didn't look away.

'Not like the sauce, then?' he said. I thought he was

addressing me, but there was a loud clang behind the counter and the woman cleared her throat.

'She said, no sauce.'

'Is that right?'

How could two people get so caught up on whether I wanted the sauce? What difference could it make to either of them? To anything?

I polished off the chips and bit into the last segment of my pie and washed it all down with the orange squash. Outside, long shadows leached into the gloaming. The neon sign centred on the wide verge at the corner flickered as though trembling in the cooling air. Across the highway, stood a hotel. Two storeys, the upper level fronted by a deep veranda, its balcony sheltering the pavement below, the whole affair painted a pale shade of aqua. Two of the downstairs windows were lighted. Another came on as I watched. Upstairs this time.

A woman exited the front door and took in a sandwich board advertising the nightly accommodation rate. For a while no cars passed through the town.

'You'll be wanting to stop the night then,' Con said to me from his station by the counter.

I got up, collected my plate, and made my approach.

'You can't look at my car straight away?'

'Afraid not,' the woman said, standing behind the till. 'Con's come in to wash up for the night. Those pies won't bake themselves.'

'She can stay here. We got plenty of room out the back.'

I put down my plate and stepped aside, keen not to stand too close to Con.

'The hotel looks fine.'

'It'll cost ya.'

'Two dollars twenty.' The woman held out her hand.

Con came and stood over me as I ferreted about in my purse.

'Not stopping then?'

'The hotel will do just fine, thanks.'

'Suit yourself.'

The door swung shut behind me and I took a lungful of the cool night air. There was no wind. A peppering of street lighting sent forth a milky haze into the dark. The trees that hugged the town loomed like ghouls.

Heading for the hotel, I crossed the forecourt and waited roadside. A second later, I was frozen like a rabbit caught in the high beam of a truck. The great, rumbling behemoth approached from the west. As it crossed the bridge the groan of compression brakes splintered the quiet. Weighed down by its load of tree trunks, the truck thundered by, headed through the town and was gone.

I hurried across the highway in case it had a mate. Approaching the hotel entrance, I started to lose faith in luck. The chips were repeating on me. No doubt fried in rancid oil. The flavours of the pie were blending with the orange squash, the entire mixture resulting in a series of unpleasant belches.

I entered an empty and wide corridor. There was a glass-panelled saloon door to my left and a plain door to my right, and stairs leading up to the accommodation. I heard voices. Pushing open the saloon door I was received by the yeasty smell of beer and three pairs of dismissive eyes as the men at the bar all turned. A silence descended. I took in the blue shirts and the suntans and returned the silence with a casual smile. The back bar was cluttered with bottles of beer, wine and spirits, packets of potato chips and nuts, a Bex powders display and a haphazard assortment of glasses. On a cabinet in the centre sat an old television, switched off. I wondered if it was colour.

'Can I help you?'

It was a woman's voice. She materialised, standing up behind the bar. Small, slight of build, with thick sandy coloured hair, shoulder length and parted in the middle. She had a round, open face that carried the nondescript features of a woman too busy doing chores to fuss with makeup. I picked her to be in her mid-thirties. She seemed personable.

I stepped forward and the men turned back to their beers.

'A room, please. If you've one spare.'

Someone sniggered.

'Okie dokie.'

She disappeared and a second later, poked her head through the saloon door.

'Follow me.'

The corridor contained a small reception desk tucked beneath the stairs. There were more doors leading off in all directions.

'Just the one night?'

'I expect so. Or should I say I hope so.'

'Aw, take no notice of them blokes in there,' she said. 'They're not used to seeing a woman in the bar.'

You're a woman, I thought but didn't say.

'You on holidays?'

'Moving interstate. Car broke down.'

'So that was you. Thought so. I'll put you in Room Four.'

I followed her upstairs. She was a brisk climber, lithe. The sort of woman always on her feet. I was panting at the last tread.

'You'll be comfy in here,' she said, flicking on the light.

She moved aside for me to enter, handing me the key as I passed by. The room was spacious and pleasantly furnished. High ceiling, faded rugs on scantly polished floorboards. Other than the bed, the room contained a free-standing wardrobe on legs, a dressing table and a couple of chairs. Long velvet curtains hung open, framing the windows. I went and stood in the middle of it all.

'You eaten?'

'I had a pie across the road.'

'Belly okay?'

'Why do you ask?'

'No reason.'

That explained it then. It was the pie.

'Breakfast at seven thirty suit you?'

'Sure will.'

'Have a good night.'

She closed the door.

I ambled about the room, ran a finger along the dressing table

top and found it satisfyingly clear of dust. Then I stood by the pair of windows. They were double hung, with nets of cream lace strung across the lower frames. The sills were set at waist height which meant I had a clear line of sight out the top panes. She'd given me the corner room, overlooking the crossroads. The iron lacework beneath the railing conjured a vintage era of horses and carts. Realising I was a silhouette backlit by the single pendant light hanging from the ceiling, I crossed the room and switched it off, returning to my lookout, knowing I wouldn't be seen.

I wasn't there long when I heard a cough, followed by a groan and a muffled scrape of something—a chair maybe—being dragged across the floor of the adjoining room. Then all went quiet. I took umbrage at having been put right next door to another guest. Wasting no time, I left my station and locked myself in my room. Over by the door I heard the distant sound of laughter coming up from the bar. It felt comforting in a fashion, yet the cheery sound seemed to reinforce my isolation.

A digital clock on the bedside table told me in vivid green that it was seven. I considered joining the men downstairs but thought better of it. Instead, I returned to the window.

The town looked lifeless. Nothing moved, not even in the roadhouse. Despite the brightly lit neon sign, the roadhouse was closed. I wished I'd had the presence of mind to grab a few things out of the car before checking in, but then again, Con had been hostile. Realising he still had my keys, I didn't like to think of all my possessions piled on the back seat, and in the boot. I felt oddly violated, intruded upon, as though something vital had been taken from me. My power. Maybe I should have stayed there, the better to guard what I had brought with me, all that I'd scraped together in the aftermath of my charred life.

I was there in a flash, back in Cockatoo, standing by another window, the one in the living room that looked out over a forested valley, on one of the hottest days I'd ever experienced.

I should have known it would turn out bad after the birds had gone. It was Wednesday the sixteen of February and at that hour in late-summer, sulphur-crested cockatoos would grace the valley with a raucous chorus. Not that day. On that day, the silken trunks of the mountain ash stood tall along the back fence of my yard, silhouetted in a dense haze. The sun, blazing red on the horizon, couldn't raise a glimmer or a shadow. The feathery fronds of the ferns were crisping about their edges. Not a rustle of a lizard could be heard in the undergrowth. High above, the tufty tree canopy was still.

A conflagration had been billowing beyond the western hills all day. A southerly was due any minute. Everyone was hanging out for the cool change. The heat wave had been dragging on too long and this was the hottest day of all. We were all craving that wolfish wind to roar through and devour the fire front, make it blow back on itself. Aching for the sigh of cool and clean air that would follow. I had the radio on. The presenter said the wind would arrive in an hour, possibly two.

I waited. Like a lot of people in town that day, I waited. What few of us knew was another, smaller fire was threading its way east through the bush up Bailey Road and heading for the town centre.

The leaves on the trees beside the road fluttered for a few moments before settling still. I leaned forward and gazed up at the canopy. Clusters of leaves on the ends of thin branches were swaying languorously. Fern fronds in the undergrowth quivered and waved. I opened my bedroom window to listen. Smoke stung my nose—the air acrid from the smoke of the Belgrave and Beaconsfield fires. The radio had said those fires were under control.

The sun dipped behind the western ridge. Then, below the gentle crackle and crinkle of the tinder-dry bush, there was a distant, roaring rush, like a far-away kettle-drum roll.

Something told me to get out of the house fast. Going outside was like entering a fan-forced oven. Breathing was an effort, the smoke raw in my lungs. It was eight-thirty and the sun had nearly set when the wind caught the thin thread of blaze that had been tracking down the hillside, transforming it into a mile-long fire front blasting down the valley with the force of a hurricane. It all happened so fast. The smoke had got so thick I couldn't see more than a few metres. Trees were falling, some uprooting. Families were running out of their houses, screaming, and heading down to the reserve. Panic-stricken men and women raced their cars helter-skelter towards the Woori Yallock Road. Suddenly, the police helicopter was overhead with its siren blaring. In minutes the firies started evacuating the

town. They did the right thing, cos that fire was raging down Bailey Road razing everything in its path.

We didn't know it then, but in just sixteen minutes, two-hundred and eighty-three houses were gone. Another twenty-four were lost in the following hours and days.

The firies had been tackling blazes all day. They were exhausted. You could see it in the way they moved. Yet they went hell for leather up and down the streets behind the shops and there wasn't a whole lot of time. There were hundreds of us who couldn't get out. We had nowhere to shelter.

Someone must have had a key to the kinder building down by the railway line. It wasn't ideal. We knew it wasn't much more than a shack, despite its fancy design, a glass-windowed carousel. But we had no choice. The smoke was suffocating us. The fire was sucking the oxygen from the air. Birds, the ones that had ignored their instincts, like us, and hung around, were dropping dead from the sky. You could hear the gas bottles exploding. Boom. Boom. Boom. And then came the fireballs, larger than a soccer ball. The endless roar of the fire, deafening like a hundred jet engines. None of us thought we would survive.

Seared in my memory was the terror of three-hundred residents crammed shoulder to shoulder into that kindergarten building. Stinking hot we were, staring out all those windows at the apocalypse. A third of us were kids. Some men climbed up onto the roof to keep it free of embers. It was a bitumen roof, and without those men risking their own lives to keep us women and kids safe, the building would have burned for sure.

They were good men.

I will never forget how good they were.

You don't forget something like that. The distress on everyone's face, the terror in their eyes, the crying, the wailing, the choking stench.

My thoughts were interrupted by headlights approaching from the west. The vehicle didn't stop. I followed it with my gaze and was about to move away from my post by the window when I saw the roadhouse garage doors open. More headlights, this time a double set, and I watched a station wagon pulling out and heading across the forecourt. As the car entered the reach of the street lights I saw it was canary yellow. Its engine rumbled and chugged. The driver, Con presumably, made a right turn and then a sudden left, and disappeared up the road to the north.

Where was he off to at that time of night?

It came to me then that I knew not a thing about Cann River, a town I'd driven through on my way up the coast so many times before. It had always been a nothing place, a welcome relief from the endless forest, a chance to take a short break, a corner sort of place where, soon after, the coastline would stop being southern. A place welcoming at first sight.

Half an hour later, and I was always glad to see the back of it.

I drew the velvet curtains, flicked the light back on and lay down in the centre of the bed. Noises from next door started up again, bonks, a moan, a cough. I tried to block them out. Told myself the next day, I would be on my way. It couldn't have come soon enough.

CHAPTER TWO

FRANKIE

I was on my belly, rifle cocked at the beast. When I saw the headlights, I cursed under my breath. The deer froze, alert, sensing. As the vehicle crested a rise and entered the hairpin on its way up to the next, its engine grunted angrily, wheels emitting a screech. The deer bolted. I didn't need to turn and watch as the station wagon drew closer. The noise, the manner of driving, were predictable. It was Con. It was always Con, disturbing the peace up in those foothills.

He was on his way up the mountain. He'd be back down in an hour or two. Pat had sent him. He never did a thing without her say so.

I couldn't begrudge him his time out in the wilderness, away from the suffocating clutches of that mother of his. She was a piece of work, that one. Moved down from the ranges when her husband died and ushered her only son into his slavish existence at the roadhouse. Rumour had it she'd received a widow's payout from the company as a salve in lieu of the proper compensation she might have got if she'd taken them to court. They knew and she knew that was never going to happen. Besides, it wasn't the company's fault Igor had fallen to his death. He was standing where he shouldn't have, on the edge of the dam wall, while behind him two men were walking by, holding a length of timber. As they passed the wind picked up. The men struggled. The foreman tried to warn Igor, but he spoke no Hungarian and Igor no English, so down the buttresses he tumbled. Con would have been about twelve at the time.

Pat—I doubted that was the name she was born with—installed Con in the café serving customers and waiting tables, and when he wasn't doing that at weekends and before and after school, he was at the bowsers pumping gas. Soon after, she pulled him out of school altogether and had him baking pies. In his twenties, he half-finished a couple of apprenticeships, one for a baker, the other a mechanic, and he'd scarcely left the area since.

The roadhouse was Con's prison. I felt sorry for him. He looked a bit strange with his cleft chin and his foot that jutted out sideways, but I didn't think he meant any harm. You couldn't begrudge the guy a nocturnal trip up the mountain, even if he had been sent out on a mission. It was all the freedom he had. Although there was no escaping he did get in my way.

I waited for the sound of his engine to fade and scanned the knoll up ahead, but the deer was well and truly gone. I picked myself off the ground. As I brushed myself down, my nose received strong whiffs of the eucalyptus oil I'd squirted on my clothes to mask my own, human smell. With the rifle in the crook of my arm, I headed off to my shack.

I'd been squatting in the abandoned timber cutter's shack for about three years. When I first found the place, it was in a sorry mess and stank of stale piss. One of the windows was smashed, and the floor festooned with animal droppings. Looked like no one had been inside for many months. The surrounding forest had long since been logged out of all its old-growth ash, and the forest-raping, timber industry had moved on.

The shack didn't seem to belong to anyone, so I cleaned it up a bit and moved in. No one to bother me up there. I hadn't done much to it since, other than repair the window, and oil the floorboards to brighten them up. I never planned to stay long enough to care. I bought a small diesel generator to power the lights, but the noise obliterated the sounds of the bush. I only cranked it up when ageing a deer in the fridge, which lately had been more often than not.

It was too early for bed, so I broke open a beer and sat back in the only chair I had, a battered wing back I'd found on the side of the road. Someone had replaced the webbing under the seat pad with a few planks of Oregon. Not that comfortable but I wasn't fussed. I rested my feet on an upended milk crate that served as a coffee table and tuned into nature's chorus, loud enough to obliterate the steady thrum of the generator. More cacophony than symphony, especially after the light seasonal rain, when the frogs tried—and failed—to drown out the cicadas and the crickets. It was autumn, and the bush chorus had quietened down after its raucous summer zenith: mating season for the cicadas.

I tuned into the various tones; I heard the faint yap of a sugar glider echoing through distant trees. Nearby, a possum burst forth its croaky growl.

I was halfway through my beer when another sound cut in, jarring. Faint at first but soon it threatened to drown out the competition. The critters were struck dumb for a while. All I heard was the vehicle, screaming down the fire track that coursed the waney ridge above my place. I knew it wasn't Con. Different engine, and Con never used that track on account of the humps and deep swales that had been bulldozed into existence to prevent erosion. Not to mention the debris. Only a complete idiot would barrel down the old logging tracks in the dark. Con could be accused of many things, but he was not an idiot.

I next heard the shriek of brakes and knew the vehicle had reached one of the track's many hairpins. There was a dull thud. Had the driver come a cropper? Hit a deer, or a kangaroo maybe? I slugged my beer and waited.

There were no more engine sounds.

I toyed with the idea of checking out the damage, when the high-pitched whine of spinning wheels hit my ears and I felt my top lip curling in response. Not long after, the vehicle thrummed its way to the main road. Whoever it was had come as if from nowhere. I wanted to hear where they were headed. The engine noise faded as the vehicle dipped behind a saddle for a stretch and I pictured the road, its uncompromising path through the rough terrain, all the wooded gullies and nature-made rock dumps, the termite mounds and stringy barks left to rot where they fell, the old-growth logged, saplings poking up in the undergrowth like hope, the blackened trunks of the larger trees where a fire had gone through. It was terrain supporting an uneasy alliance of wild and feral life.

The vehicle drew closer. It had to be a ute or station wagon, and it was heading for the town.

The hotel would be in for a fun night.

With the vehicle out of earshot, I thought no more of it. The bush came back to me in all its complexity, an aural pleasure of harsh and pleading calls.

The capacity for survival out in the wilderness amazed me. It had been a scorcher of a season and the ground was still baked dry despite the recent showers that had freshened up the undergrowth. Summer wouldn't let go. The birds, the bandicoots, the snakes and goannas were all thirsty. Plenty of water in the river, but up at the shack I was on tank water and couldn't spare much. I did put out an old dog bowl now and then of an evening, and it was drunk dry by morning. I didn't have a dog.

Cassie said I should have a dog. Maybe she was right. Still, nature had other methods for taking care of its guardians. All summer a copperhead had taken up residence under the floorboards, until it was chased away by the largest goanna I'd ever clapped eyes on. The snake was not impressed but no amount of angry hissing put off that mother of a beast. I left them to sort it out between themselves. No point interfering in nature's course unless I had to.

I made my living hunting deer. Deer were feral and had no right to occupy the bush. I had no qualms helping the cull. I had a twelve-gauge slug gun with a rifled barrel, and I was a good shot. I skinned and hung and butchered too, selling the best to a truck-driver mate with connections in the city. Rick had a refrigerated van. I gave him a fair cut and we did good business selling to high end restaurants and the odd luxury hotel. Places where they knew how to spell 'venison'.

Word had it my venison was the best on the south coast. It was all in the killing.

Fear toughens the flesh.

I adopted a softly-softly approach. Even as a kid I was a caring sort, too caring according to my mother. Back then, she reckoned I ought to toughen up if I wanted the world to treat me well. 'You're a big softy,' she would say. She wanted me tough. She wanted to make up for the fact that I didn't have a dad. Then my stepdad, new on the scene, would follow on her tail with, 'Nah, Frankie's just a big girl.'

I took that as an insult.

Howard was a pig of a man with a pork-fattened belly, which sort of completed the swinish circle in my mind. Good fortune rained on me and my mum the day he was decapitated by a sheet of roofing iron while working on a building site up north. I would've been about seventeen at the time. We were told he was bending down to pick up the hammer he'd dropped when a magpie swooped a plumber on the roof. It was all instinct after that. The plumber raised his hands to protect his head, letting go of the sheet of iron in his grasp in the process, and that was the end of my stepdad.

What was it with men and construction sites?

Howard Potter, deceased.

They put his head in a bucket and called the ambulance.

When the plumber, and then the project manager, came around to apologise, it was all my mum and I could do not to invite them in for tea and cake to celebrate. Mum kept a straight face, and I had to stifle the laugh bubbling in my tummy. Maybe it was the shock as well. No one wants to be confronted with news like that, but it has to be said that we never mourned his loss. We'd have been hypocrites if we had. The old bastard hit my mum so hard she only had half her teeth and she had to have a hysterectomy because of the pounding he'd given her guts. I would have been about fifteen when that happened. The year was 1974 and the Vietnam war had come to an end by then.

That mongrel of a man was American by birth. He'd bolted to Australia in '72 and married my mum, who was practically the first woman he'd met since back then she had a job as a cleaner at the airport. He did all that to avoid the US draft after Whitlam had abolished it in Australia. Mum said they got the first letter wrong when they named him 'Howard'.

I drank the last dregs of my beer and wiped my mouth,

before pulling on my boots and heading outside to check on the moon rise. Through a clearing in the trees I saw the forest down below, stretching towards the southern coast. Short flashes of headlights took me by surprise. I thought it might have been that same hoon. I knew my instincts agreed when my top lip reared again.

CHAPTER THREE

PEARL

S hit happens. That's been my motto in life. Seen me through thick and thin, and I'm too set in my ways to change now. It's what I told my daughter, Kylie, when her husband took off with his boss. His way of going up in the world. Shit happens, I said. She didn't want to hear it, not with two babies hanging off her. I offered to help out, but she didn't want to know. She didn't want another thing from me, she said, or even set eyes on my face.

She didn't have to make things so final.

I pushed back a cuticle with the jagged edge of a thumb nail, the pain quick and sharp. I was sitting out on my front deck, watching the last of the daylight fade out over the western rise.

I don't believe in permanence, but Kylie had held fast to that stance, for years. She'd always been tenacious. She never came down to visit me after I moved out to Peachtree. Not once. I'd abandoned her, apparently, although she hadn't given me much to stay for in the city. I thought the little twinnies would have liked it out in the country, but Kylie said the area around Cann River was too wild.

How would she know?

Then again, she was right. Of course, it was wild! There was nothing out there other than bush.

The place didn't look so lush in the autumn of '83. It'd been a long hot summer and there was little green underfoot except along the riverbank. I'd been on my own for weeks. None of the city folk who usually came out to the campsite or their shacks to fish the inlet were game enough to head into the tinder-dry forest after the fires. The whole state was traumatised. I thought it a bit of an overreaction, but then again, it had been one helluva conflagration.

At Peachtree, I felt safe enough. If a blaze did pass through, I had my boat, and the inlet was a couple of kilometres wide. As for the shack, well, I'd lost a lot more in my life than that clapped out old weatherboard. I'd lost two houses on account of a man: A house to

his debt, and a house to a flood. You get used to loss the same way you get used to a sore hip. You ignore it.

A cool breeze stroked my face. The lights were off in the house. That's the thing with being off grid. All I had was a generator and a 12-volt battery for emergencies. In the 1980s, solar power was just about unheard of. I relied on candlelight by night. It did me just fine. I had the dog for company and a large glass of scotch to keep me amused.

And to numb the pain in my tongue.

Sometimes the inexplicable happens and that was the situation with my tongue. I thought I must have gnawed it with my back molars in my sleep because I woke up with it, and only discovered the full force of the pain when at breakfast I tried to swallow some toast. A bullet of agony shot right into my ear. I nearly gagged.

The scotch worked wonders. I could swallow without discomfort, although I knew the ulcer was there. It would have taken a lot of scotch to get rid of that sting altogether. Funny how the little things hurt like the big things. An ulcer matching, say, a severed foot in intensity, if only for a pointed moment.

Sam lay at my feet. She was a staunch companion, a smart and loyal Kelpie, getting on in years so we were a good match. She'd found one of my old slippers and was having a merry old time severing heel from toe, when a rumble in the distance caused her to cock her ears. Me and Sam both sat fast, listening. I'd have heard on the bush telegraph if anyone was expected. No one came out to Peachtree at night and I wasn't due a visitor. Besides, no one I knew drove at that speed, not without a bull bar. The roos and the wombats were not given to looking both ways before crossing the road.

So, who the hell was it?

The clearing by the river that was Peachtree consisted of six rundown shacks, each on its own large block, all of them owned by city dwellers wanting to escape the rest of humanity now and then, do a bit of fishing, go walkabout in the wilderness, or take a hike along the beaches that stretched for miles and miles. Put a toe or two in the Southern Ocean that churned and pounded the shore. Probably no more than a foot. The coast had strong long-shore rips that would drag even a good swimmer out to sea. Swimming was advised only when the waters were absolutely calm, and that was hardly ever.

Croajingolong National Park was a wild, inhospitable place in every respect. Which was why, when a sedan pulled into old Fred's place across the dirt track, I went inside to fetch my binoculars. Not that I expected to make out much in the dark, but I wanted to see whatever I could. The driver had obliged my curiosity by leaving his headlights on. Wanted to see his way around. I assumed it was a 'he' and when I returned to the deck and adjusted the binoculars, I found I was right.

Sam let out a low growl. I hissed at her to stay quiet.

The man disappeared around the back. I heard a dull bang and then another. Sounded like he was breaking in. I could have run across and told him where to find the key, but I wasn't about to make his entry easy.

No need.

He'd got in anyway.

The front door opened and out he strode, all cocky confidence.

He was a small, stocky man, dressed in puffed out city gear. With his big hair, I had him marked out as a yuppie. Judging by the way he ferried the contents of his boot into the house, he wasn't that strong. Three trips later he opened the rear passenger side door. He bent in and when he stood up, I could see a sleeping child in his arms. The kiddie would have been no more than five, judging by the size. Moments later he was back at the car, and out came another one, about the same size as the first. My heart squeezed in the looking. I wanted to think the guy was just some devoted dad taking his kids on a holiday, but old Fred never let his shack out to anyone with kids, and judging by the way he'd entered, the guy was more likely not meant to be there.

If he'd been a woman, I'd have rushed over to offer my support. As it was, I felt torn between my concern for the welfare of those kiddies and wariness over that man. The father? Had to be, surely? How did he know about the shacks? A local? Not dressed like that. Someone who'd been there before, on holiday? There was no point dwelling on it. I'd phone Fred in the morning.

Sam made low throaty grumbles. I thought any moment she'd bark so I tugged her collar and yanked her inside. I had to sit with her, stroking her back, keeping her calm, while I tried to think what else to do.

I poured myself another whisky. Then I drew the curtains and locked all the doors in case the stranger went on a nocturnal walkabout. I sat there in the kitchen in the dark with my whisky and my dog, hoping daylight would bring sanity to the situation.

The dark always brought the dark along with it. I kept thinking he had to be a child abductor, a paedophile, a snuff movie maker, a serial killing psychopath about to do those kiddies unspeakable harm.

Who knew?

My mind was running away with me. I couldn't sit there speculating. I drained my glass and went over to the living room and stoked the wood stove for the night. Then I made a quick brew with the water still hot in the kettle that I'd set to the edge of the hot plate. I took my tea, black and sugarless, and *Picnic at Hanging Rock* to bed.

My bedroom was at the rear of the house, its window facing the back yard. In there, I could safely light a candle.

I put down the tea and the book and started to get changed into my bed wear. It occurred to me as I was pulling my thin grey sweater over my head that I might need to leave it on.

All I took off were my boots.

Two chapters in and I put the book down, deciding Hanging Rock was a stupid place to take a group of flighty schoolgirls. Then I thought those girls and that teacher couldn't all have simply disappeared. There'd have been traces, ripped clothing, droplets of blood, screams someone had to have heard. The ground hadn't opened its jaws and devoured them. In all, the setting, Hanging Rock, was ludicrous as it was essentially an exposed mountainside. I'd been there with Kylie when she was small. You could see and be seen for miles. Not like

Peachtree. You could walk ten feet into the bush of Croajingolong and never be seen again. It was hilly terrain, riddled with creeks and rivers, a few towering gums and a lot of thick undergrowth. Then there were the tea trees, banksias and heathland beside the coast.

Not that folk were in the habit of going missing in Croajingolong. Just that the wilderness coast could devour a person if they let it happen, and people had to show the place respect.

I wasn't from round those parts. I was a Tassie girl by birth, my family hailing from Ulverstone in the Apple Isle's north west. We were farming folk, taking advantage of the rich red soils of the northern slopes that came down off the Central Highlands and met the coast. It was a homely existence, plenty of potatoes to fill the belly, hard work out in the fields, and not much to trouble us. I had a perfect childhood. No complaints there. I loved my mum and my dad and my sisters, Clara and Flo. My younger brother was a cry baby, but I managed to ignore him until he was old enough for fishing. We'd go off for hours then, me and dad and Clive. We'd come home with dinner, and mum would have the spuds cut for chips.

My family were what folk called well-adjusted and comfortably off. We were not religious or political, none of us were gamblers, and all of us played sport. Mum loved tennis, Dad was into cricket, Clive kicked balls, with me and Clara it was netball, and Flo loved to swim, which we all said went nicely with her name. The only dent in that cradle of familial happiness was when I, the eldest, met Mal, the brickie, and we took off to Melbourne after the wedding.

My Kylie came along three years later, and that was when I discovered my darling Mal was a gambler. The day the house we'd bought and lovingly done up was sold from under us to pay off his debts, I left him. That was in the late 1950s and it was no decade to be a single mum, but I got by working in the office of the Younghusband Wool Store in Kensington. I would have been about thirty, and I only survived the workplace, and the stench of fleece that went with it, because I was a farm girl who knew how to fish and peel spuds and get her hands dirty. I toughened up quick and repeated all of Mal's tales and jokes as if they were my own. I guess that was also when I learned how to lie if I had to, if it came to saving my own skin.

I could keep other folks' lies too. Like Con and old Pat's at the roadhouse. Wild horses couldn't prise out of me what I knew about them, but I could never help the shudder that passed through me whenever one of those young backpacker girls crossed the state border in a coach, heading west to heaven knew what El Dorado was in her head. When I went into Cann River to check the mail and have a catch up with Frankie, there she'd be, the latest after the last one got away, all wet behind the ears, slaving away at the counter.

CHAPTER FOUR

EMILY

The coach heading down the coast from Sydney pulled up at the roadhouse at about midday on weekdays, and two in the afternoon on weekends. A second coach came through on Tuesdays and Thursdays at six, pick up only. That coach arrived in Melbourne at five the following morning after making numerous stops along the way. The coach heading up the coast from Melbourne arrived in Cann River at one in the afternoon, three on weekends. On Mondays and Wednesdays, the night coach came through at four in the morning.

A little before midday, Pat and Con would be poised ready to receive the Sydney-coach passengers, and shortly after they would try to hide their disappointment as they watched the raggle-taggle of coach-fatigued travellers decant and wander off to the bakery and the general store up the street. Con would angle the sandwich board listing their gourmet pies to catch the eye, but it was rarely enough to lure most, who wanted nothing more than to stretch their legs and see what else the town had to offer, or go and eat a normal pie at the bakery, the preference of regular travellers. Pat and Con enjoyed the patronage of the grannies too old to walk far, the occasional markedly weary traveller, someone with crutches or a limp, a mother eager to shut up her fussing children, and rarely—very rarely—someone lured by the word 'gourmet' that was attached to the common-as-flies, great Australian pie.

Other than those two coaches, the town, servicing a smattering of farms in the hinterland, relied for its survival on tourists journeying on the highway from here to there, keen to stop midway along a two-hundred mile stretch of wilderness; weary of the thinned-out forest of identical-looking trees, a forest stripped of its magnificence, weary too after battling the logging trucks that seemed to own that stretch of road, a road that went on and on, as though destined to never end.

Almost no one came down from the high country to the north, because almost no one lived up there, and those who did were just as likely to head in the opposite direction than come down the mountain, because the road was dirt and known to be treacherous.

To the south, some fifteen miles away as the crow flies, and about an hour by car on roads that veered first one way then another, was the coast, replete with a string of wild and dangerous beaches. The whole region had been classified wilderness for good reason. It was largely inaccessible, and it was so far from anywhere significant it might as well fall off the end of the earth altogether and be done with it.

There was, to my mind, one feature, one historical note of importance that saved Cann River and its surrounds from desolation. Nearby, was the first land of Eastern Australia James Cook had sighted when he went on his voyage of discovery in 1770. Even if he'd merely named the place Point Hicks and passed right on by.

I wish I had.

I wish I'd stayed on that coach heading for the city, but

when it pulled into the roadhouse that day in the middle of the longest hottest summer there ever was, and the passengers alighted to stretch their legs, I was intrigued by the sense of remoteness that pervaded the place. In that state of fuzzy euphoria that comes with fatigue, I wandered into the roadhouse and saw the sign advertising the need for a waitress. I spoke to the woman behind the counter and within the designated half hour of the coach stop, the driver was pulling out my backpack from the hold, and I was making my way through the roadhouse to the domestic quarters out the back.

Three months later, and I was still there. I'd arrived just about penniless and somehow the money I earned in the café, which Pat paid monthly, was always shy of what I was due, never covering much more than the rent and board she charged me. Each pay day, what she handed me, I handed back, save a couple of dollars. Pat kept promising to give me the shortfall in my wages but it never materialised.

A rough old room it was too. Windowless walls of concrete blocks painted sky blue. Cuboid, it contained a single, iron-framed bed with a thin, foam mattress and a small, wooden table with a wobbly leg. A tacky print of the Sydney Opera House had been Sellotaped to one wall. The door had no lock and the door handle on the inside didn't work—someone had tied a straw to the mechanism—which meant I had to leave the door ajar when I was inside, wedged slightly open with a sock, lest I get shut in. I placed my backpack against the door to stop it swinging open in a draught.

The room was halfway down a long corridor and opposite was the only bathroom in the place.

I never slept well. Neither did Con. He was forever up and down that corridor, visiting the bathroom. At first, I wondered if he had a weak bladder or drank copious amounts of liquid, or even if he had a medical condition. He certainly had something wrong with him other than the peculiar angle of his left foot. It took me a few nights to glean he was going to the bathroom to wash his hands. I observed his hand washing during the day as well. What I originally put down to the contradictory roles of baker and mechanic turned out to be a compulsion. I derived no comfort from the knowledge. For all I knew his hand washing habit was indicative of a much larger complex of traits and tendencies that meant he couldn't be trusted.

My conclusion was reinforced by another aspect of his nocturnal ritual. He would hover in the corridor, outside the bathroom, which was also right outside my bedroom door. I could hear him breathing. A minute or two would pass, sometimes more. I'd be lying on my narrow creaky bed, rigid, holding my own breath, alert as prey. Then I'd hear his footsteps head off and his bedroom door clunk shut. After these episodes, it would take me a long time to get to sleep and sometimes I found I was still awake when he tramped back up the corridor to repeat the whole ritual. Once, I don't think I slept at all, and counted to six the number of times he got up.

I wanted to tell Pat, but I couldn't. Pat wasn't the type of woman to take lightly a criticism of her son, and there was no way of broaching the issue without making him sound like a creep. Instead, I succumbed to quiet desperation, made worse through lack of sleep. I existed in a fog of exhaustion, my movements disconnected from my awareness. Not even Pat's incessant carping had much impact.

Earlier that April day, she'd had me on my hands and knees scrubbing the grout between the kitchen floor tiles. Then she had me scrubbing out the public lavatories which according to her had to be kept lickable clean. I thought one day she'd barge in and make me glide my tongue around the inside of a toilet bowl just to prove to her I had faith in my own work, but she never did. Really, I was her scrubber. That's all I did. I scrubbed the tables, the counter, the milk-shake maker and the pie warmer. In the kitchen, I did the dishes. I cleaned the grill and the chipper. I cleaned up the awful mess Con left behind him when he made his pies; the flour encrusted bench, the bloodied knives and chopping boards, the saucepans thick with the remains of his fillings, encrusted on the bottom and congealed about the rim, the dollops set hard on the stovetop, the oven splatters from filling overspill, and the pastry he'd managed to grind into the floor.

I was never allowed in the kitchen when Con was making those pies. Pat said it made him self-conscious. I was ushered in when the last tray of cooked pies was cooling on a wire rack. I was forced to function in the unappetising stink of it.

As I scrubbed, I would dream of home, back in Oxford, of my parents and my younger brother, Timothy. Of my heady university days reading English literature, the lectures, the seminars, the long meandering essays. I recalled my bicycle, English pubs and warm beer in quaint Cotswold villages. Cosy memories of happy days, one endless balmy summer in my imagining. The longer I remained trapped at the roadhouse, the rosier my memories, the more intense the homesickness. I would curse the day I decided to spend the money

I'd saved working in an Oxford bookstore on a return ticket to Sydney. I'd graduated and I wanted to see the world. My parents forbade me to go to India, South America, Africa, or the Middle East. In fact, anywhere I came up with was too dangerous for them, other than Australia. Nothing untoward could possibly happen to me in such a sensible country, so I secured a working holiday visa and took off.

The day was hot, and the bus heading down the coast from Sydney pulled in five minutes early. Con hadn't put out the sandwich board. He was on the forecourt serving petrol. Pat marched in from the kitchen as if by instinct, surveyed the situation and, in that gruff manner of hers said, 'Get and put out the pie board.'

I stuffed the rag that had become an extension of my hand in the pocket of my apron and heaved the hinged board outside and set it down angled at the bus, in time for the few passengers, couples mostly, to give it a cursory glance on their way up the street.

I watched a mother drag her two children to my pristine toilets, and an elderly man pause on the forecourt, scan the sandwich board and make up his mind to go inside. Behind him, a lanky and ghostly pale young man who, despite the heat, wore a beanie on his head, scrutinised the setting, taking a special interest in the trees. It was a gesture that seemed odd to me, for the trees all looked the same, forming a dense curtain around the town. The old man had made it to the sandwich board before the young man followed on behind, taking long, yet careful strides.

I went and held open the door. They both entered together, the young man dodging past the old and heading straight to Pat behind the counter. He attempted to place an order of a steak pie, which was spelt 'stake' because Con had written up that section of the board and Pat wouldn't countenance changing it.

Curious, I reached into my apron and took out my rag and wiped down the already clean tables nearby.

'There's no steak,' Pat said.

There was almost never any steak. The man looked disappointed. 'How about the hunter?' Pat said.

'You got the venison.'

'Yep.'

'I'll have that.' 'Chips?'

'No, thank you.' 'Sauce?'

'Of course.'

'Sauce, of course,' she repeated.

Pat liked to say 'sauce, of course,' although she had no idea about such things as assonance and alliteration. She had a thing about that sauce. She made it herself out of the tomatoes she grew, and it won first prize every year in the local agricultural show. Her awards were thumb tacked to the high shelving behind the counter. The sauce was sweet and tangy and intense, obliterating every other flavour on the palate, effectively extinguishing the taste, both immediate and residual, of Con's pies. He hadn't a clue because he was allergic to tomatoes.

The power of her sauce was Pat's secret, her way of undermining her son, even as she praised his pies to the hilt, and told everyone he was a master baker. She would never hear a bad word said about his pies.

The young man took his plate of pie and sauce to the table nearest the door, leaving the old man to place his order of venison pie with chips and sauce, along with a flat white coffee. He rambled on to Pat in a low drawl on how travelling made him ravenous and there was still a long way to go to reach the city, before she interrupted and told him to find a table.

The young man caught my eye and beckoned me over. He asked for some salt and pepper. I fetched a cruet set from another table. As I set it down, I took in his face, my eyes settling on the long scar running up the edge of his cheek and emerging on the other side of his beanie, on his forehead above his right ear. It was fresh-looking, red, and I thought perhaps he'd been in a road accident. His hands trembled as he doused his pie. He looked up at me and asked for a glass of water.

When I returned with it, we chatted. The way he spoke surprised me. His voice was soft, educated, the words he chose sophisticated. His name was Pete. He had large, winsome blue eyes set in a smooth, hairless, almost pretty face, despite the pallor and the scar. His mouth was full, the lower lip protruding in a slight pout. If it hadn't been for the deep timbre of his voice, he might have been mistaken for a flat-chested woman.

I asked him where he was heading, and he said he was waiting for a lift to take him to the lighthouse. I knew about the lighthouse at Point Hicks, but I hadn't been. What was he planning to do there? I thought perhaps he had a job although he looked in no fit state to work. He told me his friend and lighthouse keeper, Simon, needed to spend a couple of weeks in the city at short notice, and had been desperate to find someone to mind the lighthouse while he was away. But Pete said he was really going there to convalesce. I didn't like to ask what was wrong. I wished him a speedy recovery and left him to his pie.

I watched him from behind the counter as he battled into the pie crust, as if the effort of bringing his knife to bear on the pastry were too much. In the end, he stabbed the centre with a fork and proceeded to eat out the contents, leaving the crust untouched. After that he sat gazing out the window and sipping his water. I went and retrieved his plate and that was when he told me he was waiting for Simon to pick him up.

He was still there many hours later when a car coasted onto the forecourt, coming to a halt at a weird angle and blocking the exit. I thought it might have been the lighthouse keeper, Simon, but a woman got out and marched past the bowsers on her way inside. She looked flustered. She was middle aged, of ordinary appearance, plump about the torso; the sort of woman who'd made a career out of sitting at a desk. She hadn't seen me on my haunches wiping the floor under a table, but I disliked her on sight.

Leaving Pat to enjoy the Joan Baez she'd put on the jukebox, I snuck out to the lavatories to give them one last clean before locking them up for the night.

CHAPTER FIVE

MIRIAM

I didn't sleep well. The pie had left me with indigestion and the person in the room next to mine wouldn't keep still. Then a hoon had taken to doing donuts at the crossroads. After he'd got bored, or run out of rubber on his tyres, every now and then a truck thundered through the town as though the speed-limit sign never existed. The vibration rattled the windows. I even heard a coach pull up at about four. To add to my woes, the bed base had a squeak. I imagined whoever was next door would have been able to hear me as well, so I lay still as a board, not wanting to give any indication of my presence.

I'm not sure I slept at all. In the darkness of the night, I pictured my cindered home, recalling the acrid stench of smouldering timbers, the birds dropping from the sky, the blood curdling screams of others invisible in the thick smoke. Then there were the toys dropped in the middle of the road as children fled, toys all shrivelled and contorted. I had to make a considerable effort to replace those memories with dreams of where I was heading, of the better life I was about to enjoy amid pastures green, of sea breezes and open skies.

At dawn's first light I slipped out of bed, still fully clothed, and peered out the windows, taking in the tall trees on the fringes, their menace. The street was quiet. At the intersection, the hoon had left streaks of black in neat arcs. There was no sign of the vehicle. Whoever it was had obviously taken off to wherever they were heading, but I sensed that wouldn't be far.

Nothing in the town stirred. I stood there, watching the dark recede, eyeing the roadhouse, anticipating signs of movement. Before long, the mechanic baker, Con, came out and opened the garage door. Inside, I saw my car. The familiarity of it made me exhale with relief. I kept watch, hoping to see the driver's side door open, the bonnet lift. Instead, Con came out, closed the garage door and tramped back inside the roadhouse. A light went on inside, and another. Then sunlight shafted through a gap in the tall trees at the eastern end of town and the damp tarmac of the highway glistened. The sudden burst of sharp light hurt my eyes. I winced and pulled back.

The bedside clock's digital display told me it was seven o'clock. There was a towel, steel blue and frayed at the edges, on the chair by the door. The woman—receptionist, bar tender, whoever she was—had pointed out the bathroom three doors down on the right. I'd have liked a change of clothes, but a shower would at least freshen my skin.

All had quietened down in the adjoining room, so I took the towel on offer and my door key. Taking care to lock the door behind me as softly as I could, I tiptoed down the corridor.

A strange apprehension invaded my mind concerning the occupant of that room I had to pass on my way to and from my own. I was exhausted and overwrought. I wasn't thinking straight. The terror of the recent past pressed in on me. I didn't like being forced to stay in yet more bush during a dry and hot autumn. Such were my rationalisations.

The bathroom was large. A worn, porcelain bathtub of putrid green, deep and narrow, took up the end wall beneath the window. There was a basin and toilet to match. The tiles were pink, the floor a grey mottled linoleum. A barrel bolt locked me in. The set of taps that fed the shower apparatus didn't seem to function. I turned them on, but nothing happened, not even a gurgle or a hiss. The bath taps worked, releasing a gush of water. I inspected the bath with eye and finger. Satisfied it was clean, I inserted the plug, secured on a long chain, and waited for the water to rise to about six inches. I tested the temperature, swirled my hand in the warmth and took the fresh-looking cake of soap from the basin. Peeling off my clothes I was conscious that two doors away a stranger slept, a stranger who had helped keep me awake all night. Naked, I checked I'd secured the barrel bolt. As I climbed in the bath and felt the water clean on my skin, ridding my body of its musky, sweaty smell, I wondered if that stranger were male or female.

It was a relief to scrub away yesterday, but I didn't stay in the bath for long. The soap was Lux and I came out smelling like my mother. I'd even used a little to clean my hair. Putting on my dirty clothes felt like sin.

I heard a clatter of pans directly below and figured that room was the kitchen. My stomach gurgled. My mouth felt furry and I craved a toothbrush. But my teeth could wait. After all, my car with all my things packed in the boot and on the back seat was right across the road, and all I needed to do was eat the breakfast that came with the room and retrieve whatever I needed. Surely by then that mechanic would have figured out what was wrong with my car, and I could be on my way by mid-morning.

I deposited my towel in my room, grabbed my handbag and left, walking softly down the corridor. Passing the door to the adjoining room I heard a low moan. Part of me froze, another wanting to run for the stairs. I was confronted by an image of that man I saw the day of the fire, emerging through the choking haze of smoke, his clothes alight, his skin red and weeping.

That pleading look he had, the suffering.

The way I had to run past him to save myself would haunt me to my own passing.

I'd made it to the stairwell when behind me, my neighbour's door opened. I couldn't have been more than ten feet away. I grabbed the handrail and looked back. Out spilled the most wretched, haggard, sallow-faced human being I had ever encountered. He was thin, stooped, with hollow cheeks and eyes that bulged, a look of terror glued to his face like a fixture. Even at a distance I could see his skin was pock-marked from acne, with several unsightly boils breaking out around his mouth and on his neck. He managed an acknowledging smile as he staggered to the bathroom, and I returned a polite, 'Good morning,' thinking that the image of the man was more shocking than the burning man of Cockatoo.

Certain I was checking out, collecting my car and leaving town, I headed down the stairs grateful I wouldn't be seeing him again.

The dining room was accessed through the door to the left of the stairs. To my right, the saloon, visible through its glass panelled door, sat in darkness.

I pushed open the door. My breakfast place was laid on a small table by one of the windows. It was the only place laid in the room. I sat down with my back to the door. Outside, an old ute chugged down the highway, slowed, and swung into the road heading north.

A small glass of orange juice had already been poured so I drank it down in several gulps. I waited. Two cars swished by heading in opposite directions. Then a station wagon pulled up outside the general store, situated on the south-eastern corner of the dog-legged crossroads. The only indication the store had opened for business was the interior light showing above the painted windows. Beyond the store, off in the near distance, I noticed the pitched roof of a small church. Between the store and the church were several small shops. A sedan pulling into the roadhouse caught my eye, and I saw Con appear from round the side of the building and lumber across to the bowsers.

The woman who'd taken me to my room the night before appeared with a plate held in a tea towel. She set the plate down before me. Adequately arranged were two fried eggs, a long rasher of bacon, one grilled tomato, large, and two slices of thickly buttered toast. No sauce, thankfully.

'Sleep good?'

'Very well, thank you,' I lied. I didn't want to cause offence. 'Coffee or tea?'

'Coffee, please.'

I watched her head back to the kitchen, the purposeful sway of her hips, the way she bumped the door open on her way through.

She had the confident, practical manner born of the country life. Couldn't be easy, stuck out in a place like this, enclosed by towering trees in the middle of nowhere.

She'd flipped the eggs, but the yolks were soft. I tucked in, determined to eat every scrap. The woman came back with my coffee as I was chewing on the last corner of toast. Considering how long she'd taken to make it, I hoped it might be brewed, but it wasn't.

'You'll be off then.'

'Sure will.'

'I'll fetch your bill.'

She hurried away.

The coffee was hot, and I drank it slowly, allowing Con plenty of time to diagnose my car. The woman returned. I settled the bill with cash and handed her my key. It was just after eight thirty when I left the hotel. The roadhouse had been open getting on for two hours.

Inside, the roadhouse was thick with the meaty, slightly piquant smell of those gourmet pies Con made. I struggled not to screw up my nose on my way to the counter. Joan Baez was moaning about poor Dixie again. I was surprised to find a young woman wiping down the cabinets. She was pretty and dark-haired, with striking green eyes and milky skin. She said, 'May I help you?' in one of those cultured English accents you don't often hear in Australia and certainly not in a backwater like Cann River. I must have appeared as shocked as I felt, for she added, 'I'm a backpacker.'

'Oh, I see.'

Something icy passed through me when she said it, a resonance, a ghost. I glimpsed, inwardly, the image of a girl who went missing in Brighton. A tiny little thing. Five, the papers had said. I was twenty at the time. I had no idea who she was when the story broke, but it turned out she was my cousin.

The day I found out, we were seated in my parent's living room in Kew. It had been a suffocating day, the air thick, the sun a mean ball glaring down on concrete and tarmac. By the time we were gathered in the living room, the sun was on its descent and a light ocean breeze blew in through the double-hung windows, worrying the lace curtains that provided a discreet screen for the inhabitants of Molesworth Street from the occasional passer-by.

The house was set well back from the street, rendering unnecessary any sort of screen. Net curtains, the quintessential symbol of a bygone era along with doilies and tea cosies, a representation of a time when women with blue-tinged hair—like my mother—were expected to crochet for the edification of their home. I considered myself modern. I had no clear idea what that meant but what it didn't mean was net curtains. I'd been listening to Fats Domino in my bedroom and as the breeze tickled my back, Blueberry Hill played in my mind.

'She's getting too headstrong,' my father said, directing his comment to his wife.

We had been having an argument about my life. I sat there wondering where the old Mr Forster had gone, the one who ran about with me clasped to his back or sat me down in the spare bedroom while he tinkered with his model railway. Fell away with his hair, leaving a bald and forthright pate? Or was it buried beneath his whisky paunch?

'She's ruining her life,' my mother said, all prim in her peach dress.

I flushed. Both my adoptive parents were uncommonly emphatic and making little effort to disguise their disapproval. Something unfamiliar and strong welled up in me. Mr and Mrs Forster of Kew were not pleased to see the baby of the family relocate to an area beneath them. My mother seemed especially distraught, having raised her other children to have promising careers—my eldest brother, Greg, was a solicitor living in Prahran, Simon a botanist residing in Hobart's historic Battery Point, and Grace the wife of a geologist, happily housed in the Flinders Ranges east of Adelaide. After all that success, Mrs Forster was not prepared for this failure, not after lavishing her attention on me, an adopted baby of an unwed teenage mother. As if she had known the child would have bad blood the result of her wayward genes, through the force of her will Mrs Forster had raised me to be mild mannered. Now the look of disappointment in her eyes seemed to suggest my mother was fast realising no amount of nurturing could eradicate the tendencies I had been born with, an attitude which seemed to me by turns ludicrous, hurtful and outright insulting.

'Why didn't you mention it before, Miriam?'

Because I knew you would react like this. I didn't say it. 'Belgrave has a terrible

reputation.'

'It does?'

My mother paused and took a short breath. 'Why would you want to live there?'

They knew why. I had a job there, in a shop.

I cast my eye about the room, high-ceilinged and furnished comfortably with deep sofas, upholstered in cream damask, facing each other across an Afghan rug. Mr and Mrs Forster had taken up the matching armchairs, positioned side-by-side and facing the window. An oak escritoire was centred along the far wall behind them, flanked by two balloon-backed chairs. A portrait of the paternal grandfather hung above the escritoire, his gaze wooden and stern. On the wall to the left was an upright piano of polished rose wood, catching the late sun shafting through the windows behind me. I was feeling uncharacteristically defiant.

'It's close to work.'

'You must find a different job,' my father said.

'How in heaven's name will you meet a nice young man in Belgrave?'

I had no interest in meeting any nice young men. I was about to leave the room to pack when my mother blurted, 'Anything can happen to you out there. It's too wild. I can't bear to lose you, not after, after...'

'After what?' I asked, as politely as I could manage.

My father stepped in with an explanation of my cousin, little Nicole, and how she was the missing girl reported in the papers.

The woman behind the roadhouse counter wasn't her. Couldn't be. Nicole was found a year later, what remained of her. It was rumoured she'd been procured by some group with paedophilic habits, but nothing was proven.

Powerful feelings of protectiveness came rushing in, as though they'd been locked out of my being for far too long and suddenly wanted centre stage. I didn't know where to put my gaze. I wanted to reach out my hand, hurry her out from behind that counter, bundle her into my arms, my car, and take her away to safety. It was a ludicrous impulse, but it was strong. Yet, for all I knew she was safe, right there where she was.

'I'm here to speak with Con,' I said.

She nodded but didn't move.

Moments later, he lumbered in from the forecourt with a customer. Petrol fumes drifted in behind them.

Con took the dollars the man proffered, then hesitated as the till draw sprang open, a look of concentration appearing in his face as he calculated the change. It was an expression that made him seem peculiarly vacant.

I was left not knowing how any woman could relax in that town full of freaks.

'How's my car?' I asked Con once the customer had gone, trying not to make a study of the cleft in his chin.

'Won't start, will it?'

'I figured that much.'

'Battery's good, but.'

'It should be. I only bought it last month.'

'So, it isn't the battery.'

'Can't be,' I replied, wondering how long the inane exchange would go on.

The girl stood around, wiping down surfaces.

'It's the electrics,' he said with authority. 'The electrics.'

'Alternator's dead, I reckon.'

'And that is?'

'The machine what keeps your car running.'

'Is it serious?'

'Nah.' He shifted his weight from one foot to the other and glanced behind him at the pie warmer.

'That's a relief,' I said, following his gaze and counting the pies.

There were ten.

'Got to order the part, but.'

'How long will that take?'

'It's gotta come up from the city. I've rung through to Tony's car parts but he's outta stock till Monday.'

'Can't you order it from someone else?'

'I always use Tony.'

He stood there, implacable.

'Monday, you say.' By then I was gripping the counter.

'Monday's when he'll post it up.' He reflected, making another slow, inner calculation. Any moment, I expected him to use his fingers. 'Should be here next Thursday.'

'That's almost a week!'

'Not my problem,' he said, and walked off back outside.

'Can I get you anything?' the girl said.

I didn't answer.

Instead, I stormed out of the café and round to the garage, where Con was fiddling about. 'My car keys, please.'

He reached into the depths of a pocket. When he handed them to me, they were warm to the touch. I tried not to think about what they had been.

I retrieved a holdall, a small suitcase, and a couple of other bags from the boot, and made to cross the forecourt on my way back to the hotel.

'Cheaper to stay here,' he called after me.

I kept walking.

CHAPTER SIX

FRANKIE

The autumn chill that had settled overnight was lifting in the early morning sun. The bush was still. I heard a raven caw in the distance. Halfway up the slope above my shack, where sapling trees clung to life in the dry, where the trunks of their older companions were charred from a back burn gone wrong a few years back—the firies were reducing the fuel after a wet season to protect the subdivision of hobby farms down by the river—there was a narrow track, not visible to the untrained eye. It was up there that, when the need arose, I set a trap.

I didn't like setting traps. The native wildlife too easily got caught, but after last night's fiasco, I was in need of another kill.

I was standing over a small hind. A teenager. The muscles quivered, eyes rolling in terror at the sight of me. Its back leg was caught. I set down the hessian sacks I brought with me on my rounds and took the boning knife from my belt.

The incision was fast, deep, the little Hog hind relaxed in death.

I was glad I'd trapped a Hog. The Rusa, Chital and Fallow

around those parts all weighed in at about eighty or ninety kilos for a stag, and about fifty for a hind. Then there were the Sambar. They weighed in at over two hundred kilos. Even a hind was too much for one person to handle.

I never shot a Sambar.

I freed the leg and dragged the hind, positioning the head up hill. Then I wedged the shoulders and hips between some logs and rocks that were lying around.

I kneeled down beside the carcass, grabbed the sex organ, and, with a decisive swipe of the knife, liberated it, tossing it into the undergrowth for the goannas.

Gripping the knife, I made a short cut at the pelvic bone, then a long, shallow incision from between the back legs, running the blade up the chest and the neck to the jawbone. It was a satisfying cut. I heard the beating of wings and looked up at the branches above me.

A raven had come to watch.

I peeled the skin back from my incision. Then, making sure I didn't slit the intestines and the stomach, I made a second cut, into the muscle this time, turning the blade upwards, feeling the release. As the knife made its bloody journey up the belly, I pulled the muscle away from the organs with my free hand. It was a precision manoeuvre. I didn't want the meat spoiled. I especially didn't want to inhale the putrid stench of rotting grass and body fluids.

As it was, the heat of the fresh kill rose, and with it I breathed in the sharp metallic odour of its blood.

I set down the knife, took out my small hand saw and cut through the breast bone. With the rib cage open, I cut around the anus, tying it off quickly. I did the same with the windpipe and oesophagus, reaching in as far up the neck as I could, putting down the knife, grabbing and pulling down hard to set the windpipe free.

The motions were automatic, habitual, and I dressed the hind fast. I'd been doing the same for so long, I felt nothing.

I glanced up. The raven cocked its head.

Next, I removed the props, turned the hind on its side and cut through the diaphragm, repeating the process on the other side. Then, with the hind on its back, I reached in, finding purchase in the warmth, tugging. The guts slithered out in one lump.

I deposited the whole bloody mess in a sack, taking care to keep the bladder intact. One aroma masked another, and there was nothing as good as hind urine. A quick pick at the remaining bits of fascia and fat, a douse from the water bottle and the cavity was clean.

There wasn't much of a downhill slope, but it would do. I pulled the hind around to where the decline was steepest and cut off the head.

I was sick of seeing it. Always, when I field dressed a deer, I was sick of seeing the head. It wasn't the eye that stared or the lifeless way the head hung that bothered me. It was the inevitability of the decapitation itself.

With the head freed from the torso I was faced with depositing it in a sack. In that moment, as I took the head by the ears and shook open the sack to drop it in, an image of my stepfather's head lying in a bucket flashed into my mind, and it felt as though I was putting into that sack not a deer's head, but Howard Potter's.

The job done, I rolled the hind onto its back, propped its rear on a rock and spread the back legs. I reached for the saw. When the blade found the pelvis seam, I pressed down firmly and felt the crack. I grabbed a few rocks lying around to hold open the chest cavity and speed up the cooling.

The carcass could lie there losing its blood while I had a rest.

The raven sat, waiting. I ignored it. With me so close to my kill, the bird wouldn't bother it. I closed my eyes, enjoying the warmth of the morning sun on my skin.

About twenty minutes of blissful quiet passed. It was too early for flies.

Then I heard a vehicle heading up the mountain. As it neared, I wondered if it was the same vehicle that had been driving around the night before. The engine idled, then cut out. Couldn't have been more than a few hundred metres from away. I guessed he'd parked on the highway. There was a layby at the apex of a sweeping bend. In years gone by, it was used by logging trucks, and an old timber track led off and forked a few times. One of those forks led up to mine. Even so, I didn't expect whoever it was to head up my way. I listened. Couldn't hear a crack.

Minutes passed and not a sound.

I decided if the driver was wandering about down there, I wouldn't have heard him up where I was. But he was still out there. The vehicle hadn't started up again.

I let the minutes pass before I could wait no longer. The hind needed proper hanging and skinning and that needed to be done in the next hour.

She would have been around thirty kilos. I bagged her up and took my kill and my tools with me, leaving the trap unset and a bloody patch for the raven to pick over. With the carcass slung over one shoulder and the other two sacks weighing down the other, I didn't have a free hand.

Fifty metres from my shack, I smelled him. He was upwind with his back to me, squatting on his haunches with his trousers round his ankles, releasing his bowels. His arse was pink and pretty and what came out of it was long and hard and rank. The man had a broad back. I took in the mullet, trailing down between his shoulders.

I stood, watching. I felt the weight on my back shifting and took a step sideways for balance. My foot crunched on a patch of leaf litter. Mullet man stood up abruptly and pulled up his pants. He turned. The look of alarm in his face gave me the upper hand, but it was a look that faded into something else at the sight of me.

Malice. A glint in the eye. He saw me as prey.

I held his gaze. The feeling was mutual.

'You're shitting on my property, mate,' I said, putting the growl in my voice.

He didn't move. He was young, no more than twenty, cocksure.

He had a large face with mean features, most notable his dark, deep set eyes.

I set down the meat sacks and stepped forward. 'Get the fuck out of here.'

He took one look at my blood encrusted hand poised over my knife belt and said, 'Take it easy, mate.' But still, he didn't move.

My hand gripped the knife handle. 'I said, clear off.'

'Jeez.' He edged away.

But I knew he'd be back. Something about the swagger in his walk, the way he turned around to face me when he'd put a decent distance between us, the way he stood and stared as if to give me the message. I held his gaze thinking of his soiled arse.

I had no idea if he'd already found my shack, but if he'd got close, he'd have heard the generator. I waited a good five minutes beside his shit watching the flies zoom in for a feed, before I loaded the sacks on my back and headed home to skin and butcher my kill.

I hadn't reached the shed when I heard that engine of his revving as he headed back down the mountain.

CHAPTER SEVEN

PEARL

A sea mist had settled in overnight. The early morning battled its way through, turning the mist a pale silver, making it whirl and rise. I went and stoked the embers in the wood stove and fed Sam some of Frankie's deer offal. While Sam snuffled about in her bowl and I waited for the kettle to boil for a brew, I returned to the window and looked out through the mist at the shack across the road with its drawn curtains, and the car out front, an old blue sedan.

Nothing moved.

The kettle sang and I made my cuppa, taking it with me to my post at the window.

Still nothing.

I stood there, nursing my mouth ulcer, sipping my tea until the cup was drained.

Reluctantly, I peeled myself away and had a wash in the bathroom out the back. When I looked again the car outside the shack was gone. I rushed outside. He must have just left, and at speed, judging by the scream of the engine fading out in the distance.

I hadn't been inside old Fred's for months. The last time I cleaned the place up for him after some visitors, I swore to myself I'd never do it again; they'd left the shack in a right filthy state. The places they'd managed to smear tomato sauce beggared belief. Heaven only knew what they'd been doing with it. I scrubbed and scrubbed for hours and charged Fred an extra tenner for my trouble, after having to make a trip into town for more Gumption and a packet of scourers. Still, working for Fred put much needed cash in my pocket, so I wasn't complaining.

I didn't hang about. Curiosity had the better of me, and I was across that road as fast as a stalking cat going in for the kill, and on past the native grasses flattened by that man's car.

I tried the front door, but it was locked as I'd anticipated. I paused, listening, wondering if I should risk it. Assuming he was planning to return, then he'd be heading into town to the shops for provisions, and if that was true, it would take him well over an hour. He didn't know the road so it would take him even longer, despite the tearing hurry he seemed to be in. Those kiddies would slow him down too. Then again, he'd no doubt leave them in the car. Whatever the case, I figured I had at least a good half an hour for a prowl.

I went around the back and over to the septic tank. There, I up ended the old flower pot where Fred hid the spare key. He reckoned no one would ever find the key in that mould encrusted pot which had the look of something left out and never moved for decades. I was in the house a second later, the fly screen creaking shut behind me.

The interior was dim, the curtains closed, and the place smelled of stale tobacco and rat's piss. Fred's always smelled of rats. Fred was right not to allow kids. His place was only fit for fishermen.

There was nothing to see in the kitchen. The benches were

clear and the table in the centre of the room devoid of contents save for a vase of plastic flowers on a lace doily in the centre. I'd found that vase and the flowers at the junk stall at the Sunday market one time and bought it for fifty cents hoping to titivate the place.

The floorboards groaned beneath my tread. A wide hall ended at the front door, with the living room off to the side. A narrower hall off to my left led to the bedrooms. I went left.

The first bedroom at the front of the house contained a dishevelled mess of men's clothing spewing out a large holdall. The double bed had been slept in, the covers down, pillows askew. A similar scene confronted me in the second bedroom, the bed slept in, a suitcase opened on the floor. The end room hadn't been used. The window faced the back yard. Suspecting this had been the point of entry I went and checked. Sure enough, he'd forced open the window. That banging must have been him hammering a screwdriver to prise the latch. I went back to the second bedroom, eyed the little pink dresses, the undies and vests scattered about.

Girls.

And they would be coming back.

I went on down the hall.

They'd made full use of the living room. Takeaway hamburger wrappers and bottles of soft drink cluttered the coffee table. A blanket, taken from one of the bedrooms, lay crumpled at the end of the couch. A bottle of whisky, proudly half empty, occupied the shelf above the fireplace. I noticed an empty tumbler on the sideboard.

I went to the window, parted the curtains and looked over at my place, with my beat-up old Holden parked in the carport at the side. Did he know I was there?

I'd have to make his acquaintance and soon. Better not make it here though. I went to the kitchen, where I poked about in the cupboards. All looked as I'd left it. Satisfied I'd done enough snooping, I went outside. I was about to return the key to the flower pot, then decided to hold onto it for safe keeping. Fred wouldn't be coming down for at least a couple of months —the winter was his time at Peachtree, when the wildlife had settled down a bit—and a key would be handy in an emergency.

I heard his car in the distance when I was enjoying a second cuppa back on my front deck. I hurried inside and told Sam to hush.

A ruse was needed for my introductory visit and stoking the wood stove I came up with the idea. Cookies. What child can resist a homemade cookie? Especially chocolate and just out the oven.

I never considered myself a brilliant cook, but I was a dab hand at making biscuits. It was all in the dough and having an oven at the right temperature. I had the ingredients lined up on the bench by the time his car pulled up.

I eyed him through the net curtains, confident I couldn't be seen. Even so, when he looked around, I took a step back into the room.

He disappeared down the side of Fred's and before long he opened the front door and those kiddies were scampering inside. He came out and loaded up his arms with bags of groceries.

Sam bristled on the slam of the car boot. I cautioned her with a hiss. Not yet. I wanted my appearance on his doorstep to come as a shock. Besides, it was too early for cookies. Those girls needed to settle for a bit, play, then get bored and play up. Elevenses could be counted on to be the time when kiddies played up. I set to work on the cookie dough, an ear cocked just like Sam's, alert.

It was my grandmother's recipe: flour, butter, sugar, cocoa, vanilla, salt and a pinch of cinnamon to round out the flavours.

Grandma was my mother's mother. Alison was her name, and what she knew about herbs could have filled a book. I was the only one in the family to take an interest in her cooking, so she showed me a thing or two, glad of the company. Every Saturday afternoon, when the others were out doing their sports, I would go around to her cottage, situated down a lane not far from the farm. She even left me her recipe books when she passed. They were battered and stained, and I wasn't to look at another recipe book my whole life.

I lost myself in the kneading, the rolling, the cutting, the baking, but when the cookies were at last cooling on a wire tray, I took up my sentry by the kitchen window.

No movement.

No sound.

I didn't expect there to be, although the mist was long gone, the day now sunny and warm. With all the curtains still drawn at Fred's there was no telling what was going on over there. Those closed curtains made me suspicious. No one up and about keeps their curtains closed on the day unless they have something to hide. It couldn't be that he was pretending no one was there, what with his car parked out front. No. He was hiding something. He didn't want anyone looking in and seeing what he was up to.

What was that, exactly?

Those poor little kiddies.

The wretches had looked furtive, scared even, when they'd hurried to the front door. I was sure of it.

I moved away and stroked Sam, dozing on her rug by the stove.

With the ulcer still throbbing at the back of my tongue, I wasn't game to sample my baking. I loaded one of my best small plates with all cookies and covered them with a pretty lace doily.

Walking across with my offering, I felt furtive more than frightened. I was at Fred's front door as fast as my plate of biscuits would allow.

Before I knocked, I waited, ears pricked. I expected light footsteps running, a giggle, a squeal, but there was nothing. When I did bang my knuckles on the door, the footsteps were heavy, the voice a low growl, and the door opened only a crack. There he leaned, what I could see of him, as most of him was still hidden by the door.

'Sorry to trouble you,' I said, all breezy as you may, 'but I saw you arrive, so I baked some cookies for the girls.'

I paused.

He made no movement to open the door wider.

I raised my voice. 'They do like chocolate cookies, surely they do.

Yummy chocolate.'

I made a show of trying to glance behind him.

He didn't speak.

I wasn't about to be put off, so there we both stood wary eyed, each waiting for the other to make a move.

'Cookies!' I called.

Then one of the girls emitted a loud screech and came bounding to the door.

Defeated, the man turned to attend to the child. I stepped forward, pushed open the door and walked in, following them to the kitchen.

The child stood behind the man, and the other girl came in and hovered shyly by the door. They had to be his. They had the same hair and features.

He had a compact face, the eyes, nose and mouth bunched together in the middle. His hair was dark, voluminous and scruffy, with a fringe that hung down his forehead. He had on casual city attire, not hardy enough for the bush. No one could have looked more out of place at Fred's.

'What brings you all the way out here?' I asked, setting the plate down on the table.

'The fishing,' he said quickly.

'Is that right? I said, infusing my voice with doubt. He was no fisherman.

He shrugged. 'As good a place as any,' he said, avoiding eye contact. It was hardly the statement of a fisherman.

'I would have thought the campsite up the road better suited to the kiddies. More space to run around.'

He didn't answer. Instead, he fixed his gaze on the cookie plate.

I made my face exude a warmth I did not feel. 'Girls, my name's Pearl. I live across the road and I have grandchildren just like you. So, I couldn't resist making you some cookies. How about that!'

The girls went all coy, each where she stood, one in the doorway, the other by the man.

'That your place, then?' he said.

I gave him a steely look. 'I do fish.'

'Must be good fishing.'

'How's Fred?'

That threw him.

'Fred?'

'Fred Terkowski. This is his shack. He knows you're here, I take it.'

'Tacker, you mean,' he said, using Fred's nickname. 'Of course, he knows we're here.'

I was suspicious. Only the locals used that name. In the city, Fred was known only as Mr Terkowski.

'And you are?'

'Brent.'

I didn't believe that either.

'Well, I'm Pearl, as I said.'

I received no invitation to sit down. I was offered no tea. I stood there with my hands resting on the back of a chair.

'Well, I better be off,' I said eventually. 'If, you need anything, just yell.'

I left the cookies on the table. I knew I'd be back to collect the plate.

CHAPTER EIGHT

EMILY

When the scar-faced man, Pete, came in, looking bizarre decked out all in black with his multi-coloured beanie, Joan Baez had just stopped nah nah nahing. I had my rag in my hand, a rag masquerading as a dish cloth. It was thick and grey and frayed. I would use the rag-cloth as pretence, creating the impression of busy-ness lest Pat walked in and caught me idle and set up some other task. My rag of avoidance.

Pete hadn't seemed to notice me cleaning in a corner. He went straight to the counter where Pat was stocking the pie warmer. I was surprised to see him again so soon. He seemed less tired than yesterday when he'd alighted the bus, and I presumed his friend Simon who'd arrived late yesterday as we were closing and taken him to the lighthouse, had driven him back to town.

Curious, I inched closer and put the rag to work on some chair backs, on the seat pads too, and on the chrome frames. I overheard him place his order. Then Pat disappeared into the kitchen. I was about to approach Pete when through the window I saw that ill-humoured woman with the broken-down car struggle across the road laden with bags and a suitcase.

I didn't like her. She was frustrated, that was understandable, but she had an officious manner which I found off-putting. She had to be some sort of bureaucrat. Someone who'd sat for decades in a swivel chair. Her body appeared truncated, the result of the shapeless thickness of her torso. I hoped when I aged that never happened to me. Her thin-featured face was square too, as if to reinforce my point. Even her hair was straight and cut short. Still, as I watched her disappear into the hotel, I knew my opinion of her didn't matter. She'd be gone in a week and I'd never see her again. She was insignificant, I decided.

I knew I ought not pay such close attention to older women, especially older women I didn't like, but I couldn't seem to help it. I was always reminded of my mother and the whole point of getting away from Oxford was to be surrounded by anyone but. Yet I saw her in almost every older woman I encountered.

Pat returned to take Pete's money.

'Won't be long,' she said.

He remained where he was, with his back to me.

A blue sedan approached the intersection from the south, did a U turn and pulled up in the street. A man got out and hurried into the general store. I was about to turn away when movement on the back seat caught my eye and a child's face appeared, pressed against the window. Long hair, so I guessed it was a girl. I had no idea if she could see me, but I gave her a little wave. She didn't wave back. Instead, her face disappeared, and I wondered at parents who left their children sitting in cars while they shopped. Anything could happen. They might overheat or open a door and wander into the path of an oncoming vehicle. Or worse. All alone like that, they could get abducted. It happened. I'd read about it in the newspapers. I wanted to run across the road and berate that man for being neglectful, but of course I couldn't act on the impulse. I'd have appeared hysterical for one thing, and Pat would have yelled at me for walking off the job and docked my wages. I watched, and before too long he came out of the store laden with groceries and they were off, back down the road from whence they came, heading for the coast.

Pete went and sat at the table by the door, the same table he'd occupied the day before. He had his back to me. Pat came out and set down before him a plate of pie and chips, with sauce of course, and before she headed off, she gave me one of her looks. I pushed in the chair I'd been wiping and made my way to the counter. Satisfied, she disappeared into the kitchen.

I wiped down the already clean pie warmer. I served a trickle of customers snacks, coffees and milkshakes. I moved out the way when Con came in stinking of petrol. Things soon quietened, and I watched Pete finish eating his pie.

It wasn't a pleasant sight. He dunked his chips into the pie's sloppy, tomato-sauce riddled interior, having decapitated the pie as he had the day before, eating out the middle, leaving the crust mostly untouched. I found his method distasteful and only when he set down his knife and fork and pushed the plate from him, did I go over.

'There you are,' he said, his facing lighting in a smile.

I've been here all this time, I thought, puzzled as to how he hadn't noticed me.

'Can I get you anything else?'

'Thank you, but no. Did you tell me your name? I can't recall.'

'Emily,' I said, thinking it an odd question to ask of a waitress, but he didn't say it in a cheesy chat up way.

'Emily,' he repeated reflectively.

There was nothing leery about him. It was as though my

name mattered to him, as though he was taking a genuine interest, as though he couldn't think of another way to strike up a conversation.

'How's the lighthouse?'

'It was dark when I arrived and barely light when I left, so I can't give you a definite answer.'

'I was surprised to see you in town again so soon.'

'I needed supplies. The keeper, my friend Simon I mean, decided to loan me his car.'

'Nice of him.'

'Convenient, more like. This way he doesn't have to leave it in town while he's away.' He frowned. 'Although, you are right. It is nice of him. I should try to be less cynical.'

I liked the way he considered his thoughts. I was reminded of the first time I thought of coming to Australia. I was in second year and we were reading *Kangaroo*. No one had cared for the novel. There was a lot of criticism of D. H. Lawrence and his casual indifference when

it came to getting his book published in first draft form. Many in the tutorial found it unreadable. I struggled through it, trying to argue that in publishing a first draft, Lawrence was making a comment on Australian culture, which was, in essence, transparently unpolished. That perception evaporated in the face of Pete after I absorbed the way he'd self-corrected. I decided then and there that the others in my tutorial group had been right in their summation of Lawrence. He was dismissive and cynical if not outright contemptuous of a land he knew nothing about.

'It's good you have a car,' I said warmly, steering my mind back to the conversation. 'If it means you can drive into town and partake of these fabulous pies.'

He laughed and winced all at once.

I glanced at the hollowed-out pie on his plate, then directed my gaze back to his face. He adjusted his beanie. Something in me reached out to him. I wasn't attracted to him in the romantic sense, but I found him endearing. It was his illness too, his recovery. I wanted to ask how he was feeling, but before I had a chance, he wanted to know if I was due a day off any time soon. I told him tomorrow and his face lit up.

'Would you like to visit the lighthouse? We could explore it together.'

'I'd love to,' I said without hesitation, reaching for his plate.

'Meet me at the corner at nine.' He indicated with a glance out the window.

'See you then,' I said, walking away.

I knew I'd been chatting too long. Any moment Pat would be docking my pay.

The man who owned the general store came in for his weak coffee and Kitchener bun, having left his ancient mother in charge for half an hour. It was his daily ritual. For Pat, Mr Bruce represented the sort of loyalty absent in the rest of the community. She went to a lot of trouble creating that Kitchener bun. Every few days she made a small batch of doughnut buns and cooked them in a small fryer and dunked them in a bowl of granulated sugar while they were still hot. Then she made the mock cream from butter, icing sugar and milk. She slit the buns, inserted a teaspoon of her own homemade jam and an enormous dollop of the cream and decorated the top with a dot of jam.

As I served Mr Bruce, Pete left the café.

I spent the rest of the morning with a spring in my step. My tawdry existence in that isolated town took on a rosy hue.

I had scarcely left the roadhouse since my arrival in Cann River. The bush imprisoned me too, the highways heading north and east and west, my pathways out of that place, were all but closed off to me in my penniless state. I could have hitched but I was far too scared to do that. There was the refrigerated van that made a regular run up and down the coast, but I didn't like the look of the driver. There were the travellers, the campers and caravaners; I could have secured a ride with one of them. I could have snuck out on the pretext of cleaning the toilets and pleaded my case. I could have chosen a woman. Someone homey. After all, I was a backpacker. I ought to have had more courage, but everyone knew backpackers were vulnerable in this strange land, and there was no one I could trust.

I knew I had to get out of Cann River, fast. Cassie, who worked at the hotel, kept telling me I should be off exploring the sunburnt country before I flew home. I wondered sometimes why she didn't leave too, but the place was ingrained in her. She had a market stall and she kept bees. She knew everything there was to know about the area, which was why I took her advice on every little thing. She came in to pay for petrol later that afternoon.

Con came in with her and told me the amount.

Once he'd gone back outside and I'd given Cassie her change, I told her about the lighthouse and Pete's invitation.

She looked at me strangely and said it was good that Pete was looking after the place because it would help to ward off vandals.

'All the way out there?' I said, incredulous. Even I knew the lighthouse was a long drive from the town.

'You'd be surprised who lurks in the bush.'

As if to prove her point, a ute roared into town from the north and screeched to a halt at the intersection.

CHAPTER NINE

MIRIAM

I lumbered through the hotel door and mounted the stairs with my things, reflecting on the vicissitudes of my life. A whole week in that rat hole of a town waiting for a spare part. The hotel manager, who was drying glasses behind the bar when I found her, had feigned surprise at the sight of my return and introduced herself as Cassie. She said I could have the same room, handing me the key, which was sitting on the counter as though in anticipation.

Halfway up the stairs, my thoughts returned to that waitress. I was surprised the owner of the roadhouse let her staff wear band T-shirts, even if the one that girl had on was black. It was tight as well, cupping her pert breasts as though she were bent on showing them off. She was too pretty for her own good. Perhaps that's how she got away with dressing like that. Should have been given a uniform.

I couldn't help judging her. Despite her beauty she was sullen, at least that was the manner she used on me. Another part of me had gone all protective too, and I was determined to crush it. I supposed it was instinct, after she reminded me so much of my cousin, although that thought came as a shock in itself since I'd never felt that way before. I wasn't the mothering type.

On the landing, the bundle in my left arm slid to the floor with a clatter. I let go of my suitcase, which landed with a thud, and gathered my belongings back in my arms. At the door to my room I had to set it all down again to wrestle with the key. Once inside, I dropped the lot and slammed the door behind me for good measure. It occurred to me the man in the adjoining room might have been resting—he'd certainly looked like he needed a very long rest when I'd seen him earlier—but in that moment, I didn't care. I paused, listening, but heard nothing. I decided he must have gone out. After all, I'd made enough noise to wake the dead.

I put the suitcase on my bed and sat beside it, thinking a change of clothes would help restore my humour, although I doubted it. I was still too furious with Con for his obstructive behaviour. I knew his type from work. Passive aggressive or incompetent, it was hard to fathom. I wanted to take him to task, tell him it was no way to run a business, but I knew if I did, I would sabotage my exit from that town. You have to be nice to people if you want them to do what you want. That amounted to all I learned during the decades working for the shire council. Bullying never worked, or at best it was hit and miss and created more damage than whatever it was designed to solve. I learned that too.

I reminded myself to keep my cool. Told myself it was no big deal. I'd telephone ahead. Let the agent know I was stuck.

I created a semblance of order out of my things, changed out of yesterday's outfit into comfortable slacks and a long-sleeved top, and went downstairs to locate the phone. Cassie was still behind the bar.

'There's a payphone up the street,' she told me, 'but since you're staying here you might as well use this.'

She lifted the phone onto the counter, an old-fashioned Bakelite affair, not the push button type I was used to at work. For the sake of discretion, a quality I much admired, she walked away and attended to matters at the other end of the bar. There was no one else in the room. Too early, I supposed.

Three rings and the agent picked up. There were his usual platitudes—beautiful weather, I couldn't have picked a better spot—and upon my summary of the situation he said he'd take care of everything. I put down the receiver and glanced over at the woman, who was staring at me. She came over.

'You'll be wanting tea later, then?'

'I can always grab something across the road if it's a bother.'

'No bother. I've some fresh veggies and a nice chook. What about lunch?'

I hesitated, thinking of the roadhouse.

'You'll be getting that in town,' she said, answering her own question. 'There's the general store and a bakery further down. They do a good sandwich.'

'It's very quiet,' I said, looking around.

She didn't respond.

'The town, I mean. Is it normally this quiet?'

'Summer's over, so yeah. Only get the reps passing through, pretty much.'

'What about that man in the room next to mine? Is he still around?'

'Sure is. Why? He isn't troubling you?'

'No. I thought I might have bothered him though, crashing and banging my way to my room with my things. But I think he's out.' 'He's in.'

'Really? But there wasn't a peep coming from his room.

Whereas last night I heard him shuffling and muttering to himself.'

'He's a night owl, that one. He'll be sleeping now, I bet.'

'Who is he? If you don't mind me asking.'

'I'm not meant to talk about the other patrons, you understand.' Giving me a sly look, she leaned forward against the bar. 'But I can tell you he's from your way. Arrived the night before you rolled in, so to speak. He was in a helluva state too. Traumatised. Had a haunted look about him. Between you and me, I think he was coming down off something. Not that I want to freak you out or anything.'

She was managing to do just that.

'How long's he staying?'

'No idea. He's been using the phone a fair bit.'

I recoiled inwardly and had to curb an impulse to wipe my ear. 'Maybe he's on the run.'

'I don't know about that,' she said.

I didn't know whether to believe her. Despite all she'd said, I sensed she wasn't giving me the full picture. I thought about asking for a different room but I didn't like to burden her with extra work. Besides, I didn't fancy lugging all my things somewhere else. What difference would it make in any event? We'd both still be up those stairs by ourselves.

I bid the woman a good day and left the hotel for a wander about the town, pointedly ignoring the roadhouse and crossing the road that headed north, which splayed wide open at the intersection. As I reached the middle, a car took the corner behind me. I crossed to the pavement on the other side and watched the car disappear. About fifty yards on, the flat stretch of bitumen gave way to dirt. Whorls of dust floated in the car's wake, drifting, destined to coat whatever residential properties might be up there. Didn't look like there was anything much to see so I went on my way.

If there was one word to sum up Cann River, it was desolation. Every stitch of the place looked run down and shabby. I was reminded, briefly, of Cockatoo, although before the fires, an atmosphere of growth, of optimism, of community had pervaded the town. There were three thousand residents, and Puffing Billy went right through, drawing day trippers from Melbourne. It wasn't too far from anywhere, not like Cann River.

I faced the facades of would be shop fronts, the premises standing empty, windows whitewashed to stop the curious from peering in. On that stretch, only the general store was a going concern. A man exited laden with groceries and made his way to his car, parked on the southern arm of the crossroads. He glanced over and saw me staring, looked daggers at me and even seemed to scowl. There was something about him I didn't like, but then again, I wasn't in the mood for liking anyone.

I decided to save the store for last and headed on. After a side street, the pavement gave way to a small park, the road, already wide, widening still further to accommodate parking. Across the highway was the church I'd seen the night before, occupying the corner of another side street.

The grassed area of the park was the size of a large house block and contained a few benches and some play equipment, scantily shaded by a smattering of small trees. I sat down on a bench angled at the sun and facing the toilet block on the corner. The lavatory building was gabled and high windowed and overshadowed by a stand of maples. A touch of civic pride, if somewhat incongruous with the surroundings, and I guessed the toilet block had been built with relative opulence and style in a prominent place to encourage those travelling by to make a stop.

I surveyed the park, my gaze drawn to the low roofed houses spread thinly along the far perimeter, then to the fringe of towering gum trees in the near distance, not liking the way they enclosed the town, reduced the depth of field. To me, a refugee from the fires, they made a strong statement, as if the town were there by their grace alone.

I was about to stand when movement caught my eye, and I saw a pair of feet poking out from the base of a tree over by the swing set and the buttocks of whoever it was protruding out the other side. A lad emerged. He headed towards me before shying away in favour of a route that took him round the back of the lavatories. He looked like he'd been sleeping rough and I didn't care for his mullet. Before long, the low grumble of a car engine broke the peace, the grumble intensifying to a steady roar on the lad's revs. I saw his Ford Falcon station wagon go by, heading west.

It was then that it occurred to me the town was a magnet for unsavoury men. Another uncharitable thought, but in less than eighteen hours I had encountered a ladle full. There was the baker-mechanic Con, who was surely genetically compromised; the man in the room next to mine, drug-crazed to say the least; the scar-faced man I'd seen in the roadhouse the day before, too pale and sunken for my comfort; the peculiar man who'd glared at me as he exited the general store, he was clearly up to no good; and now a hoon with a mullet pretending to hide behind trees.

A striking contrast to all those heroic men who'd saved the lives of us women and children in the fires, a contrast that left me feeling unprotected.

I had never been given to feeling vulnerable, but I'd read about isolated towns. They could be filled with inbred types or provide havens for weird cults and hideaways for criminals. True or not, that was how I felt about Cann River. After all, I'd seen *Deliverance*—who hadn't? —and getting stuck in the backwoods of Australia was no different in my book.

Ahead of me, there was the whole day to kill. I extracted from my bag my copy of *Frangipani Gardens*, looking forward to finding out more about Barbara Hanrahan's curious painter, Doll. Then a brace of boys barrelled into the park, all shouts and high-pitched squeals, followed half-heartedly by their mother. I pocketed my book and went on my way, passing by the toilet block to the highway.

I waited at the kerb, looking both ways to make certain nothing was coming before I crossed, as it was an uncommonly wide stretch of road. The judder of compression brakes followed by a loud hiss, and a shiny old Mack truck carrying a load of logs thundered through the town, emitting on its way past a stench of diesel exhaust. I thought of my small car in Con's garage, a city car ill-equipped for the country out this far, and I envied the driver of that Mack truck, shifting through the gears as it lumbered up the hill to the east.

Safely on the pavement on the other side of the highway, I noticed I was peckish and thought to try out the bakery.

The interior needed refurbishing, although I supposed the owner might have been striving, and failing, for retro '50s. Kitsch required style and whoever had furbished the bakery had none. I nearly tripped on the cracked linoleum on my way through in the door and had to fight past the bread rack stacked with sliced white to avoid colliding with a woman, wider than she was tall, leaving with a bag of buns.

The display at the counter was exactly as I'd anticipated: lamingtons, cupcakes, vanilla slices, iced biscuits, brownies and custard tarts. The pie warmer contained the usual array of pies —meat, steak and bacon, and chicken and veg—and sausage rolls. Egg and bacon rolls were cooked to order. Also on offer, sandwiches with a choice of fillings. Nothing took my fancy, but I couldn't leave without buying something, so I ordered a sausage roll and a vanilla slice, thinking that would keep me going until dinner time.

I handed the diminutive and nondescript assistant the correct money and left with my paper bags. I felt snobbish in my assessment, prejudiced even, but some people shrink in their own skin, hiding somewhere at the back of themselves. So much so that once I was out in the street, I couldn't decide if that assistant was male or female. All I knew was I felt no inclination to go back in to find out.

The sun ambled towards morning teatime, heating the air in that bowl of a landscape, the humidity rising with it. I considered returning to the hotel to put on something summery, then changed my mind and went over to the little church.

The building was a tiny affair of black weatherboards, sporadically windowed and capped with a high-pitched roof. Set near the side wall facing away from the highway, a park bench nestled in the shade of a silky oak. No play equipment in sight. I settled in my newfound sanctuary out of the sun and the heat, content to have a few magpies for company. Knowing I would not be molested by cavorting children, I re-opened my novel. I don't know what had possessed me to enter a charity shop in Belgrave last month and scour their bookshelves, but I was glad to have a little bit of Adelaide brought to life by Barbara Hanrahan. Not that *Frangipani Gardens* reminded me of anything crass like Kitchener buns. Heavens no! It was something about the menace to be found in beauty, the shadows that lurk within vibrant displays. Flowers rot. Nothing escapes it.

The descriptions were well lit, and the beauty so tremendous you could almost smell it.

There I was, seated in a dank spot in the shade, suffering the aromas of urine and cat spray mingled with a touch of pine, forced to remain in that wild, untameable part of the country, one riddled with suspect men, and I felt I'd found good companions in Doll and Girlie O'Brien.

I read all afternoon, wandering around the church grounds periodically to stretch my legs. I ate my sausage roll and then my vanilla slice. I must have dozed too. It was late in the afternoon when I returned to the hotel to find someone, probably Cassie, had put a television in my room, along with a rabbit ear antenna.

The reception wasn't that good but after a fair amount of ear adjustment I managed to watch Hey, Hey It's Saturday until dinner.

I'd been anticipating the chicken I'd been promised, but instead she'd done a lamb roast with all the trimmings. It was delicious.

I dragged my knife across my plate for the last of the gravy, thinking the day hadn't passed too badly, when I felt a draught on my back and that sorry excuse for a human who occupied the room next to mine ruined my gastronomic satisfaction.

A shadow entered the room along with his presence. He took up a seat at the next table and sat hunched over his plate. He had his back to me, for which I was grateful. I watched him for a while, the greasy lanky hair, the crumpled clothes, the acne boils on his neck. Then I'd had enough. I didn't wait to thank Cassie before heading upstairs.

As I passed the door to his room, curiosity caused me to stop. The door was closed but I tried the handle and it turned. With a quick thrust of my hand I pushed the door wide open. An odour of stale sweat greeted me. I blenched. I wasn't keen to enter. The curtains were drawn. I flicked on the light and saw, left out on the end of his bed, a syringe, a small metal bowl and an envelope of white paper. On the floor, a holdall lay open and I caught sight of a few suspicious looking packages, like those the police showed on television when they'd had a major drug haul.

I flicked off the light and closed the door. At least the drugs accounted for his nocturnal behaviour.

Inside my own room I found I was trembling.

I was cold, that was all.

I donned a cardigan.

My mind began to race. Refusing to panic, I tried to rationalise.

The man was no threat to me. That was the thought I tried to use to repel my other thoughts, thoughts of him breaking into my room to steal cash for his habit, although judging by the size of his stash, that was unlikely. Thoughts of him raping me, murdering me for no other reason than his drugged mind felt like it. Recalling his lifeless, wretched face I doubted he had either the inclination or the strength. Even so, I had no idea how I'd sleep knowing he would be awake all night in the next room, a wall's separation away. A wall so thin you could put a fist through it.

I went to the window. Con was closing the roadhouse. That hoon's Ford Falcon station wagon drove by and headed up the road to the north. Minutes passed. Then another car drove through the town, slowing at the crossroads and pulling up at the roadhouse bowsers. A man got out. If I wasn't mistaken it was scar face. He was arguing with Con on the forecourt and then Con marched off inside, his left foot kicking out sideways as he went. Before long, that young waitress came out and approached the man. They talked. Then she went inside and returned wearing a thin summer jacket and carrying a small bag. She got in the man's car.

Stupid wench!

I left the window and switched on the television knowing I was in for another sleepless night.

CHAPTER TEN

FRANKIE

Meditation takes many forms. Butchery is one of them. A slow, methodical process of cutting. It's ritualistic. I'd executed the process so many times my mind was lulled by it. I enjoyed the precision, the artistry, and I was good at it. Which was why, whenever I radioed ahead to Rick, my friend with the refrigerated truck, he would agree to make the detour up to mine without hesitation.

That morning's kill, skinned and quartered, was ageing in the fridge, taking the place of the buck I'd shot the week before. He was laid out on the bench in neat portions, the offcuts in a bucket ready to take down to the roadhouse for Con's pies.

The lumbering chug of Rick's truck was unmistakable, even at a distance, the slowing as he made the turn off the main road, the intermittent revving as he went through the gears on his way up the track.

He pulled up in the turning circle outside the butchering shed, reversing as close as he could. I leaned against the shed wall, waiting for him to alight and open the rear of his truck.

He left the engine running.

He was a small, spritely man. As he approached, that bounce in his step gave the impression of someone younger in years. With his engaging smile and the smooth, persuasive tone in his voice, he had the manner of a sales assistant in a furniture store. Beneath that slight veneer lurked a body of solid brawn, and he wasted no time adding my load to his truck.

I gave him a hand. It was a small Fallow deer and there was a lot of it.

'He's a big one,' I said.

As if prompted, Rick reached in his back pocket and handed me a fifty.

'Bet you're pleased to see a bit rain,' he said, closing up the truck. 'I've had a visitor,' I said, making conversation.

He laughed.

'Not Con?'

'Con never comes here. Someone else. A road rat with a mullet. I caught him having a shit.'

I expected him to laugh again, but he didn't.

'You seen his car?'

'Must have parked it on the highway.'

His faced darkened. 'Frankie, I take it you haven't been listening to the radio.'

'I like my quiet.'

'You should pay more attention, living out here by yourself. You should get a dog.'

'I don't need a dog. You gonna tell me what you know?'

'Some wastrel by the name of Wayne Conway's out on bail for armed robbery. He failed to appear in court so there's a warrant out for his arrest. They shouldn't let vermin like him out on bail. This country's too soft.'

'Reckon they should bring back the death penalty, do you Rick?'

'Something like that. My mate John who works in remand

reckons Wayne was just the driver and they didn't think he'd abscond on account of his mother. She's crook, apparently. Then the cops wanted to lay more charges and that's when the story broke. He's wanted for rape, which soon became murder when the girl died in hospital from the assault. Jeez, you really need to tune in more, Frankie. I can't believe you've missed all this.'

I shrugged. 'Yeah, well, it probably isn't him.'

'There was a photo of him in the paper. Cocksure guy with a mullet.'

'Half the country's youth has a mullet,' I said, thinking of my own.

'Frankie, you really...' He stopped mid-flow as something occurred to him. He rushed off and came back moments later holding a newspaper. He riffled through the pages, and folded it open, pointing.

I was staring at my shitter in the woods.

Rick knew I could look after myself and I didn't care for his lecture. That scum, Wayne Conway, would be looking out for another victim, not a hunter, a predator, another killer like him. Besides, I knew I'd scared the shit out of him that morning.

I also sensed he'd be back.

Determined not to give the situation another thought, I waved Rick off and pocketed the cash, looking forward to an afternoon scraping every morsel of fat and flesh off that buck's hide and rubbing in the salt. Then there were the other hides in my hide tanning production line, and I thought later on I might stitch myself some moccasins for winter.

Not a day passed when I didn't reflect on my perfect way of life, one carved out for me when my mother died and left me with a house full of tat, an empty bank account and a pile of long overdue bills. By then, thanks to the friends I hung out with in the city, I knew all about taking off and hiding in the bush, somewhere the debt collectors would never venture.

After the cremation, I tossed her ashes, urn and all, into the Sydney Harbour, and let the ocean deal with the memories. I couldn't. She'd left me too young, and it had all been so sudden, although excruciatingly slow for her—the way folk were forced to live by the medical profession was astonishing—and I'd wanted to put as much space between my future and a past riven with her bruises and delirium.

Sometimes real life wasn't worth facing.

On my way back to the shack, I narrowly missed treading on a death adder that had curled itself in a nice tight ball and looked like a stripy knitted sock.

CHAPTER ELEVEN

PEARL

I'd have to drive into town to phone Fred. There was no phone line out at Peachtree. It was part of the attraction of the place. And since it was Saturday there was no point in calling. Fred was never in on a Saturday.

It was noon by the time I'd cleaned up the kitchen after the cookie baking, fed the chooks and harvested the day's pick of veggies. I felt restless, aware of that man who called himself Brent and the two girls across the street. I couldn't peer out of the window all day. It was giving me a headache.

The day was warm and still and the sun had a bit of bite to it. Thinking a spot of fishing would calm me down, I packed a sandwich for afternoon tea and fetched the spin rod. The waters were cooling, the flathead slowing down and the bream yet to start schooling. I was guaranteed a nice tailor. I took along a couple of Sguidgy Bloodworm wrigglers for the bream in case I got lucky, and some wire trace for the toothy tailor.

I had the small jetty at Peachtree all to myself. My little rowing boat which I kept tied near the riverbank rocked gently back and forth in the tannin stained waters of the river. I eased myself in with my rod, backpack and bucket, and untied the mooring. Enjoying the motion, I let the boat drift before unfastening the oars and rowing downstream.

The rowing was effortless, the river soon opening out into Tamboon inlet. Other than the pelicans, the lagoon was empty. All summer I'd suffered the competition, locals and recreational fishermen from all over, visiting for the easy pickings. They were greedy buggers too, always catching more than anyone could eat, killing for the sake of it, killing the big bream, the breeders, forty-year-old fish that should be left for the spawning.

I liked to fish the flats. Casting, dragging the lure on the silty bottom two metres below, keeping a slow roll going, putting in a couple of slight twitches every few seconds, it was slow, rhythmic, meditative. The bream generally took the bite on my twitch and that day was no exception. The first few catches were small and I threw them back, but as the afternoon ticked by, I caught a bigger one. I unhooked his mouth, slapped his head against the side of the boat and tossed him in my bucket.

Satisfied, I stopped the slow roll and held the rod loosely in my grip. The soft laps against the boat soothed me and after I'd eaten my sandwich, I went all dozy in the sunshine.

My gaze settled on the tangle of bush embracing the shore. I saw a kookaburra perched on the high branch of a tree. I admired its proud beak, its plumage. Then something occurred to me and I was alert in a flash.

Brent was a liar and a quick witted one at that. On the community noticeboard outside the general store was a poster advertising Fred's shack. He'd put it there last year, hoping to catch passing trade. No one came. I couldn't understand why he hadn't stuck up a photo of the inlet and a fishing rod, but regular fishermen were not the types to pay Fred's rates. Instead of an idyllic scene, he'd provided a grim, black and white photo of his shack. The day he'd taken the shot, the skies were closing in. The photo made the setting appear more desolate than it was, his mud map daunting to all but the most intrepid. He'd got the scale wrong. If he'd set out to put people off, he couldn't have done a better job. He'd given his phone number in the city and a name: Tacker's shack. That must have been where Brent got the name from and the location. Unlike the regular tourist, the place would have suited him fine.

I felt tension on the line, gripped the rod and started reeling. It was a flathead. The afternoon's relaxation broken, I left it thrashing about in the bucket with the bream and rowed back to the jetty, feeling the pull of the water this time, as the river emptied out into the lagoon.

Back at my place, I washed, scaled, gutted and filleted the bream and the flathead, and by dusk it was all frying in the skillet with a touch of garlic and rosemary. While I waited, I pulled aside the net curtain to get a better view of Fred's. I no longer cared if that man who called himself Brent could see me. I let Sam out the front too, to have a good sniff about. Let that guy know I'm not vulnerable, unprotected.

I ate slowly, taking small bites and keeping the contents of my mouth to the ulcer-free side. There was no avoiding the pain on every swallow, but the fish was superb, as ever it was. With my belly full, I spent some time sharpening my filleting knife on a whetstone, taking pride, enjoying the long, measured strokes, the sharp, gravelly sound. It was the sharpest knife I owned; bone handled, my grandmother's knife, my pride. Once I was satisfied it could split a hair, I wrapped it in its special blue cloth and put it back in the drawer away from the other knives.

Another glance out the window and I saw that Sam had found something. He was standing at the base of a large gum tree over at Fred's, looking up, tail not wagging. That was no bird. I went out to the front deck. At first, I didn't see it, they disguise themselves so well, and it was only after I stepped off my deck and walked round to line up my sight with Sam's that I saw what it was: The largest goanna I'd ever clapped eyes on.

Damn thing would be after my chickens. That was my first thought. I don't know why I kept chickens. They were such hard things to keep alive. Snakes, foxes, eagles and bloody goannas, everything was attracted to them. I thought of getting my rifle, just to give the beast a fright, but I didn't want to scare the kiddies.

I thought the lizard might move on overnight, but I'd keep my eye out. I called to Sam and called to her again, and eventually she came trotting back.

There was no movement that I could see over at Fred's. Not a flicker of light shining through the cracks in the curtains. I ushered Sam inside, poured myself a whisky and waited.

The moon was up before I tried the short wave.

I didn't use it much, preferring not to hear the gossip coming through all that crackle and hiss.

There was no response. I tried a few times over the course of half an hour before I gave up, deciding Frankie wasn't around.

I listened to a couple of other channels. There was a lot of talk among the truckies about some hoon out on bail who'd failed to appear and there was a warrant out for his arrest. A person of interest in a rape and murder case, apparently. Along with the discussion, came complaints about the justice system and I soon lost interest in the whinging. Since when had the justice system ever been fair or perfect? Our judges were too soft, and the cops were useless or corrupt. Everyone knew it. The result was men like Brent got to do whatever they liked.

No consequences.

There had to be consequences.

I switched off the radio and went back to my chair by the fire.

CHAPTER TWELVE

EMILY

The sky-blue walls of my cuboid room were an insult to my imagination, the paint colour mocking my freedom, the blue skies I craved. I lay on my bed, reflecting on the injustices that had befallen me through the course of that day.

I'd suffered a run of stroppy customers, all of them wanting the steak pie we rarely had. Their poor attitude had left me feeling ragged. Pat ran the roadhouse with quiet tyranny, never letting me out of her sight, always criticising under her breath. I could never measure up to her exacting, if fluid, as-the-fancy-took-her standards. Then there was Con. Whenever he came in for a customer's change, it was as much as I could do not to bolt for the toilets with my rag-cloth. Con wasn't properly adjusted somehow. It was more than just his hand washing. I couldn't work out what was wrong with him other than that he was not that intelligent. Something that should be there was missing in him and what remained was muted, shut down. He only had the pilot light on.

I scratched an itch on my scalp, thinking about how I would

while away the hours before sleep, when I heard his voice calling out my name.

I sat up, senses alert.

'Hey, Em,' he said again, this time outside my bedroom door.

'Yeah?' I said, wary.

'Someone here for you.'

I went through to the cafeteria and on outside to find Pete leaning against a bowser. His friend's car was parked in the bay behind him.

Beneath his beanie, his face came alive when he saw me. He shuffled forward.

'Want to come out to Point Hicks tonight?'

I hesitated, glancing at Con who was looking down at his feet. I thought Pat would bustle outside to discover the goings on, but she didn't appear.

'I was in town,' Pete said casually. 'I thought, no harm in asking.'

I held his gaze, grinning. 'Wait just one second.'

I wasted no time collecting my jacket and stuffing a few things in a small canvas bag. We were off heading south into the forest before sanity kicked in and I mused over what had possessed me to be so spontaneous, so reckless. Then again, I'd been cooped up in that roadhouse for so long it felt natural to want to cut loose. Besides, with Pete, even though I hardly knew him, I felt I could be myself. He had Joy Division playing on the car stereo, as if that confirmed it.

As Ian Curtis pleaded with his girlfriend not to walk away in silence, the forest, all contorted and dark limbed, stampeded towards us and hurtled by and it felt like the car was doing the cleaving.

At the bends, Pete slowed, and the bright lamp eyes of wildlife watched at the roadside. On and on we went, on first one rutted and pot holed track and then another. It was disorienting. It occurred to me if anything untoward happened, I'd never find my way back.

Joy Division kept playing. When one album ended another began.

'I had no idea it was so far,' I said, raising my voice above the music.

'Seems further in the dark. I have to take it slow round the bends. You never know what might be lurking on the other side. But even in daylight it takes over an hour.'

His remark reinforced a sense of togetherness, just me and him in the car and all that nature in the black beyond.

When he wrote *Kangaroo*, did Lawrence have any idea at all of the scale of Australia, the overwhelming vastness of the bush? I know my parents hadn't before I came here. I recalled showing them where I planned to visit, starting in Sydney and working my way down to Melbourne, and my mother had pointed at the top of the map, over by Darwin and said, what about here, or there? And I had to explain that it would be like a day trip to Siberia.

Accustomed to the pocket handkerchief that was England, I found the emptiness of the country oppressive. I was used to there being a village over every rise. I couldn't say I liked Australia. I wanted to. I wanted to appreciate it, understand it, acclimatise, but I felt too in awe, too alienated and exposed and trapped by it all at once.

'What do you do in Sydney?' I asked when the second album came to an end.

'For work? Sound engineer.'

'Interesting.'

'It was.'

'Will you go back to something else, then?'

'That's the plan. How about you?'

'I read English at Oxford.' It sounded so pretentious and irrelevant.

'And the future?'

'My parents want me to teach.'

'Boring.'

'I know, but what else do you do with an English literature degree.'

'Write.'

Write? I couldn't take his suggestion seriously. Not least because it seemed like awfully hard work.

Pete didn't put on more music, yet he seemed disinclined to say more. His eyes never left the road.

I thought about how Lawrence had slapped down his Australian novel and sent it to his publisher in its raw first draft from. How arrogant that was. How presumptuous. Then I considered Iris Murdoch and Penelope Lively, both Oxford-based acquaintances of my mother, and how I'd never measure up to their talent and insight. You need experience to be a writer and so far, I'd had none.

'What do you make of Australia?' Pete said. 'Seen much of the place?'

'Only Sydney. Then I made my way south, stopping off here and there. It's a stunning coastline. So many beaches and the sapphire ocean.'

The ocean leant perspective. Tucked inside dense forest, all that was lost. I felt foregrounded. In anticipation, I waited for the land to open up to the sea.

We crossed a low wooden bridge and wended our way for about a mile, then we passed through a low gate and he stopped the car.

'Open your window,' he said and as I did, I could smell the sea and hear the waves breaking on the shore. He got out and shut the gate behind us.

The track was narrow, just a car width, and although I couldn't see the coastline for the coastal scrub and small trees, I felt it there. The track climbed a steep rise, levelling out and snaking its way on, and at every corner I expected to see a clearing and some buildings, but there was more road. Then we rounded a bend and I saw a bright light flash up ahead. We'd arrived.

We passed a few old sheds laid out in a clearing and went past the back of a cottage, entering a short driveway flanked by high dry-stone walls. On the other side of the wall beside me I saw the outline of another cottage.

When I opened the car door, I was greeted by the crash and rush of waves breaking on the rocks. It was unexpected. Although I knew the ocean was close, the day had been still, windless.

'Swell's up,' Pete said, as though reading my mind.

My eyes adjusted to the dark. The lighthouse towered, not ten feet away, a tall white cylinder, thicker at the base, the intermittent flashing of its light illuming the promontory and the ocean beyond.

I rounded the front of the car and followed the path of light cast by Pete's torch. We went down through a gap in the wall and across a small concreted area to the front door of a flat-roofed, corrugated iron shack.

Inside, a small kitchen opened into a cramped living area. A door at the end presumably led to a bedroom. The strike of a match and Pete went around lighting candles.

The place took on a warm hue, but I felt unsettled. The bungalow was low ceilinged and dingy. I looked around at the shabbily furnished room with no idea why anyone would want to stay there.

'Is there a reason why you aren't staying in the one of those cottages?'

'Simon is doing them up.'

'You are out here all alone, then.'

'That I am.'

Apprehension stirred at the edges of my mind. I wanted to look at my watch, see how long the journey had really taken, plot my escape should I need to make one, but I sat there, trapped. When I left the roadhouse, I had some ill-informed notion there would be a village, a hamlet, even a few farms nearby, but there was nothing at all. I'd not seen one single dwelling between Cann River and Point Hicks.

'Visitors do come and stay out here though,' I said.

'The last lot left a month ago. Not expecting anyone else.'

'I can't think why anyone would want to holiday in such a remote place.'

He laughed. 'You don't like remote?'

'All I've seen is endless forest.'

'That's because you haven't left the highway. UNESCO declared this area a biosphere reserve in 1977. You are in one of the world's most significant natural environments. Alpine rivers tumble to the ocean. The beaches are wild and go on forever. There are lagoons, massive sand dunes, amazing rock formations and as for the wildlife, it's rich out here, rich.' I must have looked agog, for he said, 'You really need to get out of that roadhouse more often.'

'Don't you get lonely?'

'I have the birds for company. The ocean, the wind, the whales and the dolphins.'

'But it's so primitive,' I said, gesturing at the candles.

'There's no shortage of supplies. The lighthouse is powered by electricity, but the cottages and this bungalow are yet to be re-connected. All part of the renovations. Anyway, there are tons of candles.'

'What about if something happens. I mean, if the car breaks down. I don't know, a catastrophe. Anything.'

'Relax. Regarding the car, there's an old and reliable diesel station wagon in one of the sheds. And Simon has a short-wave radio for emergencies. You see, remote and isolated it might be, but not entirely cut off from civilisation.'

'Where's the loo?'

'Outside. There's a door to the left.' He handed me a candle and a box of matches. 'The wind will blow it out.'

He was right. I hadn't even stepped outside the door when I was thrust into darkness.

The bathroom was tacked on the side of the bungalow. I groped my way to the door.

Inside, the bathroom smelled of disinfectant. I relit the candle and saw it was basic. There was no lock on the door.

I exited on a sudden blast of wind that had whipped round the side of the lighthouse and on down the path past the bungalow, funnelled by the high stone wall. The gust reinforcing the inhospitable atmosphere of the place. I went back and joined Pete, reminding myself that lighthouses were, by definition, situated in isolated places beside treacherous waters. What else had I expected?

Seated on the couch, I allowed myself to be comforted by Pete's presence, his engaging smile. He seemed eager to please, to make me feel at home, comfortable and safe. Music played softly in the background. Jazz this time.

'Batteries,' he said, following my gaze to the transistor radio. 'It's why I was in town this afternoon. I'd forgotten to buy batteries.' A voice cut in at the end of the song. Over it, Pete said, 'Wine?'

He pulled back the curtain that hid the shelves beneath the sink. A few bottles of wine were lined up alongside a cask and a bottle of whisky. He opened a bottle of red and poured two large glasses. He handed one to me before returning to his own at the table and taking up one of the wooden chairs.

I took a long sip of the wine and sank back into the couch, glass in hand, allowing myself to feel the liberation from the roadhouse that Point Hicks afforded. Pete watched me. There was nothing in his manner to make me suspect he desired me. Then he started talking. He was casual, engaging, funny, coming up with yarns about his brother, explaining how he knew the lighthouse keeper, Simon—an old school friend. On and on he chatted. He told me Simon had come into an inheritance and it had been himself who'd encouraged Simon to renovate the keeper's cottages.

'You're meant to be convalescing,' I said with sudden concern, wondering if he would ever remove that beanie. 'Isn't it hard to keep the lighthouse?'

'There's nothing to do except flick a switch.'

'Really?'

'For two weeks, anyway. He's got it all sorted.'

Pete seemed evasive, or perhaps distracted. We'd come to the end of the wine. He yawned.

'You can have my bed if you like.'

'I'm fine where I am,' I said, keen to stay put. I didn't want to sleep in a sick man's bed and besides, the couch was closer to the front door.

He went through to his bedroom and returned with a couple of blankets. I made up my bed as he went about blowing out the candles. He bid me goodnight, switched off the radio and left the room, taking the last lit candle with him.

Alone in the quiet, the roar of the ocean felt close. The lighthouse light brightened the thin curtains intermittently. The raw force of the setting crowded in on me and it took me a long time to get to sleep.

When I woke, my neck was stiff.

I threw off the blankets, slipped on my shoes and tiptoed to the sink. I filled a glass from the water pitcher, drank it down and went outside.

The air was cool and still. The ocean had settled and was no longer a roar. I went to the top of a short flight of stairs that led down to the lighthouse, centred on a concreted concourse cut into the hillside. Hard against the western retaining wall was a rainwater tank.

Close as it was, in daylight the lighthouse imposed itself on its surroundings. It was a long cylinder, tapering as it rose. Facing the bungalow was an old blue door. Three small windows, deep set, were positioned one atop the other at intervals. I stepped down and walked around the base.

More small windows were set at similar intervals up the length of the structure. Facing south was a much larger window, multi-paned. Above it, and girthing the lighthouse, was a concrete lip.

From where I stood, I couldn't see past the lip. Keen for a better view, I followed a path that led down through low shrubs to the rocks at the water's edge. A few steps on and I turned to look back up at the lighthouse, taking in the light itself, encased in a dome, and the low iron railing that skirted the edge of the lip. The view from up there would be tremendous. Looking back around, I took in the giant boulders at the waterline, many tinged an earthy orange. A pair of seagulls glided above the ocean. Birds I'd never seen before, pretty birds, cawed and preened and flew off.

I could see why Pete had chosen to convalesce there. The energy of the place was exhilarating, compelling, mysterious. I imagined James Cook in his tall ship, sighting the promontory, surveying through his telescope the rocky and wild coast and, seeing nowhere to pull in, sailing on by.

Thinking I'd explore the lighthouse interior, I headed back.

I tried the door, but it was locked. Disappointed, I thought I'd venture off for a wander on the higher ground behind the cottages, when Pete called out. I could smell frying bacon in the air.

'Hey, there you are,' he said as I entered the bungalow. 'Take a seat.'

Pete had arranged eggs, bacon, fried tomatoes and mushrooms on my plate, with a hunk of white bread and butter, a pitcher of orange juice and freshly brewed coffee. A banquet. I felt thoroughly indulged at the sight of it. I was transported back to Oxford, to my parents, to my life. A wave of nostalgia consumed me. I picked up my knife and fork without bothering to ask how he managed to keep all that food from going off without refrigeration.

He dived into his with the appetite of a starved animal, shovelling in his food and gulping it down. I struggled to keep up. We were clearing the table and stacking the plates beside the sink when he said, 'Big climb ahead of us, so I thought we should eat well.'

'Best way to get your health back, too, I suppose.'

It was an innocent remark. I caught his gaze. He studied my face, hesitated, then looked down at the floor.

'I'm not getting my health back, Emily,' he said despondently. 'I'm dying.'

The cup I was holding tumbled into the sink.

'You can't be,' I whispered, thinking him young, far too young to die. 'What of?'

'Brain cancer,' he said flatly.

He removed his beanie, revealing a hairless, scarred scalp.

'But you told me you were convalescing.'

'It's true. Partly. I'm recovering from surgery.'

'Maybe they'll find a cure,' I said, wanting to inject a positive tone into the exchange.

'Not in time to save me.'

I hesitated, not knowing what else to say. 'I'm so sorry,' I said after a long pause.

'Don't be. I'm resigned to it.' He returned his beanie to his head. 'Life's short for everyone. It's just a bit shorter than most for me.'

'I suppose that's one way to look at it.'

'I'm making the most of the strength I have left. I climb the lighthouse stairs most days and look out at the view. I've seen so many gorgeous birds. I hope to see a whale before I'm gone.'

'Don't say that.'

'Back to the city, I mean. I'm not dead yet. Leave that,' he said, gesturing at the dishes. He reached for a bunch of keys hanging from a hook on the side of the cupboard above my head. I set down the dish cloth and followed him outside.

Entering the lighthouse, it was as though I had crossed a threshold into another reality. There was a strong smell of the ocean, fishy and salty. The light was dim, my eyes adjusting. I'd expected to see a spiral staircase—what else would there have been? —but with stone steps and a central column, the sort you can't see far around. Instead, the interior contained an ornate iron staircase. The treads were painted a dark red, the risers white. Beneath each tread, a handrail strut was capped by a chunky black knob.

The staircase spiralled up steeply. It was cantilevered into the wall and where the central column might have been, there was nothing but air. Even standing at the bottom, the void was breath taking.

Pete led the way, his pace measured and slow. Our footsteps echoed on the treads. We passed the small windows I'd observed on the outside, set in deep recesses, and I paused to peer out, each time at a different portion of the view. At first, I gripped the rail, but after a few turns of the spiral, I began to want to lean into the wall.

About halfway, I could hear Pete's breath, which matched my own. I thought I was fit, but as we neared the top, my legs were burning and my chest felt tight.

When we reached a flat section, positioned before the large window I'd seen at ground level, we stopped to catch our breath, gazing out at the ocean way down below.

'One hundred and sixty-two steps,' he said between gasps. 'It's the equivalent of a ten-storey building.'

'That's quite a stairwell,' I said, glancing behind me down the spiral to the very distant bottom.

He laughed.

Another turn of the spiral and we reached a second platform. There was a door ahead, up a few steps. Another door on our right led outside. Pete extracted his keys.

The view was everything I'd anticipated. I felt heady at first, but my mind soon adjusted, and my balance restored itself. Even so, I kept my back close to the wall of glass behind me. To the east the rugged coastline comprised a series of small bays and long, gently arcing beaches. To the west there were two small bays then a long stretch of beach. Wooded hills and heath descended to meet golden sands. Plastered to the hillsides here and there were massive dunes. They looked like giant sand carpets.

Pete leaned his elbows on the railing. Pointing out the landmarks, he gave me the potted history.

Lieutenant Zachary Hicks had spotted the land from aboard James Cook's first Pacific voyage in the Endeavour. Cook named the promontory Point Hicks in his honour. Observing the coast, I sensed something of what Cook might have thought as he veered off and up the eastern seaboard, looking for a likely place to pull in and ending up in Botany Bay.

The lighthouse was built a hundred years later, in 1887, Pete said, after many other ships had sailed past and met their fate.

The wind freshened unexpectedly, and he ushered me inside.

'It isn't safe out there in a strong wind,' he said, locking the door behind me. 'And it can pick up just like that.'

He went past me and led the way down.

The descent used a different set of leg muscles and by the time we reached the bottom, every part of my thighs and calves felt strained. I marvelled over Pete's strength. He might have been pale and clearly not in rude health, but his body had not given up on him. We rounded the lighthouse and took the path I'd found earlier, strolling down in single file past clumps of sedges to an area of flat and pale rock fringed by boulders at the water's edge. We scrambled on.

'That'll do,' Pete called as I went further.

I looked back. He was standing on a higher platform a few metres behind me.

I heard the wave before I saw the spume and stumbled back, narrowly avoiding getting wet.

'The tide's high,' he said. He looked so serious, standing there all scrawny and caved in. 'I don't want you to get swept away.'

My heart went out to him. That he was protective of me I found overwhelmingly endearing. We stood together for a while, watching the water surge and draw, each lost in our thoughts.

'It's so desolate,' I said on our way back. 'Do people really come out here on holiday?'

'Australians love their bush. The wilder, the better, for some.'

Lawrence really should have ventured further than he did, much further I thought, and I began to consider the hurried way he'd written *Kangaroo* as something of a travesty.

I spoke of the book to Pete. He hadn't read it.

In the bungalow, he handed me another book. 'You should read Patrick White,' he said.

'*The Cockatoos*?' I said, reading the title.

'Don't worry. It isn't about birds.'

'Thank you.' I held the book in my hand. I didn't want to return to the roadhouse, but as the day wore on I knew I had no choice. After a pleasant lunch of tinned fish and pickles on rye, I could scarcely stomach the thought of returning to the stench of Con's pies.

CHAPTER THIRTEEN

MIRIAM

It was Sunday and I felt like murder. I'd had a hellish night. Didn't sleep a wink. I couldn't switch off my mind, knowing I had a drug addict for a hotel neighbour and his bonks, footsteps, moans and grunts hadn't help one jot. I wasn't sure I could endure another night of the same. My eyes were sore, and my head ached and swam all at once. I couldn't concentrate.

Down in the dining room I ate my buttered toast and sipped the weak coffee Cassie had made. Then I shunted my scrambled eggs about my plate. When I was considering taking another mouthful, she wandered in and shot me and my breakfast a look that told me she was keen for me to finish. I hesitated with my fork to my lips, holding her gaze. I might not have wanted to eat that morsel of egg, but I was in no mood to be rushed.

'It's market day,' she said, walking over. 'Happens once a month.'

'Oh, I see,' I said vaguely.

'I have a stall selling honey. I keep bees.'

'Bees?'

'Plenty of pollen in the bush.'

'Is there much trade for local honey?' I said, casting an eye out the window at the empty street.

'You'd be surprised.'

I drained my cup and kept eating, regaining my appetite.

'Sleep okay?' she said.

'I was going to talk to you about that.'

'He's a restless one, that's for sure. He isn't bothering you?'

I raised my eyebrows, inhaling to speak, but she went on. 'We get a lot of troubled souls passing through here. Something about the crossroads, my pa used to say.'

'Oh, yes?'

'Ma says different. She says the place is cursed, ever since Gran Parks cleaved her husband in two, right down the middle of him.'

My eyes never left her face. I thought she was winding me up. It sounded like a tall tale to me.

'Put half in the cold room,' she said reflectively. 'The other half she fed to his dogs.'

I scoffed. It was a reflex.

She looked defensive.

'He deserved it, make no mistake. Used to beat her black and blue. The whole town knew it, but no one did a thing. Too scared. Too scared he'd turn on them as well.'

'That's outrageous. What about the police?'

'The cops didn't care. They don't get involved in domestics.'

I began to realise she was telling me the truth. At least, she believed in what she was telling me.

'How long ago did all this happen?'

'Way back. Not long after the war, ma says. The thing is, old Gran Parks has caused a lot of trouble ever since. Her ghost,

I mean. Seems to affect people. Mostly the newcomers. The townsfolk are immune to her, I guess. People say her energy is trapped here by the bush.'

Now she sounded ridiculous and I switched off. Although it was all the more reason for Con to hurry up and fix my car. Not that I believed in ghosts.

Cassie leaned against a nearby table, clearly not planning on leaving without my plate. I polished off the last of my eggs and handed it to her.

'See you at the market,' she said.

'What about that man?' I pointed upstairs.

'Dan? I took a tray up about an hour ago.'

It must have been while I was running the bath, for I'd heard nothing.

CHAPTER FOURTEEN

FRANKIE

O utside my shack, mug in hand, I felt nature on my skin.
I took in the forest, the dark spaces between the trees,
the haphazard arrangement of limbs, logs and undergrowth, the
tangle of nature. I listened to the chirrups, the squawks, the
chatter, and the steady drone of my generator beneath it all.

My tea had gone cold. I tossed the dregs on the soil at my
feet. A stray bull ant went over for an inspection. I watched its
sly movements before kicking up dust with my boot to shoo it
on its way.

The sun arced towards its zenith. I went back inside and
grabbed my boning knife, satchel and car keys. Con's meat was
in a bucket on the passenger seat, covered, but on the way
down to Cann River I could smell the bloodied flesh.

It was with some disappointment that I made my way to
the highway in my old white ute. When I'd gone out that
morning, I found the trap I'd set along that track was empty.

I hadn't set it to snare a deer. None came by that way. It
was too close to my dwelling and they could smell me.

I'd set a man trap. It was for that murdering hoon, Wayne

Conway. I was wondering why he hadn't returned. Perhaps he'd absconded from the area, headed on up or down the coast. Instinct told me he was still around, lurking. There being no better place for him to hide.

I needed a lure, some way to entice him back.

I pulled up round the back of the roadhouse a little after eleven. I entered with my bucket of venison off-cuts, expecting to find that new backpacker in the kitchen, down on her haunches with her head in the oven, cleaning up after Con. Instead, I was greeted by the stench of pie filling sputtering on the stove. I set the bucket down on the bench and poked my head in the café. Pat was behind the counter serving Mr Bruce from the general store. That god-awful Baez song she always played filled the café with jangles and twang. I coughed. She glanced over. 'Oh, it's you.' She took a tenner out of the till.

I pocketed the cash. A measly ten bucks for all that meat, but that stone of a woman had no blood in her.

I went across to the general store and stocked up on essentials. It was Sunday and the general store was usually closed, but Mr Bruce didn't want to miss the trade of market day. His prices were inflated but it was never worth the petrol to shop elsewhere. The tyranny of distance meant we all used less squares of toilet roll in Cann River. Mr Bruce's mother served me. She was a squint-eyed woman and the transaction took a lot longer as a result. Not trusting the cash register's capacity for adding, she peered at the price of each item and wrote the amount down in her slow hand. She was even slower adding up.

Market day fell on the third Sunday in every month, and everyone had come in from the outlying farms and localities to see what was what and exchange the latest. All the usual traders were there: The Country Women's Association with their cake stall and raffle, the Cann River Clickers displaying their knitted and crocheted bits and bobs, old Bill and the second-hand items he'd snaffled from charity shops, Annie the greengrocer, Sal and Sol's art stall, and Cassie with her own home-produced honey.

I recognised faces among the browsers, said g'day to some, picked out those passing through. A middle-aged woman attracted my attention. Stocky, square-set, and dressed more for the office than the market, she stood apart from the rest, surveying the stalls. I caught her eye and offered her a welcoming grin. She was disconcerted by it and looked away, heading for Cassie's stall. Irritated, I made to join her. As I neared, I overheard Cassie say to her, 'You came.'

'Not much else to do,' the woman said sourly.

'Hey, Frankie,' Cassie said, her face lighting up at the sight of me.

'How's it going, Cassie?' I said, stepping round the stall to give her a hug.

The city woman handled the honey tubs, before examining some of my wares that Cassie kindly sold on my behalf—deer skin bags, wallets, moccasins and tool belts mostly. The woman went back to the honey.

'You should buy some,' I said. 'Beaut flavour.'

'Is that right?' she said.

Cassie put her hands on her hips.

'Frankie, this is Miriam. She's staying at the hotel.'

'Is that right?' I said, mimicking the woman's hostility. 'On holidays?'

'Her car broke down.'

'Bad luck.'

'Con's fixing it.'

'Even more bad luck.'

I offered up a laugh.

Miriam was not impressed.

I turned to Cassie. 'You should have told her about Steve.'

'It was too late. Con had ferreted her car away in his garage before I knew a thing about it.'

'Not like you.'

There was a brief moment of silence. Miriam stifled a yawn. 'So, you'll be here for a fair while,' I said, holding her gaze, taking in the dark circles under the eyes, the harried look of her.

'Till Thursday. That's when the new part will be arriving.'

'Friday, then.'

'Friday?'

'You seen how fast Con works?'

I couldn't help teasing her even as I began to warm to her, deciding she was my kind of woman, no nonsense and no frills. Even if she came across a tad stuffy.

I took a tub of honey. 'Any sales?' Cassie checked her notebook. 'A bag.'

A bit of maths and she handed me a ten-dollar bill.

'I better be getting on,' Miriam said.

It was a figure of speech. Realising she was stranded in town with no car and bugger all to do, I suggested a cuppa.

Miriam was about to decline when Cassie said, 'Go on. Frankie's an old mate.'

Miriam seemed to relax. Leaving the market, we strolled over to the roadhouse making small talk. It wasn't until we were seated with a cup of Pat's stewed tea that she revealed why she was so tired. Some drug-addicted guy with bad acne and a stash was holed up in the room next to hers.

'I can't sleep,' she said. 'He's doing my head in.'

I listened, attentive, questioning. I had no idea why I wanted all the details—which room she was in, which was his, whether she had ever seen the guy up and about during the day, at what time he surfaced—but I gained a clear picture of the acne-infested addict and his nocturnal goings on. Miriam had only encountered him at her breakfast—his dinner; and at her dinner—his breakfast.

'When you found the syringe, did you notice anything else? A bag?'

'I didn't take it all in, but yes. There were packages as well.'

'Large?'

'Hard to say. I guess.'

I didn't say anything more. Didn't want to alarm her. I'd heard just that morning on the radio that a guy was on the run from a bikie gang. The cops had raided a house after a shooting, and they found nothing. No cash. No stash. They made a number of arrests but laid no charges. There was a public outcry, which was why I'd heard about it. Police said without evidence, their hands were tied.

It was a safe assumption that the guy in the hotel was their man. Sounded like he was hiding, thinking he might have gotten away with it and too drug fucked to figure out his next move. I felt a sudden sympathy for Miriam, lumbered with him for a room neighbour. I sipped my tea, toying with recommending to Pat she invest in an extractor fan to deal with the odour of Con's pie fillings. Thankfully, she hadn't put her Dixie song back on the jukebox.

Across the street a car pulled up, an old rust bucket of a Holden. I watched the driver get out. A woman. She strode to the phone box, exited almost immediately and marched into the general store. She came out not long after carrying her mail and went and stood by her

car, reading one of the letters. She looked pissed off. It was Pearl.

CHAPTER FIFTEEN

PEARL

Across the road at Fred's, the goanna was still up the tree.
Nature's guard. That wasn't the reason I felt reluctant to
drive to Cann River. I didn't like to leave those kiddies and that
man for one second, but I had no choice. I couldn't recall them
saying the word daddy either, which had been troubling me all
night.

I left Sam in the house and locked up, something I never
did, but the stranger, the so-called Brent, had me on edge. I half
expected to return to a scene of carnage.

I travelled that dirt road and all of its twists and turns faster
than normal, kicking up dust, but the drive into town seemed to
take all morning. With my belly churning and my head ringing
like a belfry with my misgivings, I pulled up outside the general
store, planning to use the public telephone in the street outside.

I picked up the receiver, only to find some vandal had
tampered with the apparatus, no doubt trying to access the
coins. The only other phone available for public use was Pat's.
There was a phone at the hotel, but Cassie reserved that for

patrons, and besides, I never went in there. Didn't like the clientele.

I went into the general store and collected my mail, a bill for the rates and a letter from Kylie. My daughter never wrote me letters. Sensing something was up, I tore open the envelope on my way out the door and went and stood by my car to read it.

She opened with the usual reproach. That she couldn't understand why I had chosen to live out in Cann River. A few lines about how scummy Melbourne had become and then, she dropped the bomb. She was moving to Queensland. She was upping sticks and taking my grandkids to Queensland. Not even southern Queensland, which was reachable, but right up north to Daintree. Who the hell lived in Daintree? She said she'd met some fella and they were opening a bed and breakfast. What a joke! What a hypocrite, too, accusing me of moving too far out. Why did she have to be so vindictive?

I stuffed the letter in my pocket. The revelation was all consuming. I almost forgot why I'd gone into town. The roadhouse, with its row of windows looking out beneath a low roof, held a welcoming appeal. As I crossed the forecourt and I saw Frankie seated at a table, that welcoming feeling grew all the stronger.

She was talking to a woman I'd never seen before. I thought it strange. Frankie was a loner, like me. I acknowledged them both as I headed for the counter.

The place stank of Con's pies. He must have had another batch on the go. Smelled like it was burning.

'What do you want?' Pat said in that unambiguously insulting tone typical of her.

'I need to make a phone call.' 'Local?'

'National.'

'It'll cost you.'

'It's a dollar, you said.'

'One fifty.'

I reached in my trouser pocket and withdrew the coins, slamming them down on the counter to make my point. She pointed at the wall phone.

'Help yourself.'

I dialled.

The phone rang and rang.

I tried again.

No answer.

Maybe Fred had gone out for a late breakfast or early lunch. Or he was sleeping off last night. I'd have to try again later. Which meant I had to hang around in town. Pat was watching me.

'I can't get through,' I said.

'You want your money back?'

'I'll try later.'

'Sure.'

I left Pat to serve the customers who'd walked in behind me and were taking an age over the meat pie choice. I felt like making it easier by telling them the steak they were indecisive about was almost never on the menu—not unless Con got lucky rustling a stray calf—and they might as well go for the venison because Frankie made some cash that way and the hunter seemed to give everyone indigestion. Then I thought, why bother?

'How're you doing?' I said, pulling up a chair at the end of Frankie's table.

Frankie looked at me inquiringly. 'Good thanks.'

'You going to introduce me?'

'Pearl, this is Miriam. She's staying at the hotel.'

'My car broke down,' Miriam said, eyeing me warily.

'Shit happens,' I said. 'I suppose Con's fixing it.'

'It's only the locals who know about Steve.'

'She's here for a while then.'

'Till Friday.'

'Thursday.'

'If you say so.'

Whatever. All I knew was I didn't mind the look of Miriam. She was the sort of woman I would have picked for a daughter, and not that feeble creature I'd spawned. Miriam was solid, big boned and forthright. She wore casual city clothes. Only, she looked as though she hadn't slept for a month.

'Those hotel beds no good?' I said with a friendly smile.

Miriam avoided my gaze. Frankie gave me the story of Miriam's hotel neighbour, of how he was most likely on the run from a bikie gang and the police after a drug bust gone wrong. Miriam's face changed from outrage to horror in the telling.

'I had no idea he was a drug dealer,' she said.

'What else would he be?'

'Maybe you should take a room here at the roadhouse,' I suggested, trying to be helpful.

'She won't be any better off, Pearl. You know what those rooms are like. Pat keeps them shut up like tombs and douses them with air freshener to mask the smell of mould. They never get aired and they never get heated.'

'Only trying to be helpful.'

'I reckon she's safer where she is.'

'You're probably right. That guy isn't the only low life we have to watch out for,' I said.

'You've heard about Wayne, then.'

'Who?' I said, puzzled. 'I'm talking about the guy staying in Fred's shack.'

Mindful of the customers, I kept my voice low and explained the situation so far. Fortunately, those taking seats to eat their pies chose tables well away from ours. There was no sign of the backpacker waitress.

'Does he look all city trendy with high top hair?' Miriam said.

'You've seen him?'

'Yesterday. He was parked right where you are now.'

Frankie and I exchanged glances.

'He reckons Fred knows he's staying in his shack,' I said, 'but I know he broke in.'

'Hence the phone call,' Miriam said sagely.

It didn't need saying.

'Thing is, he's got a brace of kiddies with him.'

Frankie leaned forward.

'Maybe he's abducted them.'

'Kidnapped even,' said Miriam.

'Could be.'

'I've not heard anything about a kidnap,' Frankie said. 'I reckon I would have heard.'

She was right. Frankie spent a fair bit of time on that short-wave radio of hers.

'Abduction then.' Miriam raised herself up. 'Is he the father, do you think?'

I recoiled. She was taking too much interest, the sort a social worker would take.

'I reckon he is. Look, I'm probably being paranoid. That's why I really need to speak to Fred.'

Without giving her a chance to respond, I asked Frankie about that guy Wayne and she filled me in on the details. A robbery gone wrong, the driver failing to appear, new charges brought. Miriam looked as shocked as I felt. None of us was comfortable with a murdering rapist on the loose.

'I've seen him,' Miriam said, her voice now a whisper. 'I was in the park. He appeared from behind a tree, then took off.

That car of his makes a hell of a racket. And I saw him doing donuts the other night.'

'He's definitely hanging around then.'

'Have you told the police?' Miriam said.

I'd wondered when that remark was coming.

'The police?' I said, making sure I sounded incredulous.

'You must be joking!' Frankie slapped a hand down on the table. Miriam froze.

'She doesn't know about this place,' I said softly.

'Ain't that the truth.'

I filled Miriam in on the local cop, singular. If he wasn't propping up the bar at the Cabbage Creek hotel, he was at home, sleeping it off.

'Jeez,' I said, changing tack. 'We have a drug dealer on the run, a murdering rapist on the loose, and a child abductor in hiding. Cann River hasn't been this lively in a while.'

'We don't know that last one for sure.'

'We don't know any of it, for sure.'

'Wayne's a safe bet. As is Miriam's drug dealer.'

'He's not my drug dealer.'

'You know what I mean.'

'I think they are all a safe bet. No one brings little kiddies out to a place like this after the summer holidays.'

'The question is, what do we do about it?' Frankie said.

'What are the odds?' I murmured, my mind drifting.

The last of the clientele filtered out the door and Pat sauntered over with a small notepad. I ordered a coffee and a bowl of chips to share.

'Sauce?'

'Of course.'

'Anything else?'

'Nah.'

I thought to mention the smell which had taken on a

charred undertow. I was astonished Pat hadn't noticed. Presumably she was used to it. She took away the empty cups. We were silent for a while, as was the jukebox. Then I asked Miriam where she'd come from. For my trouble, I received a blow by blow account of the bushfire that had razed her house. Poor woman was plainly still upset by the disaster, but I didn't feel all that sympathetic.

The hot chips, doused with Pat's sauce, changed the mood, and we all leaned forward, elbows on the table. I took a chip from the edge, dunked it in the sauce and nibbled at an end, careful to shunt the food to the ulcer-free side of my mouth. I only risked two chips. Watching the others eat, I sat back and opened up about Kylie's latest. The verdict was unanimous. She was selfish and inconsiderate and likely as not I'd rarely if ever see my grandkids.

I was about to try Fred again when a car pulled up in the forecourt and a young girl got out, looking all flushed with love. Miriam followed my gaze.

'The waitress. A backpacker from England.'

'Aren't they all.'

'Pat always uses backpackers,' Frankie said, addressing Miriam. 'Cheap wages and dear accommodation. Silly things don't know any different.'

'She won't last long. They never do.'

'Why would they?' Miriam said. 'They're here to see the whole country.'

We all watched the girl enter the café, trudge across the floor and disappear into the kitchen. Everything about her indicating she did not want to be there.

CHAPTER SIXTEEN

EMILY

W hen I walked across the forecourt, I heard Pete drive off back to the lighthouse, and it felt like I'd been on day release and was re-entering my incarceration. Worse, that woman from the hotel, Miriam, had made some friends, that pair of ferals I'd seen a few times, and the three women were huddled around the table beside the entrance door, like witches. Or rather, an old witch and her two novitiates, for one of the women had snow white hair and a weather-beaten face and looked ancient.

Con was nowhere to be seen. Pat poked her head into the cafeteria, checked to make sure it was me, and disappeared back into the kitchen. I'd only just put my bag down on my bed when she yelled at me to get to work.

It was my day off, but I wasn't about to argue with her. I sauntered into the café, found my rag-cloth and disinterestedly wiped down the counter, my nasal passages revolted by the stink of burning pie filling—something else for me to clean. In my side-vision I caught Miriam waving at me. Cloth in hand, I went over.

'Hey, Emily, isn't it?' she said, all polite smiles. 'Sorry to bother you. I can see you've only just started your shift.'

'What can I fetch you?' I tried not to sound cold.

'We're after three coffees.'

I eyed the half-consumed bowl of chips in the centre of the table. I was about to walk away when Miriam spoke again.

'That guy you were with. He's the one who was in here before? The one with the beanie and the scar on his face?'

'His name is Pete. What about him?'

'Only, I wondered...'

'What? If he was a serial killer, you mean?'

'Woah. She's only asking.'

I glared at the woman who spoke, taking in her skunk mullet, the shaved sides leaving a bushy stripe of thick black locks trailing down her neck. She was a hulk, long boned and muscle-bound, seated with her legs apart a fair way from the table, yet managing to lean against it with her back perfectly straight. It was a posture that showed off her armpit hairs. She had to be at least six foot tall.

'If you must know,' I said, backpedalling, 'he's staying at Point Hicks while his friend the lighthouse keeper is in the city.'

'He's a lighthouse keeper too, then,' said Miriam.

'No. He's a good friend of Simon and he's convalescing.'

'Convalescing? At Point Hicks?' The witch had spoken. She was wiry, thin lipped and mean-eyed, her white hair, long and wavy, unkempt, and there was nothing in her manner that was likeable.

Miriam, the least vile of the three, took up the theme, warming to it, as though she relished in having knowledge they didn't. 'Not only does he look pale and drawn. He's sort of hollowed out and he has a scar running right round the edge of his face.' The way she coursed a finger round her own as she spoke made me want to slap her. 'That must have been the surgery.'

'Surgery for what?' skunk mullet said.

'He's lucky to be recovering,' said the crone. 'After an operation that big. Sounds like they peeled off his face.'

'All right,' I said, exasperated. 'Not convalescing. He's got terminal brain cancer. Satisfied?'

The women made noises as though shocked, yet none of them seemed sympathetic. I felt awkward, realising I'd betrayed a confidence.

'Sorry, I shouldn't have said that. I don't think he wants anyone to know.'

'Dying is a private affair,' the old hag said, as though she knew all about it.

'He's a sweet and kind guy,' I said. 'Harmless as a fly.'

'Simon has short wave, too,' the crone added, directing her comment to the other women more than me. She held out her hand. 'I'm Pearl. I live down at Peachtree Creek. It's not that far from the lighthouse.'

'I'm Frankie,' skunk mullet said. 'We don't want to alarm you, but there's a guy hanging around the area you should know about.'

'Three, in fact,' said Pearl.

'I don't think the child abductor is any threat to Emily,' Miriam said.

'Okay, two guys.'

'By the sound of it, that guy in the hotel is too drug screwed to be any threat,' said Frankie, reaching for a chip. 'Besides, Miriam said he never leaves the hotel.'

'One then,' Pearl said with irritation.

'But I'm serious.' Frankie held my gaze. 'He's jumped bail for armed robbery.'

'And he's wanted for rape and murder.'

Frankie shot Miriam a censorious look. 'I wasn't going to tell her that.' She looked back up at me. 'He drives a blue Ford Falcon station wagon and he's a hoon with a mullet.'

I thought for a moment. 'I've seen him.'

'Doing donuts at the crossroads, I bet.'

'He's been in here?' Miriam asked.

'Not when I've been around, thank goodness. I've seen him go into the general store a few times.'

I was finding their scaremongering hard to take seriously. Pearl caught me rolling my eyes and gave me a dismissive look.

'Honey, my advice is stay here at the roadhouse until he's caught. Con might be a bit different, but he'll look after you.'

'I will, probably.'

'Probably?' Frankie sat up. Her breasts jiggled beneath her shirt.

'She's smitten,' Pearl said with a snigger.

'With a dead guy?'

'He isn't dead,' I said, instantly defensive.

'Yet.'

Pearl reached out and placed a weather-beaten hand on my arm. 'Remember, Simon has a short-wave radio. He keeps it in the end cottage, in a room at the back. He put it there as the reception's better. If you do go out to Point Hicks again, just remember, okay? The door is never locked. Simon has it there for emergencies.'

'We all do,' Frankie said.

In my side vision, I glimpsed Pat entering the café heading for the jukebox. She had the key and at least five times each day she played her favourite song. I had no idea what it was about 'The Night They Drove Old Dixie Down' she loved so much, but she adored it.

'Three coffees, ladies,' I said loudly, wanting to appear busy. 'I'll bring them right over.'

'Emily?' Pat said as I approached.

'They want three coffees,' I said and barged past her to fill the kettle.

CHAPTER SEVENTEEN

MIRIAM

Two coffees, one not long after the other, and I was feeling the effects. I left Pearl at the roadhouse to make her phone call and Frankie waiting to cross the highway and wandered up to my churchyard bench. Intense as it was, the smell of Con's pies had whetted my appetite and despite the chips I'd scoffed at the roadhouse I stopped by the bakery for a sausage roll and a vanilla slice. The morning had taken an unexpected turn and although I didn't anticipate meeting Pearl and Frankie again, I warmed to them both, as unlikely as that seemed to another part of me. They were the sort of women my adoptive parents, the upright Mr and Mrs Forster, would have found horrifying.

Frankie was a bush-loving hippie with a punk haircut, and I didn't much care for the armpit hair. There was a metallic smell to her too, and she came across as masculine. Although her pendulous breasts hanging unsupported beneath her ill-fitting shirt were anything but. Altogether she was not my type, yet there was something about her I felt I could trust.

I had the same feeling about silver-haired Pearl. She

smelled salty, as though she'd just come out of the ocean, and despite her diminutive size, from her rugged features I could tell she had a lot of life experience under her belt.

Both women were tanned and weather-beaten. I looked down at my own skin. The pallor spoke of a woman chained to her desk. I yearned for a different sort of life, not one to compare to Frankie's or Pearl's—they were rough—but one spent in the fresh air. I vowed to myself to get out into my new garden and make an impression the minute I took possession of my new home.

I pulled the sausage roll up in its paper bag, wrapped the paper around its midriff and took a satisfying bite.

It was reassuring to learn my own instincts and misgivings were not askew. I could tell by Frankie's reaction that I was right about that drug addict. I wondered why she hadn't mentioned Wayne straightaway. She hadn't wanted to alarm Emily with the full story, but she was happy enough to tell me and Pearl. Well, she'd alarmed me on two counts. A drug addict was one thing, a dealer on the run another. Not that I anticipated he'd attack me, even though I knew he had a stash and the cash. It was the others after him that had me worried, rough and menacing bikies who might turn up at any moment. There'd be a bloodbath if they did, and I didn't want to get caught in the crossfire. I'd had enough drama to last me a lifetime. I could still hear those gas bottles exploding in the conflagration of Cockatoo.

Then there was Wayne. He was even worse. No one was safe with him on the loose. It was a wonder the police were not already on to him. Why hadn't Frankie reported him? Both women had an aversion to the police, but it didn't make sense. Lots of folk despised the police yet they still resorted to their services when the need arose. Then again, Pearl did say the local cop was worse than useless. Should have been retired if he'd had an alcohol problem as bad as she described. During my second coffee, she regaled me with the story of his failure to arrest a Trevor Bartlett, who'd beaten his wife so badly she was in hospital for over a month. Broke her jaw and several ribs. The local cop didn't do a thing.

I popped the last of the sausage roll in my mouth and folded the bag in half and half again. A bird of some kind strutted about after the crumbs. I ignored it.

Pearl said around Cann River, justice was served in other ways. She took relish in telling me that Trevor had a seizure six months later and died. Natural causes, she'd said. I noted that both Frankie and Pearl had sniggered when she said that.

What was it with those two?

Justice has a way of landing the right way in the end.

Frankie had said that. Not that I felt comforted by the comment. I resolved to contact the authorities later that day, when I found a private moment and a telephone.

Somehow, even thinking of making that call felt like betrayal. Frankie and Pearl would know it was me, too. I reminded myself I'd only just met them, I owed them no allegiance, and besides, their attitude was abhorrent. Satisfied that my higher, bureaucratic self would hold sway, I reached for my vanilla slice.

Worsening an already menacing situation, we had a child abductor in our midst, if Pearl's impressions and analysis were reliable. When I imagined those little girls, I couldn't help also seeing my cousin and that tragic day all those years before. It was back then I realised men could not be trusted, and I vowed to keep them all at arm's length. My life would be safer that way. The presence of that child abductor reinforced my decision to make that call to the police, although I hoped I wouldn't be perceived as deranged, reeling off so many suspected criminals.

The ordinary goings on in the town were taking place a few steps removed from my head space. If I'd wanted to, I could have watched the bakery doing a steady trade. I could have taken in the exchanges of cars in parking bays as one set off and another took up the space.

The market proved to be the magnet Cassie needed it to be. For the first time since I'd arrived, Cann River felt normal, like any other small country town. I tried to latch on to the sense of it, tried to instil in my mind a measure of calm, of patience. It was to no effect. I knew I'd have to go back to the hotel and tough it out next to that drug dealer. It occurred to me as I polished off the vanilla slice that I should accept Con's offer of a room at the roadhouse despite what Frankie said, but I quickly gave away the idea, knowing I'd be trading one set of dire circumstances for another. I didn't fancy lugging my stuff across to another room, especially if it was mouldy; I had to think of my health. Besides, for all her reserve, I felt I had an ally in Cassie. She'd never let anything untoward happen to me. I was sure of it.

I sat on the bench, ruminating over all that Pearl and Frankie had said, until a full bladder saw me on my way.

CHAPTER EIGHTEEN

FRANKIE

S tanding at the crossroads was never my idea of a pastime, although that was what it was turning into, with first one, then another car trundling by. When the road was finally clear and I was about to step out, I felt the rumblings of a truck. Then I saw the metal beast, crossing the bridge and speeding into town. I anticipated the compression brakes to kick in any second, as they did, and eyeing the monster with its mean brow and menacing jaw and its load of logs on its back, my upper lip curled. I didn't move until the truck had disappeared on its way up the coast.

Only then, did I saunter across the highway, making a point of appearing to onlookers a woman with it all in her stride.

I stood for a while with my back to the hotel, looking across at the roadhouse and the general store. Normal businesses in a normal town, but for the last few days Cann River was anything but. For a few seconds, I pressed against the bricks of the wall, my senses alert. It didn't feel good to have a drug dealer upstairs, disturbing the energy of the place.

I strode over to the kerb of the road heading north, my

road, and this time walked straight across without having to wait. As I neared the park, I was no longer able to pull off an easy-going manner. Not with the trouble stirring in me. Whatever kindness lived in my heart was hardening over with hate. It had been a long time since Cann River had attracted so much scum all at once. Evil was in the air. I could smell it.

Market day was a short-lived affair. The park was beginning to empty of browsers and Cassie was already packing up.

'Good sales?' I said, joining her behind her stall.

She laughed. 'Not bad. I sold two pairs of moccasins. You better get stitching, Frankie.'

She boxed the rest of the honey pots on the table. Then she unzipped her wallet.

'Here,' she said, and handed me thirty dollars. 'Keep the wolf from the door, eh?'

We both laughed as I pocketed the cash. She'd already taken her cut. People paid good money for hand-stitched, deer skin moccasins, especially when they were hairy, like mine.

I helped her fold up the table and load her ute. The other traders were packing up; the park would soon return to its vacant state. I watched a car head off west. It was old Joe, secretary of the Red Cross, returning to her farm out Cabbage Tree Creek way.

'You got a sense something's not right again?' I said.

Cassie was the town radar. She shut the tailgate and secured the latches before giving her answer.

'Gran Parks,' she said slowly, 'I saw her last night, in the saloon. I can feel her energy right through the building, especially in the kitchen.'

I wasn't surprised. Even standing out in the street, I'd felt her presence.

'That guy you got staying in the hotel. You want to get rid of him.' 'You're probably right.'

'Send him on his way, Cassie.'

'Can't.'

'Can.'

'Can't. His uncle owns the hotel.'

'Stan?' I thought for a moment. 'Malice really must run in families.'

'Sure does. Stan's old Parks' third cousin.'

'I didn't know that.'

Something in me stirred; we both knew old Gran Parks was stirring too.

It took a moment to absorb the family connection, from Gran Park's husband, to his third cousin, Stan the absentee landlord, to Stan's nephew, Dan. All that bad blood.

'We're stuck with him, then,' I said. 'Can't boot out family.'

'I don't think he'll be any trouble. He's terrified.'

I pictured him there in his room, a blubbering wreck of a human. In a brief moment of amusement, I saw Miriam, uptight next door, trying to get some sleep.

The afternoon sun was warm on my face. I squinted into it then lowered my gaze. Cassie started chatting to another stall holder. The conversation unfolded as I'd expected—not enough passing trade, too many tyre-kickers, and the audacity of couples in caravans who thought it okay to haggle. Uninterested, I closed my eyes and let my mind drift.

When I heard the customary, 'See you next time,' I opened them again and a jolt passed through me. In my side vision, I caught Wayne skirting the park. He was heading our way. In an instant, I saw in his approach an opportunity.

I went around to the other side of the ute, making sure I was in his line of sight. He seemed intent on ignoring me, but I knew from the way his face had tightened that he'd seen me.

He was downwind of me. I waited until he was close enough before raising my voice.

'I better be on my way,' I said, looking over at Cassie. 'A funeral waits for no one and it's a hell of a drive.'

She gave me a puzzled look.

I went on, keeping my voice loud. 'Good job my sister's up there looking after my place.'

'Your sister?'

'Pretty, young thing though. Probably shouldn't be staying up there all on her own.'

It was a crude attempt at a lure, and I wasn't sure it would work. I went back around the ute and held open my arms to give Cassie a hug, offering up a quick explanation before I pulled back.

'You have an okay time down there, Frankie.'

I left her and returned to my ute, taking a good while buckling up before heading off out of town, giving Wayne enough time to make his way to his car. His was parked in the main street in full view of anyone official who might, on the off chance, be looking for that number plate. For a guy on the run he sure was taking some risks. We were pointing in the same direction. I pulled away, keeping an eye out in the rear vision mirror. As I crossed the bridge, I saw the Falcon turn up the road heading north.

I pulled over and sat in a layby beside the river. It was a boring couple of hours. I listened to the radio. Dozed. Thought about Pearl and that shifty sounding guy at Fred's and pondered her options on her behalf. Wondered how Miriam would handle her drug dealing neighbour until Friday. Decided that Pommie waitress had an awful lot to learn about life. She had naive plastered all over her. A girl like that wasn't equipped for a place like this. There she was hanging out with a beanie-headed drop kick, going by the way Miriam had described him, what with him claiming he was dying of brain cancer, too. I didn't buy it. At least, I didn't buy his innocence.

The sun was making its descent in a clear sky when I drove back through the town and on up the road north.

I rounded the last bend before mine and there at my turn off was the blue Ford Falcon, obscured by a screen of small trees.

CHAPTER NINETEEN

PEARL

Once Frankie and Miriam had left the roadhouse and Joan Baez had stopped her caterwauling, I went over to the phone. Pat poked her head round the kitchen door and gave me a cursory nod. Judging by the smell emanating from the kitchen, Con's pie filling was incinerating on the stove. I got another blast of it as Pat closed the door. Judging by the crashing and banging of pots and pans, Pat had at last discovered it.

Again, the phone rang out. I held back the impulse to slam the receiver in its cradle and went and sat at a table, thinking I'd give Fred another try in a bit. Shit happens, I told myself. That's how I'd always lived my life and I wasn't about to change.

That attitude had helped me through the tough times.

Helped me not to get bitter.

Reflecting back, I first adopted the phrase when my house got flooded out. I was in my mid-twenties and newly married to Mal the brickie.

It was his idea to buy a house in Flemington. Low on its

stumps and on the low side of the street, and when a big fat cloud burst over Melbourne that December, the floodwaters in the vicinity funnelled into our block and under my front door. I was knee deep before I could bat an eyelid. The house was ruined in an instant.

In the days that followed, I spent many a frantic hour trying to salvage what little I owned. Meanwhile, all Mal did was sit back and wait for the insurance. I should have left him then, for it was a sure sign of his attitude.

Instead, when the money came through, we bought a renovator in Moonee Ponds. Place was built back in the last century, and we had a lot of fun adding the cheap extensions. The flood had done us a favour in many ways. Or so I'd thought until Mal's gambling forced the sale of the Moonee Ponds house, and I got to watch all our efforts benefit his debtors.

Losing houses was one thing, losing a daughter another. Kylie was on her way to Daintree with my little grand kiddies and she didn't even think to swing by for a visit to say goodbye. My belly lurched in the imagining.

Emily caught my eye from the other side of the café. I made an effort to arrange a smile on my face so as not to scare her off. The silly thing looked worn out and terrified, although a bit stuck up. She would have been a few years younger than my Kylie. I couldn't hold age against her, but just then I wasn't predisposed to any woman below the age of thirty, other than Frankie.

I watched her dodge around tables with a cloth in her hand and something in me softened. You really shouldn't be spending time with a guy you don't know in a place as remote as that lighthouse, I thought, especially with a murderer on the loose. I wanted to say it. I wanted to insist, reach for her hand and beg. But what good would it do? More likely she'd bristle and get all defiant and do the opposite. Since when have twenty-somethings ever listened to wisdom?

She was heading my way and as she came closer, I beckoned her over.

'You know how to use a short-wave radio?'

'I won't need to.'

As I'd thought; uppity and defensive and contriving self-assurance. Talk about naive. Seemed I had the measure of her, but that given, I remained compelled to advise her.

'You don't know that,' I said. 'That guy, your new friend, is dying. He might have a seizure. They do have seizures you know. Brain cancer does that.'

I had no idea if that was true, but it seemed plausible and it had the desired effect. Emily stared at me, wide-eyed.

'What if he needs urgent medical assistance?' I went on. 'He really shouldn't be out there all on his own either.'

'That's probably why he's asked me to be with him,' she said, as though the thought had just occurred to her.

'Fair enough,' I said, doubting it. 'Do you have a pen and paper? I'd like you to write this down.'

She stood there, making no indication of movement.

'Go on.'

Reluctantly, she went and fetched pen and paper from the counter.

'That's quite a stink coming from the kitchen,' I said.

'Con's burned the pie filling.'

'Pat not happy then.'

'She's livid.'

'Emily, isn't it?'

She nodded her reply.

'Emily, round here, we all use the same transmission frequency.' I reached out for the notepaper and wrote it down for her. 'You'll find the headphones. Put them on.

There'll be a fine tune dial somewhere. Use that if the channel is scratchy. Take the handset and press the side button and talk into it. That's all there is to it. There could be a lot of other buttons and knobs. You're not to touch any of them. Got it?'

'I think so.'

'Make sure you do. I don't want to alarm you, but I've a bad feeling about Cann River right now. I don't want anything happening to you.'

'I'll be fine.'

I held her gaze. 'That is what I am trying to make sure of. Humour an old woman, would you? And write this down as well.'

I handed her back the notepaper. She held her pen, poised in obedience.

'Peachtree is to the west of the lighthouse. That's where I am. If there is an emergency and you need to make a run for it, head west.'

'West.'

I thought she might not know where west was, so I said, 'Face the ocean and head to your right. That's west. You'll need to go back along the track you come in on, though, and take the first walking track to your left.'

'Left.'

'It's called West Beach Walking Track. That will take you to a small and rocky beach. You'll need to walk up and over a bit of headland to reach the main beach.' Hopefully it would be at low tide, I thought, keeping that to myself. 'That next beach goes on a fair way. You have to keep walking until you near Clinton Rocks.'

'How will I know I've got there?'

'You'll know. They're huge and bright orange. Before the rocks, you'll need to exit the beach and head inland on another track. It won't be easy to find. You'll have to look out for it. I reckon it's about a hundred metres before you get to the rocks.'

Her face wore a perplexed look. I ignored it.

'After that, follow the track until you reach an intersection. Take a left and keep on walking. That track leads down to mine.'

As she scribbled down my instructions, I saw that the notepaper was too small.

'Will I know which house?'

'No, but I'll see you coming, don't worry about that.'

'How far is all this?'

'All up it's about fifteen kilometres.'

'Fifteen? That's quite a hike.'

'You're young and fit. It'll take you four, maybe five hours I'd say.

But like I said, it's only in an emergency.'

I didn't know why I bothered telling her how to find me. I knew she'd never make that trek. It was probably to clear my conscience if anything happened to her.

'I'm your closest neighbour out there,' I added, hoping to reinforce my point.

I didn't mention how soft the sand was, or the size of the waves that pounded that shore, or the sudden squalls that came in off the Southern Ocean and blasted the beach, blowing sand in your face. I told her about the rainbow lorikeets, the honey eaters, the falcons and even the owls she might see. She told me she knew about the birdlife already from that walking corpse she called a friend.

The café door swung open and in walked a doddery old man. The girl stuffed the pen and paper in her trouser pocket and turned to serve him.

Thinking I'd wasted enough time hanging around in Cann River, I tried Fred one last time. Still no answer. Pondering my next move, I forewent retrieving my dollar fifty for the unmade call and left the roadhouse. There weren't many options. Then it occurred to me to ask Miriam to make the call on my behalf. After all, the hotel had a phone and she had nothing else to do.

I headed down past the general store, following the direction she took when she'd left the café. Outside the bakery, I saw her leaving the churchyard. I stopped and waited. She deposited some folded paper in a bin beside me, a look of surprise appearing in her face.

'Hello, again,' I said warmly. She returned my remark with a cautious smile and a sideways glance at the Sydney coach making its way to its pit stop at the roadhouse.

'You wouldn't mind doing me a favour?' I asked, barrelling in without so much as an excuse me. Even as I spoke, I thought I could probably have handled that a bit better.

'If I can,' she said slowly.

'I can't get hold of Fred. He's still not picking up his phone.'

Her expression changed in an instant.

'Give me the number,' she said without hesitation.

I rummaged through my purse and wrote it down for her on the back of an old receipt.

Plucking it from my hand she said, 'How will I relay a message to you?'

'Call Cassie. She has the only short wave in town. Here,' and I reached for the receipt and her pen and scribbled down the number.

She took it back in a similar fashion, holding it between her thumb and fingers.

'Cassie seems to be the hub of this town. Out of curiosity, where is her place?'

'Never a truer word, Miriam. She has some acres down past the church.' I wasn't prepared to be more specific.

'How do you people live like this? If you don't mind me asking? Isolated, I mean.'

'You get used to it. We all have our reasons for being here.'

'I suppose they'd be solid reasons too.'

I didn't think that remark warranted an answer. We walked back to the crossroads in silence and I left her to it.

Back at the shack, I found Sam asleep by the stove. The fire had gone out. I relit it and fetched more kindling and a few logs from the wood shed. Then I went back out and picked some greens for my dinner.

Brent's car hadn't shifted by the look of things and Fred's was all shut up as ever.

I needed to take action but until I heard from Fred, there was not much I could do.

Except retrieve my plate.

With the fire ablaze and Sam content to toast herself in its radiance, I ambled across the street, eyeing the tree in Fred's front yard on my way by. Seeing the goanna, halfway up, content to cling on and wait for a meal, I smiled, feeling something like solidarity.

The so-called Brent opened the door before I knocked. I knew he'd been watching me. He was quick witted too. He had my plate in his hand.

'This what you've come for?' he said, shoving it at me.

I snatched it from his grasp. I didn't care for being treated like a nosy, meddlesome old crone, and that was exactly the vibe I got off him.

'Actually, I came to warn you,' I said, before he closed the door in my face.

He was instantly unsettled. 'Warn me?'

I pointed behind me up at the tree.

'You better come out and have a look.'

'Just tell me.'

'Suit yourself. There's a goanna up that tree. Do you know much about goannas? I suppose not. I'm telling you, don't let those kiddies play outside alone. She probably won't attack a human—chickens are more their thing—but you never know, and those kiddies are awfully small.'

'A goanna?' he said with sneering scepticism. 'I thought you were about to tell me about a big bad wolf.'

'Look, smart ass, come out here and see it for yourself.'

I took a step back. He just stood there.

'Come on.'

I gave him the impression I wasn't going to budge. Curious, he took a few slow steps outside and gazed up at the beast.

'Bloody hell,' he said. 'I had no idea they could get that big.'

'They're carnivores too. Born killers. Wouldn't want those kiddies of yours to come to any harm.'

'Thanks'

He seemed to relax.

'It's what neighbours are for,' I said, reinforcing my sudden advantage. 'We look out for each other.' I paused. 'Tell me, do you lot each fish?'

'I do, but the girls won't touch it. I blame their mother. She hated fish too.'

He said hated. Past tense. I wanted to ask what had happened to her, but instead I said, 'Really?' keen to press forward with my inquiry. 'You sure you can't tempt them?'

'Not a chance.'

'But what about you? Sounds like you do.'

'Why do you ask?'

'There's bream out there. And tailor. Flathead are a bit quiet at this time of year. Aren't you here for the fishing?'

One of the girls let out a wail.

'I better see to that,' he said, and made to hurry inside.

'If you need anything, just shout,' I said to the closing door.

CHAPTER TWENTY

EMILY

I watched the roll of Pearl's buttocks as she walked away. I knew she meant well but that would never make me like her. She was rough and ready, her accent painfully broad, her manner abrasive. Although, I preferred her to Miriam. Pearl didn't come across all bossy and pompous and she had some decorum, unlike that hairy-arm-pitted Frankie, who might as well have been a man, even with her pendulous breasts hanging unsupported beneath her shirt. As far as I was concerned, Frankie was terrifying; the sort of woman who resembled a thug. I didn't think I was exaggerating, even though she was probably very nice once you got to know her, and I supposed living out in the mountain wilderness would make anyone a bit rugged in their ways. But still.

I suspected I reacted most strongly towards her because she was about my age. At least, much closer to my age than the others. Yet it hadn't escaped my notice that they treated her like an equal, and me like a child.

Alone in the café, I tried to ignore the stink of burnt pie filling, adopting my usual pretend cleaning routine.

They really ought to prop open a door.

My hand glided the cloth over the tables and my mind wandered back to Point Hicks. I recollected the incredible landscape, the orange coloured boulders, the rugged coastline that stretched on and on, the creamy white sand of sweeping beaches, sand fringed with the bush that rose up at its edge, and the enormous sand dunes we passed on the way back. The pull of the place was intense, and I began to understand the allure of Australia and why its people chose to holiday or even live in far flung and inaccessible places. The spirit of the land was a siren call.

Ever since I'd learned about colonisation and empire in school history, I'd conceived of Australia as provincial in all the various meanings of that word: A backwards backwater, parochial, blinkered and unsophisticated, I'd believed Australia to be distinctly racist as well, a nation that majored in mistreating its own indigenous peoples. A nation with a ludicrously overinflated sense of its own importance, manifesting most distinctly in comedic fashion in Dame Edna Everage of Moonee Ponds. Back in Oxford, Australia was viewed as a land filled with Skippies and corkscrew hats and vegemite-smeared faces. A land known for exporting its talent. When I told my friends I was going to visit, they were unanimous in wanting to know why, when the rest of the world was there for the choosing. I could hardly tell them it was to satisfy my overprotective parents.

Point Hicks had changed me. I went from table to table, straightening chairs and sweeping up crumbs, with a fresh new impression of Australia in my heart. I didn't want to think about child abductors and drug dealers and murdering rapists. I pushed all that from my mind. I didn't want to think about Pete and his cancer either. I craved the open expanse of the ocean, the panoramic view from up the lighthouse.

Freedom.

I tidied some leaflets in a wire display, thinking I needed to leave Cann River as soon as I could and head on to the city and beyond. I almost had the bus fare and once Pat paid me, I hoped to have the rest. The way she fiddled with my pay and extracted her exorbitant rent and board was corrupt and my resentment was growing by the day, eating away at my good nature. I vowed I'd quit after one more visit to the lighthouse. I'd get paid and be on that bus.

Meanwhile, I was doing my best to stay out of Pat's way. That afternoon, her mood was sullener than usual. Despite it being my day off, she hadn't taken kindly to me staying over at Point Hicks and had put me to work the moment she set eyes on me. It transpired she was annoyed with herself for allowing me free time on market Sunday.

She was also livid with Con for burning the pie filling. He'd forgotten to turn off the stove when he'd gone out to serve petrol. Pat's diminished sense of smell meant she hadn't noticed.

Earlier, from my location near the counter, I'd overheard them arguing in the kitchen. Pat was growling at him to get a move on.

'Make more.'

'There's not enough meat, Ma.' He put on that whining, complaining tone that made him sound like a ten-year-old. 'I can cook up Frankie's venison.'

'We have plenty venison. Go get more meat for the hunter pie.' Her directive was vicious.

'There's no point doing that till dusk, Ma.'

'You useless, like your father.'

'Don't say that. I got a kangaroo last week.'

'It was wallaby. When you got it, half was gone.'

'I can't help the dingoes.'

'You get out there. Come back with sack full.'

Dingoes? Half a wallaby? Revulsion took hold as it sunk in that the meat in those hunter pies was road kill. It warranted a phone call to the public health department or whoever it was in charge of such things. In the meantime, I vowed never to sell another of those pies.

That proved a challenge when the coaches pulled in the afternoon. The bakery was closed on Sundays, so the decanting passengers all headed into the roadhouse. A queue soon formed, and I was stuck explaining to each and every one of the travel weary passengers that there was no steak pie, but the venison was very nice. About half went for the hunter. All I could do was urge them all to have Pat's homemade tomato sauce and blot out of my mind the knowledge of the carrion slurry those pies contained.

CHAPTER TWENTY-ONE

MIRIAM

I t was ten that evening before I reached Fred.

I first tried his number that afternoon, the moment I entered the hotel. There was no one about and the bar was empty, but not closed. I took the liberty of going behind the counter to make the call. The number rang out, so I went upstairs.

All was quiet in the adjoining room. I settled on my bed with Frangipani Gardens, determined to finish it. The hours slipped by and when I turned the last page, the sun was setting and things were stirring again next door.

Looking forward to moving from Adelaide to rural New South Wales, I put away the Barbara Hanrahan and took out of my bag the Miles Franklin. *My Brilliant Career* was a novel I should have read long ago but hadn't. In my youth, I'd been put off by the depressing sounding ending, but then a colleague at work kept raving that it really was a feminist novel since the protagonist was independent and strong-minded. Besides, Sybylla had chosen never to marry, just like me. A sensible choice, and I did hope the author thought so too.

I straightened my clothes, ran a brush through my hair, and tucked the Franklin under my arm. After ensuring I'd locked my door, I headed down to the dining room. No sooner had I taken up my seat than Cassie marched in carrying an oval plate in a tea towel.

It was steak and chips and I gave her a pleasant smile as she set the plate down before me.

'Enjoy your meal.'

'Thank you. I believe I will. I should probably mention...' I trailed off as she rushed back to the kitchen.

I inhaled the sweet aroma of the hot chips and adequately charred beef rising from my plate, smells that conjured memories of happy times in Cockatoo. The meat juices oozed and mingled with the chips and I marvelled at how Cassie had managed to cook me a perfect steak without ascertaining if I liked it rare or well done. I liked neither, and she'd managed a satisfying medium-rare. Perhaps it was luck. She didn't strike me as a chef and probably knew only one way to cook a steak. I took up my knife and fork.

Some time later, Cassie re-appeared with a breakfast tray and I heard her footsteps on the stairs. I was grateful. It meant I would miss the appearance of that drug addict. Although, I knew the longer I remained up and about, the higher the odds I'd encounter him.

The meal turned out as good as it smelled. Without doubt one of the best steaks I'd had in a long time. Afterwards, I cornered Cassie, who'd returned to the kitchen when I was eating my last chip. I explained the situation Pearl was facing with her unwelcome resident at Fred's. When I asked permission to make use of the telephone, Cassie assented without hesitation. I felt justified in making my earlier phone call and thanked her.

'Don't make it too late, honey. I'm in bed by ten-thirty.'

'I promise I'll give up the ghost by nine.'

The look she gave me was disconcerting. I couldn't figure out what I'd said.

I took *My Brilliant Career* to the saloon. It was empty. I tried Fred again, slipping behind the bar for the phone, taking it to the counter and heading back round to make the call. No answer.

I considered telephoning the police but hesitated, unsure whether to dial triple zero or the local station. With the receiver poised over the cradle, the saloon suddenly felt chilly and I broke out in goose bumps. I left the phone where it was, my book on the small table by the door, and went upstairs to fetch a cardigan.

Surveying my room, I took in my soiled clothes mounting up on the chairs. I didn't want to trouble Cassie, but I thought a small wash wouldn't go amiss. I didn't mind doing it myself. The idea of smalls, hand-washed in the bathroom basin and left to hang here and there on hangers and chair backs did not appeal one bit. I snatched from a pile the green cardigan I used to wear to work on cool days and made to leave the room. As I pulled my door closed and inserted the key, I heard shuffling in the other room.

He was well and truly up.

I didn't care to hang around in the corridor a second longer, in case he emerged.

I'd made it to the last treads at the bottom of the stairs before I heard his heavy and slow footsteps above.

I was in the saloon the next instant.

This time I was not alone. Cassie was serving a bearded man. I'd not seen him before. He was accompanied by three others congregating over by the dartboard. The old man who seemed to live in that hotel when the bar was open was propping up the other end of the bar, nursing a beer. His eyes never left me. Not given to interacting with hardened drinkers, or any sort of man in a bar, I gave him the briefest of smiles and turned away.

'She's still here then,' I heard him say to Cassie.

'Con's fixing her car.'

'I heard.'

She ignored the insinuation and came over with a large glass of red. I opened my purse. She waved it away. 'On the house.'

'Thanks.'

She didn't bat an eyelid at the phone on the counter either and I was relieved about that.

The wine was cold and sharp and not unpleasant. I sat for some time before heading to the counter. I picked up the receiver and dialled Fred's number, already lodged in my mind as a temporary fixture. It was an easy number to remember. It had a lot of threes in it. The line rang out.

Cassie looked at me inquiringly. I shook my head. Before I had a chance to return to my seat, she came over. Searching for a topic of conversation, I said, 'I heard that guy moving about upstairs.'

'Dan? Yeah, he's up. I took a tray to his room earlier.'

'I saw.'

She made him seem normal, his addiction and his stash an everyday occurrence and nothing she or I should be troubled by. Maybe it was normal in Cann River.

I settled into my seat by the saloon door, well away from the men in the room. I was glad I'd had the presence of mind to bring the Franklin down with me earlier. I had my wine and my book and in any other situation I would have felt at peace, but the need to contact Fred nagged at me, as did that drug dealer Cassie referred to as Dan. With all those men in the bar, even if I wanted to I was no longer in a position to call the police.

Miles Franklin's traditional writing style didn't have the same captivating effect on my attention. I needed to concentrate on what was a more demanding read.

I persevered. Cassie came and went. I drank my wine and went to the bar for more. I got up about every fifteen minutes and tried Fred. The men were engaged in a languorous conversation, interspersed with long pauses and the odd grunting laugh. Thankfully, I was ignored. As the evening dragged on, they left in dribs and drabs. Eventually, I was alone.

Soon after, a shadow crossed the windowed saloon door. Then the door opened a crack. I braced myself but no one entered. The door closed on its hinges.

I heard voices out in the hall. One of them was Cassie's, the other, male. I listened, but I couldn't make out the words that were being said. The talk was informal, more banter, and I couldn't imagine Cassie talking like that with a stranger. On the contrary, I had a strong sense they knew each other. Their exchange had an air of familiarity, confirmed when she laughed.

I had no evidence that it was Dan, but I knew it was. Perhaps Cann River was sharpening my instincts. A few hurried sentences later and the man raised his voice. I was sure I heard Cassie say, 'Better not draw attention to yourself.' A door slammed, and I saw Cassie head off up the street, followed by Dan's heavy tread on the stairs.

I waited, straining to hear the closing of his door. I thought I heard it but couldn't be certain. I kept waiting until I was sure he wasn't hovering about in the corridor.

Common sense told me to give up on Fred and make a dash for my room while all was quiet. I polished off the last of my wine and took it to the bar, where I tried Fred one more time. I wasn't expecting him to pick up. When he did, I jumped in surprise.

I wanted him to tell me he knew all about that man and his kids. I wanted reassurance, but all I got in response to my brief account was a string of expletives and a plain talking, 'You tell Pearl to tell that dog turd to sod off out of my house, and tell her to squeeze some rent out of him when she does.'

'Should I call the police?'

'Just talk to Pearl. She'll deal with it.' He hung up.

My mind was racing. Pearl was right about that man. I rummaged in my pocket and found her scribbled note and dialled Cassie's number. The phone rang and rang before she answered. She sounded breathless. I presumed she'd just arrived home.

'Oh, it's you,' she said upon my introduction.

I relayed Fred's message and asked her to radio it through to Pearl.

'Surely this is a matter for the police?' I added.

'They won't do anything,' she said flatly.

'But they must.'

'You reckon? I don't want to contradict you, Miriam,' she said in a low voice. 'But here isn't the city. Out here the police are worse than useless. Leave it to Pearl. She'll handle it.'

I couldn't find it in myself to contradict her. I had no way of knowing if she, or if Frankie and Pearl, were right. All I knew was I had to play by local rules or I'd get offside the only allies I had in that small town, and if working in local government had taught me anything over the years, it was never get those closest to you offside.

I left the phone and made a beeline for my room, which felt like a haven of tranquillity after the stress of that evening.

As though to reinforce the hard-edge of Cann River, a truck thundered by. Must have been doing well over the speed limit, judging by the window rattles. Seemed everyone abided by the lawlessness of that place. Even those passing through.

CHAPTER TWENTY-TWO

FRANKIE

The highway was quiet. Not many used that stretch of road, not on a Sunday evening, not even the logging trucks. I took the boning knife out of the glove box and put it on the passenger seat, regretting I hadn't thought to take the gun with me into town. Then again, I didn't like to carry a rifle around, even if it was hidden under the back seat. I couldn't justify it. I was a deer hunter, and there were no deer in town. I wasn't some crazed nut on the rampage. I didn't want just anyone feeling threatened by me. Only someone. Him.

I was all stealth, creeping along the track. I picked my way over twigs and leaf litter, a predator.

On the fourth bend, where the track narrowed between two full-grown stringy barks, I saw him.

He was lying on the ground, his foot caught in my trap.

I left him there and crept back to fetch my ute.

I drove along the track, veering at a cut through that branched off and arced around the narrow pass between the trees where Wayne lay, re-entering the track about ten metres on. I used it so rarely it wasn't visible to the untrained eye. I pulled up and opened the door, my palm folding around my boning knife.

Wayne was hollering. I don't know who he'd expected, but when he saw me, he cowered. Then terror gave way to indignation.

'You fucking lunatic,' he yelled, which did nothing for my own mood. 'Get this thing off of me.'

'Why would I do that?' I said, standing over him, taking in the trap clenching his thickly booted ankle.

'You stupid whore!'

My forehead broke out in sweat. It was his choice of word. No one called me a whore. No one should call any woman a whore. I'd carried that conviction in my soul ever since the dark days of my father, Howard Potter. It was a word that carried the force of a fist. A word that had dogged me into adulthood.

The word blinded me. I left him there and made my way back to the ute, brushing past tree trunks, breaking through the undergrowth. Panting, I leaned, palms flat against the tailgate, head bowed.

I'd never been a whore. I was the smart kid. That had been my trouble all through high school. Made me a target in the school playground. Things quietened down when my class got wind of my dad's decapitation. For a while it was all, 'Wanna come over to my place for the weekend?' and other offers of shallow sympathy. I never went. Instead, I left school soon after and became a women's libber, largely thanks to Germaine Greer and a women's liberation march that ended with a concert in Hyde Park. I was seventeen years old on the day of the march and I happened to be passing. Others were passing too, but I stopped and took it all in. The year of Howard Potter's demise was the same year that the first women's refuge opened, along with a rape crisis line. Looking back, I found that ironic. A year went by and I was rolling up my sleeves and getting involved.

Through the activism I was able to distance myself from my mother's decline. I could never understand why she didn't pick herself up, but she'd had one too many beatings and she was so downtrodden there was no helping her. I tried to look after her. Even after I moved out I visited and made sure she had the basics. I was loyal until she died and left me in the shit. She had debts heavier than a Sambar stag. That was my inheritance. I couldn't pay them. By then I was what people called feral. I lived off the dole and scavenged what I could. It was only another step to up sticks and go bush.

In the hinterland of Cann River, I led a good and honest life. I troubled no one and no one troubled me. I had it all set up. Mostly I stayed calm, centred, satisfied.

Then someone like Wayne appeared.

Anger reared in me even at the thought of him and I slammed my fist into the tailgate. Pain, strong and sharp, bolted through my wrist.

I needed to get a grip.

I inhaled, steadied my breath and my thinking, looked around at the trees, tuned into the birdsong, the rustles and scuttles of the bush. It was no use. Wayne's moaning breached the peace, and all my reason and steady calm were gone.

My vision blurred. I'd lost the good-natured part of my self. That weasel, Wayne, had raped and murdered an innocent female. It wasn't only a heinous crime, it was insulting. He wasn't feral. He wasn't wild. He wasn't any sort of animal, and he was definitely less than human. What the hell that made him, I had no idea.

I put the boning knife back on the passenger seat and returned to Mr Wayne Conway.

I knelt down beside his foot. I gripped the jaws of the trap with my bare hands, pulling it apart. The idiot just sat there, complaining.

'Get your foot out.'

He shunted away on his butt, clasping his calf.

I let the trap jaws snap shut.

He gasped.

I stood over him.

'Get up.'

I kicked him. Not hard, but enough to make a point.

He scrambled to his feet and edged away, tripping over himself, losing his balance, self-correcting. I watched. I wasn't going to touch him.

Then I changed my mind and made a grab for his mullet, yanking back his head.

'Let go of me, you dumb whore.'

At that I hurled around and kneed him in the groin.

He grabbed his appendage and hobbled to a nearby tree. Using the trunk as a prop, he keeled.

Laughter burst out of me, a single, sharp explosion.

I was breathing deeply, enjoying the rush, the heat of the blood in my veins. I went over and pushed him on.

'Walk.'

He offered no resistance.

He limped, hunched over, one hand nursing his crotch. I went up behind him and pushed him on, past my shack and the butchering shed and down to a small clearing. In the centre of the clearing was an abandoned spot mill. It was fully kitted and in good working order. I used it from time to time. It came in handy when I had to deal with a fallen tree. When not in use I kept it covered with a large tarpaulin. But it was always good to be prepared. That night, the tarpaulin lay folded on the ground. The contraption looked all the more menacing in the fading light.

I gave Wayne another push. He resisted, turning back. I grabbed his arm and wrenched it up behind his back.

'Keep walking.'

'What're you doing? Mad bitch.'

I grabbed him by the hair again and leaned into him, forcing him to the mill. Once his thighs pressed against the rack, I kicked the calf of his bad leg just behind the knee, using the momentum of his stagger to force his fall.

Before he had a chance to resist, I reached over for my leather straps and fastened him down. I'd made the straps out of last year's deer skins and held onto them thinking they'd probably never sell on Cassie's stall. It felt good putting them to use.

Sweating, breathing hard, I hovered over that murdering rapist strapped to a spot mill in the middle of a forest that had itself been raped by loggers who'd used that very machine; it was poetry.

Gran Parks would be proud. I could feel her presence, spurring me on.

Confident he couldn't wriggle free, I headed back to the shack, ignoring the yells reverberating through the trees. It had begun to feel like a game. The more his terror increased, the greater my satisfaction, and I understood what it was that fuelled retribution in the human heart. Suddenly, every single bad deed done by every single man on the planet had condensed into Wayne.

I had no pity when I heard his whines and screams that echoed through the bush.

I had no pity when I returned and came up behind him and fired up the mill.

His screams were all the more desperate as time wore on. I marvelled at his vocal capacity, the varying tones he used to convey his fear.

'No one about to hear you, mate,' I murmured.

The situation was surreal. I could see myself from afar, as though I was watching an actor play my part on my behalf. I turned off the mill and walked away.

Outside my shack, I sat, squat on my haunches. Minutes passed. Maybe an hour. Then, torch in hand, I strolled back down. The torchlight caught Wayne's face, pale with terror, eyes bulging, yet still he yelled insults. The mullet-headed hoon stopped the moment he heard the mill's motor fire up a second time.

'What the hell!'

I smiled. The smell of diesel obliterated the stench of his fear. When the blade made its whine, I watched him writhe and strain and blubber.

Then he begged.

I let him beg.

The whine went on and on, the blade, able to slice a tree trunk, indiscriminating.

The blending of the two sounds, the one determined, constant, the other fluctuating, landed in my brain like irritation.

Despite what Gran Parks would have me do, I was never going to slice him in two. The thought of all that blood spattering my clean spot mill was enough to put me off. I considered leaving him there all night, but there was a chance he'd wriggle free and I didn't fancy the reprisal.

I switched off the mill and unfastened him. Stunned, he made no effort to move, so I heaved his quivering flesh off the rack.

'Wait there,' I said, and he did. He obeyed me as a child obeyed its parent, and I went about covering up the mill with the tarp and tying it down.

'You going to let me go?'

'Nope.'

I dragged him by his mullet up to my butchering shed and pushed him inside. He made a single whimper and I heard the thud of him falling to the ground. I padlocked him in. Then I went back to where I'd found him on the track, slung the trap in the ute and drove back to the shack.

Inside the shack I couldn't hear Wayne. The evening returned to normal. I lit the stove. I fried myself a venison steak and cracked open a bottle of beer. The tension eased and fatigue set in.

My recent acts were not what Germaine Greer and the women's liberation movement had in mind when they campaigned for women's rights. Still, I thought they'd salute my efforts in a private moment. It was all very well trying to fix up the laws of the land, raise awareness and put things like equal pay on the table, but when it came right down to basics, men took out their rage on women with impunity, and somewhere along the line there had to be some redress. It was the wisdom of Gran Parks.

I flipped my steak, waited for the blood to ooze through the surface, then slid the animal flesh onto my plate.

CHAPTER TWENTY-THREE

PEARL

Furious with Kylie and her move to Daintree, I thundered home, kicking up dust, skidding on the gravel as I rammed on the brakes and swung the car into my driveway. I had enough fire in me to light the whole of Croajingolong.

Two door slams and I was in my kitchen with Sam looking up at me, startled. The fire was out. The day was warm but inside wasn't. I set about fetching wood and kindling. By the time the firebox blazed, my own rage had lessened. It settled down even more when I threw Kylie's letter on the flaming logs. It smouldered then caught alight, turned to grey ash and disappeared.

I couldn't make my daughter disappear. Damn Kylie and her wilful nature. I sat back in the battered armchair feeling I'd been cut off from my own blood. Axed. It occurred to me I could head up there. Turn up in Daintree in my old jalopy and insist on having the spare room. Only, she'd turf me out. I was sure of it. That was assuming she would even let me in the house in the first place.

Shit had happened, that was certain, shit had happened as

if God himself had done a great big dump and the whole damn lot of it had landed right on top of me. Adding insult to injury, my ulcer had flared up after those two chips I'd eaten at the roadhouse and my tongue had begun to throb.

I got up and poured myself a whisky, draining the glass in a single gulp before pouring another.

My attention turned to that Brent across the road. His car was still there which meant so was he, and those kiddies. But there was nothing I could do until I heard from Fred.

I went over to the short-wave radio and made sure the volume was as high as it would go.

All I could do was sit and wait, my eyes darting to the radio on every crackle.

A few hours later, I fixed myself an omelette and salad greens. The ulcer had settled down again, my tongue numbed by the whisky, but I avoided my usual salad dressing, just in case.

Day faded into night. Grim, I sat by the fire, wrapped in a shawl like the grannie I should have been, working my way down the bottle of whisky, getting up now and then to put more wood on the fire.

I mulled over the past, my mind lurching from Kylie, to Mal and then back to my folks in Tassie, landing at the feet of my grandmother. I missed her. I could have done with her wise talk, her kindness. I began to feel maudlin. Decided it was the whisky doing my thinking. I reached down and gave Sam a pat. A woman's best friend was her dog. Loyal to a fault and never took issue.

Cassie's message came late. I was beginning to nod off in my seat when I heard the crackle and then a voice.

'Pearl, are you there?'

I got up and reached for the handset. The shawl fell off my shoulders.

'Yeah, I'm here. What's the news?' I had to focus on my speech to stop the slur.

'Not good, I don't think. Fred's never heard of that guy across from you.'

'Thought not.'

'He said no one should be in his place and to get some rent off him before you get rid of him.'

'Those were his words, hey?'

'As relayed to me by Miriam, yes. She said Fred said he wants that guy out pronto.'

'I'll deal. You rest up, Cassie.'

'Good luck.'

'I don't need luck, honey. But thanks, anyway.'

I was in for a restless night. I switched off the radio, drained my glass, and screwed the cap back on the whisky bottle. I took the glass to the kitchen and gave it a quick rinse. Then I peered out the window. There was nothing to see, but at least I had a new focus.

In fact, I had a mission and I looked forward to it with relish. That so-called Brent might think he was a smart operator, and I bet he thought an old hag like me was no threat to anyone. If he did, he thought wrong. My veins were filled with my grandmother's blood and my heart beat to her rhythm. Never mess with a white-haired fisherwoman living the hermit's life down by the river. Maybe his mum never read him fairy tales. If he even had a mum. There was something wanting in his manner, of that I was sure, and those kiddies needing rescuing.

I got myself ready for bed and lay back, staring into the dark, knowing I would have a long morning ahead of me.

CHAPTER TWENTY-FOUR

Pat made Con close the roadhouse on the dot of six. She was still furious with him over the burnt pie mix. She told me she'd made a goulash with potato dumplings and didn't want it to spoil, but I didn't believe that was her reason. I suspected she wanted to hurry Con out on a quest for more road kill.

Her mood had improved since their earlier altercation, slightly. She was counting the day's takings while I cleaned out the pie warmer. I had to rub away at some spilled gravy on the tray at the bottom that had formed a hard lump. I wasn't allowed to use abrasives in case they marred the interior gleam.

Every hurried rub, I did with resentment. I'd already cleaned the bomb site that was the kitchen after Con's baking, eyeing off the tray of incinerated pies tossed in a heap in the open topped bin. Pat made me clean the oven too, to rid it of the caked-on gravy spills that had turned charcoal black and clung on as though they'd been welded. I was allowed to use a scourer and cleaning agents, but the task was still laborious and seemed to take an age. Every so often Pat would hover behind me, peering in and saying, 'Missed a bit.'

After that, I'd had to tackle the offending saucepan with its half inch of caked on pie filling, replete with congealed carrots and ribbons of flesh.

I eradicated the last of the gravy spills and closed the pie warmer. Behind me, the till drawer clapped shut. Pat went and switched off the lights. With the café closed up for the night, we went through to the kitchen and sat down to the food Pat had prepared. Around the table were three chairs, arranged in a T. She took the head of the table, as usual, which meant I had to sit opposite Con.

Pat served. I received three dumplings, a ladle of goulash and a small mound of cabbage. Con received more than double my portion and Pat's plate scarcely had anything on it. We picked up our knives and forks in silence. Con dove in, Pat picked around the edges of her food and I struggled through mine, hoping—although I knew it was most likely in vain—that the meat in the goulash was shop bought beef. It did taste like beef. I swallowed each mouthful, chasing it with a forkful of cabbage or dumpling. I struggled through everything on my plate, for I knew there was no point in attempting to leave a morsel. Pat brooked no waste. To add to my chagrin, Con ate as he always did, with the manners of a hog, elbows on the table, shovelling in his food, chewing with his mouth open.

I kept my head bowed. He was impossible to watch.

When he finished, he belched.

'Thanks, Ma,' he said, leaving his plate where it was and going over to the sink to wash his hands.

Con and Pat left the room as soon as they were finished. It was down to me to clean up. Thankfully, Pat was a tidy cook. Her saucepans had unblemished sides. In ten minutes, I was done and sitting on my bed reading Patrick White.

I was grateful to Pete. I thought it might be the last thing he ever gave anyone. It was a gloomy thing to imagine.

I warmed to the author's wit. I liked the almost Dickensian characters he imagined. With names like Nesta Pine and Goodenough and Shacklock, how could I not? I sunk into his short stories as though they were a cultural eiderdown, plumped with little bits of poetry and astute observances. I gained a much better sense of what constituted Australian society, although White found the country as provincial as I, his tone gently mocking and ironic. At the end of a story I closed the book thinking the title apt, for the characters were indeed a large mob of squawking cockatoos.

Although, thinking about it, there in Cann River, where there was an abundance of bird life, there was no human equivalent of the cockatoo or even a parrot anywhere to be seen. The place, as far as I could tell, was full of ravens and blackbirds. The locals I'd encountered were sullen and laconic, battling through from one week to the next, or they were strange or bat-shit crazy. Maybe the nice and ordinary folk never left their properties, but truth be told the only happy resident I'd met was Cassie. I recalled, dimly, the smiling faces of the people I'd met up the coast, the sunny reality, buoyant, fresh, alive. Cann River, I thought with sudden gloom, smelled of Cons' pies, of animal urine and rot, all musty and rank.

From somewhere in the building Pat's voice, low-toned and gravelly, broke the silence. Moments later, I heard Con in the corridor outside my room. Breathing. There was a soft creak as he entered the bathroom. The whoosh and tinkle of water in the basin. That went on for some time. Then footsteps, the door creaking shut, the breathing as he stood there. The dog let out a soft whimper. It occurred to me he was patting the dog.

After a short while, he went back to his room and I continued reading. I chose stories at random, and after devouring the final two, I came to 'The Night The Prowler'. Not long after, I decided I'd had enough and put the book down. The story was forty-five pages long, and I knew I'd strain my eyes if I kept reading as I'd already consumed one hundred, which was my limit.

I wasn't sure where my fixation with numbers of pages came from, but I suspected it arose through the pressures of studying numerous university set texts. Besides, I wasn't so taken with that particular story of White's. A woman vomiting into a washbasin was more than I could stomach after the goulash, and all the smells of the roadhouse which had congregated in my room. When I thought of it, the comingled odours were already making me feel queasy.

I switched off the light and lay in the darkness. For a short while all was quiet. Then I heard a slam, the rumble of the garage door and Con's station wagon revving and chugging. The sound faded away as he headed off up the mountain. It was all familiar. I used to feel relieved when Con left, knowing I wouldn't have to endure his hand washing for many hours. No more. I lay there unable to sleep, knowing why Pat had sent him out.

CHAPTER TWENTY-FIVE

MIRIAM

The first rays of dawn infused the room with a dim, grey light. It was a signal to my nocturnal neighbour, and all went quiet in the next room; the bonks, the moans and the tossing about, gone. His nocturnal noises were replaced by the raucous chorus of cockatoos, shouting their heads off in the nearby trees, as though a new day had never before occurred, and they were rendered ecstatic and had to tell each other all about it.

I didn't share their enthusiasm. I felt more haggard than ever. Another night of intermittent sleep, interspersed with long spells listening to the goings on next door. I couldn't shake off my apprehension. I didn't dare put on the light in case he saw it and sought companionship, or worse, saw it as an invitation to molest me in some fashion. For he must have known about my presence in the adjoining room. He'd seen me in the corridor and in the dining room.

The fatigue added to my harried state of mind. My hopes of a bright new future that had buoyed my journey from

Cockatoo had stalled in Cann River with its roadhouse and hotel, and its dubious collection of local women and equally dubious collection of men. It was as though I had never left my charred past. Instead, I was forced to pick my way through the blackened remains of memory, hemmed as Cann River was, by a skirt of towering, flammable trees.

I sat up in bed, gazing blankly at the wardrobe with its single mirrored door, and there I was, hair askew, eyes puffy, mouth set. Ash Wednesday blazed in my mind as though the conflagration had taken place the night before, and I could smell the acrid fog, feel it stinging my nose, my eyes; the heat of that day scalding my skin while those around me burned alive in the fire.

The screams.

Oh, god, the screams.

It was rumoured at the time to be arson. The suspect duly shunned by the community, but I doubted he'd ever face justice. The trauma of that day flared inside me, and the fear I'd felt back then intensified in the gloom of the morning, before giving way to outrage and indignation in the face of my present. I was furious that a down and out drug dealer with a serious habit could infiltrate himself into me, a threat. I felt trapped and it was only Monday. I was a prisoner, at his mercy for the next three nights.

I dragged myself out of bed, rummaged around in my suitcase for clean underwear, and grabbed yesterday's pants and shirt off the chair. I didn't bother to be quiet. It felt good to be stomping around, a sort of revenge, however insignificant. If I was disturbing him, he never let on. It was as though he was dead to the world. Even the loud bang of the door as I went to the bathroom didn't evoke a reaction.

The gush and the splash. The steam and the soap. Washing

away my restless night did little to refresh me. At seven, I took up my place in the dining room and knocked back the orange juice Cassie had already poured hoping food would do what fresh warm water hadn't and I'd gain at least a measure of energy for the day.

While I waited for my food, I watched the events of the morning unfold at the crossroads. Not that there was much to see. The roadhouse was lit and there was a station wagon on the forecourt. Con had left the garage door half open, revealing the rear bumper of my car. Seeing it there provided no comfort. A deep rumble shattered the quiet as a logging truck thundered into town, its compression brakes hammering as an afterthought.

Cassie bustled in with a plate of eggs, bacon and thickly buttered toast in one hand and my coffee in the other.

'Just leave it there when you're finished. I'll clear up after,' she said, setting down the plate and cup before me.

'You seem in a hurry.'

'Sure am. Got a delivery back at mine in half an hour and I need to set up.'

I was about to ask what of, but she was already rushing away.

The food made me feel better and worse all at once. All that protein and fat and carbohydrate gave me much required energy, yet I felt sleepy, despite the coffee. It was set to be another long and tedious day.

I decided to hassle Con, make sure that spare part was on its way.

My constricted existence, back and forth across the highway; a hotel, a roadhouse, a park and a churchyard all that occupied my time, and the whole situation pressed in on me. As I polished off the last of my toast it occurred to me with a burst of optimism that I could get a bus out of town and come back for the car on Friday. I calculated the logistics of the idea and factored in the five hours to my destination, which wasn't my actual destination, for my house was another hour's drive from the coach stop. It would be dark on my arrival. I was instantly deflated as I realised I'd have no way of getting from the village to my house. There was a night bus, but it only came through on Mondays and Wednesdays and I'd already missed my chance. When I considered all my personal possessions still in my car, I was more deflated still. I knew I'd never leave my belongings with Con in Cann River. It was bad enough being a highway's width from the contents of my car, let alone several hundred miles. Besides, even if I managed all that travelling, I'd have about one day there and I'd have to turn around and come back. It wasn't worth the effort.

Con was out on the forecourt rolling up the air pressure hose. I seized the moment, left the hotel, crossed the highway and marched across the forecourt.

'G'day,' he said and made to walk away.

'Any chance you can remind Tony to post up my spare part?' I said brightly.

He stopped and gave me a puzzled look. 'Phone Tony?'

'That's what I said.'

'He'll do it.'

'I'd like confirmation that the part has been sent, please.'

'I can do that for you.'

'You will?'

'Um.' He thought for a moment. 'I just have.'

'I don't follow.'

'I already told you. He's posting the part today.'

I clenched my jaw. 'But I want confirmation.'

He shrugged and slumped away, leaving me standing by the air pressure hose wondering at the stupidity and

THE LEGACY OF OLD GRAN PARKS

belligerence of the man. Surely, he knew what 'confirmation' meant?

I marched into the café and found that young girl, Emily, at the counter.

'Hi, what can I get you?' she said with fake cheer.

I considered ordering another coffee to wake me up a bit. Instead I asked to speak to Pat.

'She's out the back.'

'Well, go and get her.'

The girl blushed, and I realised I'd been too abrupt. When she returned, I offered her a brief smile. She responded in kind. Pat came out moments later.

She looked me up and down and said. 'What you want?'

I wasn't about to be put off. 'Con's friend Tony is meant to be posting up my spare part today. I want to confirm that is going to happen.'

'It will happen.'

'That's what Con seems to think. Look, Pat, you might know that. Con might know that. Tony might know that. But I don't. I won't know for sure unless I hear it from the horse's mouth.'

'The horse?'

'Can I have Tony's number? Please? I'll call him myself.'

'Tony won't like that.'

'Too bad.'

Pat riffled through a small pile of business cards and sundry bits of scrap paper, extracting a soiled and limp piece of lined paper with a number scrawled on it in red pen. I thanked her for her trouble.

'Can I get you anything?' Emily said again, this time for Pat's benefit.

'No thanks, honey.' I checked to make sure Pat was out of

earshot before adding, 'You really should get out of this place. Which way are you planning to head?'

'West.'

'Pity. If it had been east, I could have given you a lift.'

Emily didn't appear as disappointed as I thought she might.

CHAPTER TWENTY-SIX

FRANKIE

It was set to be an interesting day. The sun had risen in a murky sky and the air was still. I stood by the wood stove, mug of tea in hand, warming my shins. Mid-autumn and I kept the fire going overnight to take off the chill. Without the fire, the cabin would be frigid. Other than in summer, the sun barely made an impression on the windows throughout the course of its daily passage.

I'd slept well. It had taken a few moments of wakefulness to recall the unwelcome company of Wayne, locked in my shed. When I did, I hurled myself out of bed and filled the kettle.

I used the two-ringed camping stove to boil the water and cook my rice porridge. It was a morning ritual. I kept the heat nice and low. Rice porridge was apt to burn on the bottom and I wasn't having my shack stinking of burnt milk. Con's cindered pie filling had been bad enough.

Ten minutes later, I spooned the porridge in a bowl and laced it with molasses. A woman needed her iron. I sat down and took my time, feet up, chewing slowly, enjoying the sweet, creamy smooth coating in my mouth.

It was only when I was chasing the last grains of rice around my bowl that my thoughts returned to Wayne. I supposed he'd be hungry too, not that I cared about his welfare, but I scraped the rest of the porridge into a bowl and drizzled on the molasses.

I sculled my tea, pouring the dregs down the sink.

I slung my rifle over my shoulder on the way out the door, not wanting to give Wayne the impression I'd softened.

Outside the shed, I set down the porridge and unlocked the door, keeping my rifle to the ready. I expected him to come hurtling out, but when I pushed open the door all that exited was the stench of human urine. I found him wedged in beside the fridge in the far corner. The fridge was a double door Kelvinator, large enough to chill a deer. It whirred and droned. No doubt Wayne had huddled against it for warmth. He sat there, nursing his sore ankle. He'd taken off his boot and as my eyes adjusted to the interior gloom, I saw that his ankle was swollen, bloody and bruised. He looked up at me with that expression of fright and disbelief.

I leaned my rifle just inside the door. Seeing he was in no hurry to get up I collected his breakfast and set it down on the floor near his feet. The shed reeked. My mood darkened with the knowledge that I'd have to scrub out the space before I did any more butchering. I returned to the doorway, my rifle at my side.

He looked at his bowl with instant disgust. Neither of us spoke. Minutes passed. Then he picked up the spoon and started shovelling the porridge into his mouth. I figured he probably hadn't eaten in a while.

'What are you doing setting man traps like that?' he said between mouthfuls, talkative now as his belly filled. 'Are you mad or something?'

My upper lip twitched. It was as though he thought I was

his equal, and we could have a banter about ways of causing others harm.

'It was only for you,' I said.

'Me? Why me?'

I didn't answer. I didn't think his remark warranted an answer. I watched him finish his food. Contempt bristled in every cell of me. 'Whaddya tie me to the spot mill for?'

'I was having a lend of you, mate.'

'Damn straight you were.' A nervous laugh spilled out of him, as though I'd reassured him I was joking. His confidence grew. 'There was no need to lock me up, but.'

'It was dark. I didn't want you getting taken by wildlife.'

He looked at me, trying to gauge if I was serious.

'How's the leg? You able to walk?'

'I reckon.' He tried to stand, winced and slumped back down. 'Hurts, does it?'

'What do you think?'

'Need a doctor, maybe.'

'I'm not seeing no doctor.'

I left the rifle where it was and crossed the shed. My eyes never left his face. I reached down and grabbed his arm. 'Get up.'

He leaned forward and pushed up on his good leg, steadying himself. The moment he gained his balance I wrenched his arm up his back, letting him know I was still in charge.

'For Christ's sake!'

I waited, keeping him there, wanting him to feel my power before releasing his arm. He hobbled forward, moaning, and sat down on the only seat in the shed, a rickety three-legged stool. I observed him, letting a few more moments pass, allowing him to gather himself up, not giving him long enough to run with an idea.

'That really hurting you?' I said, crossing the shed and blocking the exit.

'What do you think?'

'You need painkillers.'

'Damn straight I do.' He inhaled as though to add an insult to the remark before letting out the air in his lungs in a sudden moment of common sense.

'I know where you can get strong painkillers,' I said, careful to keep my tone hostile. 'Real strong. No doctor. No chemist.'

'Yeah?' His eyes lit with greed more than a desire for pain relief.

'At the hotel. There's a guy staying there. A drug dealer on the run. I've heard half the state is after him. His stash is that big.'

'Of what?' He sounded part interested, part doubtful.

'Just your kind of painkiller, I'd say.' I swished away a fly that thought it had been granted easy access to my shed, and then I took hold of my rifle. Wayne wasn't threatened by it. 'I've been told it's smack.'

'Yeah, right.'

'He's hiding out in one of the upstairs rooms. Weird guy apparently. Up all night and sleeps all day. Paranoid by the sound of it. He never leaves his room.'

'How do you know all this?'

'I got talking to the woman in the room next to his.'

'Which room is that?'

'She's not your type, buddy.'

He gave me a puzzled look, his slow brain trying to figure out how much I knew about him. I was quick to add, 'Hers is the corner room overlooking the crossroads.'

I went and picked up his empty porridge bowl and handed him his boot.

'You can't stay here. I've got deer to hunt and this is where they're butchered.'

His freedom took a while to sink in. I was standing behind him.

'I really thought you were gonna kill me,' he said, struggling to get the boot on.

I laughed. 'Just get going. Strong lad like you will make it back to the highway, no problem.'

I watched him limp down the track wondering how he'd manage to drive. About half an hour later I heard his car engine fire up and I decided that ankle of his couldn't be that bad after all.

I had no idea if my ruse would work or what the outcome would be if those two met, but it seemed to me I'd thrown one stone to rid Cann River of two blackbirds. Old Gran Parks would be pleased.

CHAPTER TWENTY-SEVEN

PEARL

The mouth of the inlet was open, the tide running high. The ocean pushed against the outflow of the Cann river and the lagoon was full to its edges. Despite the cool, I was in my boat on sunrise, rowing out to the further reaches of the northern basin, where the waters were deep.

Away from the river flow, the water was glassy, my boat and oars upsetting the calm, sending off ripples. All was still in the bush that enclosed the inlet. Towards the inlet's mouth, where the southern basin met giant sand dunes, there were granite slopes and rock platforms interspersed with brackish marsh. There was good fishing to be had down there, but not for an old woman in a small rowing boat. Not when the tide ran into the open mouth. Tides turn.

I reached the long tapering spit that separated the basins when the waters were low. Towards the middle of the inlet the spit was broached by the higher water level. Taking advantage, I pulled in my oars and settled in for the morning's fishing. The sun warmed my back. With a Squidgy Wriggler for bait, I cast and dragged and waited. I was in no rush. I gazed into the bush not ten metres from my boat, and picked out a wild dog, sniffing the air. It was mean and mangy looking and hungry. Probably not a swimmer.

The salty sea air, the sun on my face, the mantle of bush wrapping the lagoon rendering private the brackish waters and the gentle rocking of the boat, and my mind drifted, lulled.

Out there beyond the sand bar spoke of exposure. I thought of Emily, trudging down the long stretch of wild beach from the lighthouse to Clinton Rocks. All that soft sand, with the thick bush and the sand dunes rising up high to one side of her, the ocean thrashing on the other. I never told her low tide was best as then she could walk on the wet and firmer sand. I doubted she knew much about tides. I doubted she knew much about the Southern Ocean. Lately the swell had been large and the southerlies had been driving three-metre waves at the beach. They had a habit of breaking close to the shoreline too, each a gaping mouth threatening to swallow the onlooker. It was better she didn't know any of that unless the time came, and she was forced to do it.

I don't know why I kept thinking about her. She was nothing to me. Just a pretty, young backpacker making foolish decisions. I supposed it was a lot easier to think about her than my grand kiddies being taken thousands of kilometres north by Kylie and her new life in the tropical rainforest of Daintree. It was a lot easier to think about Emily than those two kiddies in the care of that man who called himself Brent. Emily would most likely not come to any grief, I reasoned, even with a murdering rapist on the loose. Yet I couldn't remove from my head the image of a lone woman battling her way along that beach.

I told myself Emily was nothing to me, yet she was becoming something even if she was only a replacement for all the anguish.

I felt the pull of the rod and began the slow reel. The bream was a good size, neither large nor small. I enjoyed the cool, slimy feel, the way it wriggled for freedom, its gills flapping in desperation. It was all to no avail. I reached for the mallet I kept for the job and dealt it a couple of swift head blows before tossing it in the bucket.

I caught a couple more bream before rowing over to the southern basin where I hoped to catch some tailor. I cast the lure off the back of the boat, and pulled it in slowly, pausing intermittently. It took about ten casts before I felt the bite. A feisty fish with teeth like daggers and once I'd unhooked the barb, I slit its throat and let it bleed before putting it in the bucket with the bream.

Satisfied with the catch, I replaced rod for oar and rowed upstream. The going was strenuous. By the time I entered the river mouth my arms ached from the effort. For an old crone with darts of anguish in her heart and niggles that twinged in her bones, it was a pleasant, muscular sort of ache.

Gutting and filleting required method and focus. I liked to take my time. It was late morning when I'd finished. I cleaned my knife, took out the whetstone, and sharpened the blade. The motion of the blade, the slow sharp sound, put me in a kind of trance.

Emily was forgotten. Instead, I pictured my grandkids, their little bodies growing bigger every day. Their angelic faces. Their sweet smiles. I had to make that drive. The missing would be too much if I didn't. I told myself when things settled a bit, I'd go up there for a visit.

Then I pictured myself on the road. Driving north. Four days' worth of driving under normal circumstances. My old jalopy wouldn't make it. Not without a service. I wouldn't make it. There was no servicing me and I was all out of luck. Kylie knew that. She knew I didn't travel well. I'd suffered travel sickness my whole life and the most I could manage was a few hours at a single stretch. She knew that and that was why she'd taken off up there. She was doing it to hurt me, to punish me for being a bad mother.

I put away the knife and leaned back against the bench. I was not a bad mother. I'd done everything for that child and given her everything I could manage.

It was never enough.

She'd taken her father's side in the fallout from the marriage. She'd forgiven him straight away, quick to adopt his view that the only reason he'd gambled was because I'd driven him to it. Meek and mild me. I was meek and mild back then too, despite the tough, farm girl exterior. The fact that Mal gave up the gambling habit soon after we'd sold the house and I'd left him, didn't help Kylie's perception. Which was so plainly warped, but there wasn't a thing I could do to fix it. She was entrenched.

Maybe that was why I was feeling an attachment to Emily. Maybe she represented the daughter I never had. Although, I would not have wanted a daughter like her. She was too callow for her own good.

Over by the wood stove, Sam stirred and pricked up her ears. I glanced out the window but there was no movement.

The day's catch, and I had a nice platter of filleted fish. All thoughts of Emily and the grandkids faded, and I fell back into full awareness of the plan I had devised the night before.

Fish pie. Who could resist my grandma's recipe? Only those who disliked fish. I knew Brent was a liar, but I believed him when he told me his kids despised fish. He could have had no motive for lying. It seemed I'd hit on a source of deep resentment he held for their mother, as though she'd set about getting her children to dislike fish as some sort of vendetta or vengeance against him. What sort of woman would do that? Certainly, no woman I'd ever met.

The blood of my grandmother pumped through my veins. By hook or by crook, she would say softly when we were alone. She'd say it when she was cross. At the time, I had no idea what she meant. It wasn't until much later that I discovered it was her way of dealing with those who had wronged her in large and small ways. In some ways, her and Gran Parks were similar.

My grandmother said a fish pie should contain a variety of flavours to round out the taste of the fish. Dill, parsley and tarragon were preferred herbs and a selection of diced vegetables never went amiss. I put in onion and carrot. In the white sauce, lashings of black pepper and a good dollop of mustard. Plenty of butter in the mashed potato topping. In all, it was a hearty and delicious combination of flavours. My grandmother would have been smiling over my shoulder. It was her recipe and I was following it to the letter.

Only one ingredient was missing. I pulled on my rubber gloves and went outside armed with scissors and a bowl. The roadside herb was flourishing that autumn. I picked a nice bouquet.

It was a method as old as history.

I chopped and stirred in the last ingredient and proceeded to assemble the pie in its dish. With every spoonful, the cautious part of me kept telling the steadfast part that I had no evidence that the Brent character was bad other than that he'd broken into Fred's. The cautious part kept berating the steadfast part as I baked another batch of cookies for those girls. When I pulled the cookie tray from the oven and set it down beside the pie, observing the fare with an admiring eye, the cautious part of me gave up and slumped off, defeated.

I placed the cookies in a fancy tin thinking they would fill those little tummies nicely.

Late that afternoon, I ferried across to Fred's the cookies in their tin, and the fish pie, still warm in its dish and draped with a fresh tea towel. I hoped the pie contained enough poison to kill an elephant, but I really didn't think it would do anything other than give that imposter a whopping bellyache. I wouldn't have minded being rid of him. I'd have relished taking those girls back to their fish-hating mother, but despite being steadfast in my plan, I knew it was wrong.

Then, I reasoned out my innocence. I was following instructions. I was following the instructions laid down by Gran Parks and my grandmother, and I was following Fred's directive. He wanted that man called Brent gone from his premises. I was doing everything in my power to make that happen. By the time I reached the front door I decided I was blameless. I was doing what I was told.

Seeing me laden with fare, Brent was more willing to let me inside and I followed him through to the kitchen.

He stood by the sink as I deposited my gifts on the table. He seemed more amenable, almost relaxed. He probably thought he had an idiot old granny for a neighbour, the sort who couldn't harm an ant.

'You shouldn't have bothered,' he said, eyeing the food.

'No trouble at all. I caught way too much fish for just me,' I said brightly, unfurling the tea towel and revealing the pie with its crusty potato top. 'It would be a shame to let it go to waste. Call me a dotty old granny, but I just can't help myself when it comes to baking.' I laughed, keeping the tone light and pleasant. The uniquely appetising smell of my pie infused the room. 'Besides,' I said, 'you look like you could do with a good feed. The country air and all that.'

In my side vision, I spotted the girls. I gave them one of my winning smiles.

'I made some more cookies, too.'

The blonde came forward. I held out the tin. She took a cookie and ran off. The other child, the redhead, followed suit.

Black-haired Brent remained where he was, one ankle casually crossed over the other.

'The pie's a bit rich for them,' I said, just in case he thought of giving them some. 'I cooked the fish in wine.' I hadn't but he'd never know. 'It's my grandmother's recipe. I do hope you like it.'

'I'm sure I will.'

'You planning on staying long?'

'A few more days.'

'Where are you heading?'

'North.'

'Not back home then.'

Something like hate flashed into his face.

'We're moving to a new home,' he said, flicking his fringe out of his eyes with a toss of his head.

I wanted to ask him what the girl's mother thought of his decision, if she was still alive to be asked.

'I hope it all works out for you,' I said, making every effort to sound genuine. 'I'd better get back. Got the other fish pie to get down me.'

CHAPTER TWENTY-EIGHT

EMILY

There was something about that Monday that brought things to a head. A new cynicism had filtered into my being and it came from a variety of sources. The three hags—the skunk mulleted Amazon, the white-haired witch and the indomitable old maid—with their cautionary tales about bad men from out of town, had me thinking that they'd overlooked another, because they'd been focussing in the wrong direction. Pete was my salvation. He was the one, the only one who'd offered a realistic alternative to my caged existence at the roadhouse. Miriam's casual suggestion that she might have given me a lift if I'd been heading the same way as she didn't count because it was vacuous. Besides, I doubted her sincerity. Without Pete, I was stuck in that roadhouse, suffering the weirdest human being I'd ever encountered: Con.

The way his mother hemmed him with her mithering seemed little short of toxic. To a degree, he was a product of her oppression. He was also his own product, born of all the cells in his being. With or without her, he was an oddball. The sort that would have been labelled and put in a special unit or centre, or even locked away somewhere. Really, on some level Pat was doing him a favour. At least in Cann River, he had a measure of freedom, even if it was collecting road kill.

The morning got off to a strained start after Miriam had demanded the telephone number of Con's spare parts mate in the city. When one controlling woman confronted another controlling woman, things never went well. After Miriam had marched off, Pat was angry, her mood leaden. She couldn't take out her wrath on Miriam, who was a customer after all, and she couldn't carp at me when there were other customers in the café, so she took it out on her son. To make a tense atmosphere worse, Con was not having a good morning making his pies. I wasn't surprised, with Pat standing over him, complaining that she didn't want another burnt batch.

I heard all the goings on in the kitchen from my location behind the counter. First Con had trouble with the pastry. He'd made it too wet and, by adding more flour, the ratio of fat was wrong and it didn't hold together so well. Then he forgot to stir the pie fillings, this time managing to burn the venison. There was a lot of crashing down of utensils and slamming of cupboard doors. In a voice that could cut steel, Pat dished Con advice on masking the flavour. The hunter was no better. I was making a customer a coffee when I heard a spitting sound, which must have been Pat because she was quick to yell at Con for adding too much salt and told him to grate a couple of potatoes into the hunter mix. I could only imagine what state the kitchen would be in by the time he was finished. I dared not look for fear of attracting Pat's ire to myself.

Whenever Con was baking, it was down to me to take care of the bowsers, should anyone pull up needing petrol. I didn't grumble. It was good to get outside, even if to inhale petrol fumes and not fresh air. The lack of passing trade meant I only went out a handful of times before the sun had risen high enough to warm the forecourt.

After filling the tank of a Holden, I went in with the cash, depositing it in the till to the sound of a sudden gush of water in the kitchen. He was washing his hands. That, and the smell of baking signalled the end of Con's culinary chore. I wiped the counter anticipating the presence of Pat for the lunchtime rush, bookended by the arrival of the city-to-city coaches, when a car swung onto the forecourt and pulled up on the far side of the bowsers. My heart beat a little faster. It was Pete.

I watched him cross the forecourt. As he drew nearer, I thought he looked markedly sicker than yesterday. Perhaps that climb up the lighthouse had worn him out, although he said he did it every day. Maybe the cancer had decided to gather its forces. Whatever the cause, my heart reached out to him. As he opened the door, I averted my gaze, not wanting to appear intrusive. By the time he stood at the counter I was shunting about the clutter on the narrow bench below the servery, making space for an imaginary plate of food.

'Hello, Emily.'

I couldn't help the colour rising in my cheeks.

'Pete. Good to see you again. What brings you into town so soon?' My words sounded formal and polite, despite the warmth behind them. 'Is everything okay?'

'I came to check the mail. Simon's expecting a parcel.' His gaze darted back and forth from my face to the menu board on the wall above me. 'And to eat one of those pies. I'm famished.'

'The venison's good,' I lied, reflecting back on the fracas in the kitchen earlier.

'I fancy the hunter.'

'There's none left,' I said quickly, without looking round at the pie warmer.

'I spot one, right there,' he said, pointing.

'He said he wants a hunter pie, so get him one. What's the matter with you?'

I froze. Her voice came from the other side of the servery. She had the hearing of a bat.

I couldn't disobey her. Without catching her gaze, I took the pie out of the warmer and slid it onto a plate. I could see her head and shoulders, framed by the servery, a ghoulish portrait of someone's little loved aunt. I willed her away, but she stayed there.

'Sauce?' I said to Pete. I had the bottle in my hand, poised to squeeze. When he gave me the indication, I squirted a great dollop right into the vent in the crust.

'Now ask him if he wants tea or coffee,' Pat said. She still hadn't moved away.

'I was just about to,' I said, annoyed at the defensive ring in my voice.

'I'll grab an iced coffee from the fridge, thanks.'

'In this weather?' she said.

Pat always tried to get her customers to have tea or coffee. She made more profit that way. Pete handed me a five-dollar bill and I gave him his change.

'In this weather,' he said, winking at me as he walked away.

Although he didn't really walk away, he shuffled, setting his plate down on his chosen table in the far corner, well away from the entrance door, before heading for the drinks fridge. It appeared he wasn't able to carry both his food and a carton of cold milk.

'Take him a straw,' Pat said.

I didn't mind receiving that directive as it gave me an excuse to go over.

Observing his pie with its red sauce oozing from the lid, I wanted to mouth, 'Don't eat it,' but I knew it wasn't my place, and besides, he seemed to enjoy the hunter pie.

He looked up at me when I gave him his straw as though trying to read my face.

'She likes to humiliate you,' he said quietly.

I didn't dare answer.

'How do you put up with it?'

I shrugged. 'I have to get on,' I said and walked away.

Pat's warring mood had set in for the day, and I knew as I neared the counter that she hadn't finished berating me.

'Customers are always right, Emily,' she said, with that growl in her voice I'd come to despise. 'You remember that.'

She was standing in the kitchen doorway and as I went past her, I cowered inwardly. I thought she would slap me.

Instead, she disappeared, returning with a tray of pies to replenish the warmer.

Within moments, I was confronted with the lunchtime rush, little more than a slow trickle of diners wandering in, all of them wanting various combinations of pies and chips to eat here or take away.

Pat put Joan Baez on the jukebox then went and fired up the chipper and I could hear over the music the sizzle and hiss as she plunged in a basket of frozen chips.

Two customers wanted to order a hamburger with the lot, but hamburgers were off the menu. Like the steak pie, they were a rarity. A middle-aged woman, looking like a relic from the Seventies in a hideous red kaftan, insisted on having a hamburger with the lot, but without the burger, and I had no choice but to call Pat to see if it could be done.

She came out, took in the woman in her kaftan, and ran through each of the salad items, and the egg, bacon and cheese, to confirm what was required. The woman was tapping her fingers on the counter and bobbing her head in time with the beat.

'Good music.'

Pat gave her an appraising glance. Order in hand, she made to head back to the kitchen.

'How much will it be?' I asked her on her way by, as discreetly as I could manage.

'Charge her the same.'

'Even without the meat?'

'She's having everything else,' Pat hissed.

Embarrassed, I took the woman's money and asked her to stand aside while I served a family of four who wanted two hunter pies and a large serve of chips. When they said they didn't want sauce, I all but insisted. They added four milkshakes to their order, and I was occupied with milk and syrup and the high-pitched whine of the shake machine.

Throughout the course of the so-called lunchtime rush, my eyes kept wandering over to Pete, who was hunched over his plate, scooping out the contents of his sauce-adulterated pie crater. I did my best not to dwell too much on the filling.

During a lull, when the customers were seated and no one was out on the forecourt, I reflected on all the meals Pat had prepared in the two months since I had been there, wondering if she'd served road kill in any of her fare. Pat wouldn't serve us the pies. She said they were reserved for customers. She fried a lot of chips and we ate eggs in all kinds of ways. Bacon too. It was definitely bacon and came out of a sealed packet. I'd seen the packaging in the bin. Roast chicken, which was plainly itself with its legs and wings intact, and her goulash, which I decided had to be beef although I couldn't prove it. Then I recalled the bolognaise she made on Fridays. It had a funny twang to it, which I had put down to the sauce but with my new knowledge, I wasn't so sure. I almost heaved in the imagining.

I noticed Pete drawing his knife and fork together and went over to fetch his plate.

I caught Pat in my side vision returning to the jukebox, and Joan Baez started up again.

'She really likes that track,' Pete said with a dry laugh.

'Drives me insane, and just about everyone else, I swear.'

'Johnny Cash does it better.'

I hesitated, not wanting to show my ignorance.

'You never eat the pie case,' I said, picking up his plate.

'Too much pastry gives me indigestion.'

'Then why order a pie? Why not have something else? A woman came in just now and ordered a hamburger with the lot, minus the burger, which we don't have. It looked quite good.'

'I suppose I've been taken in by the gourmet factor. That hunter pie has quite a kick to it. Unusual. At least, I've never encountered anything like it. I've become a bit of an addict.'

He laughed.

I couldn't bring myself to laugh with him. I was about to make my way back to the counter with his plate when he caught my arm.

'I'm heading back to Sydney on Wednesday.'

'So soon? I thought you were here for two weeks. Is something the matter. Are you...?' I couldn't complete the last question.

'Simon's plans have changed and he's coming back early.'

'Can't you squeeze into one of the cottages?'

'They really aren't habitable, Emily.' He held my gaze with sunken eyes. 'Don't look so crestfallen.'

'I wanted to visit the lighthouse again.'

'That's why I'm here.'

'I thought you were checking Simon's mail.'

'That too. But I came in here to see if you wanted to come back with me this afternoon.'

'I'd love to,' I said, refusing to heed the warning voices instilled in me by that cast of hags. A dark mass entered my side vision and I sensed Pat staring at me from the kitchen doorway.

'Are you in a hurry?' I said. 'I'll have to ask if I can have the time off. I'm meant to be working.'

'I'm in no rush.'

I braced myself for the confrontation. In the kitchen, I marched straight over to Pat and came out with my request in a blunt fashion. She refused to let me go. I engaged in a long stretch of wheedling. I felt like a child pleading with its mother for permission to go stay at a friend's house. Pat remained resistant. Then, as though it had only just occurred to her, she said, 'All right. But you lose two days' pay.'

My jaw fell open. Forfeit a whole two days' pay! I could hardly believe she'd do such a thing, even as I knew it was typical of her.

'You will be gone this afternoon and I bet you won't come back until tomorrow lunchtime. That makes two days I lose you.'

'You don't know when I'll be back. I could be back tonight, or before opening tomorrow.'

'Bah!'

'You can't dock two days' pay,' I said, struggling not to shriek. 'I've already worked all morning.'

'I want you back by eight, do you hear me? Eight in the morning at the latest. Then I decide if you lose one day's pay.'

'All right, then.'

'Be back by eight. You clean up Con's kitchen mess then.'

I was shaking with indignation. To not only lose my pay but be confronted with Con's filth on my return? It was the closest I'd come to packing up my things and walking out for good.

.   .   .

Miriam

I decided to wait in my room until twelve, thinking that an appropriate time to inquire about the spare part. I faced a tedious few hours. I determined to get through a large chunk of the Miles Franklin, although I'd been toying with not bothering with it, but that seemed wrong somehow, as though I were doing the author a disservice. Not that she would know. She was no longer alive, and the dead can't speak or influence this world, no matter what people say.

All that nonsense Cassie had spouted about Gran Parks cleaving her husband in two and cursing the town with her legacy in the process. It sounded like make believe. Where was the evidence? If Cassie had any, she wasn't letting on.

I sat up on my bed, ankles crossed, and laboured on with Sybylla and her frustrations, hoping the rural idyll I'd chosen for my life didn't turn out as dull. It was as much as I could do to keep my eyes open. Franklin had done a marvellous job conveying the tedium Sybylla faced. Too marvellous. I must have dozed for the next I knew it was ten to twelve. I grabbed the note Pat had given me and headed downstairs.

The bar was empty. Cassie might have been around, but I didn't bother asking her permission to use the phone. She'd put it back behind the counter. A swift passage through two doors, and I dialled the number.

The phone at the other end rang and rang. I pictured a car parts store, the grubbiness, the concrete floor, the men in overalls at the till, shelves running at right angles to the counter and stacked high with blue boxes of all shapes and sizes. I dialled the number again, and a third time for good measure. No one answered.

Did they close for lunch?

First Fred, now Tony. It seemed I was doomed to spend large chunks of my time in that town attempting to make phone calls. I looked around, eyeing off the spirits lined up on the back-bar shelves. But a drink wouldn't make Tony answer his phone.

I tried one last time. I was putting the receiver in the cradle when Cassie came in and I gave a little start.

'You after Fred again?'

'Sorry, I should have asked permission. I'm trying to call Tony about my car's spare part.'

'Con's mate in the city? Is that the number?'

She gestured at the tired scrap of paper by the phone. I handed it to her. She studied Pat's scrawl for a moment, then frowned.

'I bet she's written that down wrong.' She searched about in a small hutch beneath the counter where an array of business cards leaned on their sides, and pulled out an old invoice, folded in two and impregnated with black grease.

'See,' she said, pointing at the top corner and comparing the two numbers. 'Pat's written an eight instead of a two.' She handed me the invoice. 'I'm glad I caught you. I'm having the rest of the day off. Going home to put my feet up. I've made you a chicken salad. It's in the fridge.'

'What about the bar?'

'It's closed Mondays.'

Impatient to make my call, I bid her a pleasant afternoon, and picked up the receiver. This time the number I dialled answered on the third ring. I explained as succinctly as I could the situation, but there was no need for details. As soon as I mentioned Con, the man on the line who I presumed to be Tony reassured me the part was on its way. The relief I felt made me lightheaded. I succumbed to an upsurge of joy. I was infused with anticipation of a bright new future, my charred past behind me, and Cann River soon to be well and truly history.

Buoyed at the prospect of my imminent release, I took myself off for a walk. Ignoring the coach that had pulled up on the roadhouse forecourt, its passengers decanting and milling about, I went and took a circuit around the park and a detour to the bakery, before settling on my preferred seat in the churchyard. I was determined to get to the end of the Miles Franklin to see if Sybylla would ever have her brilliant career, but I suspected not. I resonated with Sybylla's refusal to marry, but her self-doubts were tiresome. She lacked confidence. I wanted to yell at her, 'You go girl!' But then again, I lived in a different age. Women had more freedom and more choice in the 1980s.

I drifted back to my own young adulthood, to my defiance and determination to live my own life. My adoptive parents were good people, my father certainly not a drunkard like Sybylla's, and they never stood in my way once they realised I was immutable. I'd disappointed them in not providing them with grandchildren, but I had led a satisfying life. Not a brilliant life, but certainly satisfying until calamity struck, and I was rendered homeless.

All afternoon I sat in the churchyard reading, for the most part undisturbed by sight or sound. The sun began to sink behind the trees before a nip in the air caused me to close my book.

The town was lifeless. Barely a car had passed by in all the time I was there in the churchyard. Other than the one o'clock coach rumbling through the town, the only vehicle breaking the peace was the occasional logging truck hurtling down the highway with impunity. When I strolled back to the hotel there were no people about in the street.

It wasn't until I'd reached the bottom of the hotel stairs that I realised I would be alone in the hotel all evening, with that drug dealer in the next room.

I tiptoed through to the kitchen for my dinner, then on to the bar, entering silently through the door that led behind the counter. There I selected a bottle of dry cider. The hiss as I opened the bottle, the chink of the cap as it fell in the bin, the fizz as I poured the cider into a glass, and I was alert to other sounds, from elsewhere in the building.

Glass in one hand, plate in the other, I slunk up the stairs, cringing at every creak. I scuttled past the dealer's door to my own. I had to put my drink and dinner on the floor and fumble in my bag for the key. My heart beat hard and fast. I inserted the key and turned it slowly. The lock made barely a sound, and neither did the door. I was inside my room with the door locked before I realised I was holding my breath and exhaled.

I put the food on the dressing table and sat on the bed with my cider. It was only five thirty, perhaps a little too early for the dealer's transition, but I was convinced I heard movement in his room. Footsteps. A creak of bedsprings. Then, silence.

I sipped my cider and continued reading. A few pages on and I put away the book and polished off the cider. I sat there, bored, frustrated and uneasy all at once. I thought of switching on the television and decided against it. I must have dozed, for when I next opened my eyes the room was in darkness. My bladder was full and despite all the liquid I had drunk, my mouth felt dry. I rummaged in my bag for a bottle of water but found it empty. I'd drained the last drops at the churchyard and forgotten to refill it. A sudden crash and I was alert in an instant. It sounded as though a piece of furniture, perhaps a chair or something heavier, had thundered to the floor. One explosive yell, followed by a loud cry, and another single, heavy thud. Then it all went quiet next door.

Sounded like the dealer had suffered a drug-crazed fit and collapsed.

Concern prickled, ever so briefly, giving way to irritation. I was tired of his antics, of his almost inhuman habits, and in a moment of blind courage, making no attempt to hide my own footsteps, I grabbed my bag and the empty glass and made my way to my door.

In the hallway, I paused and asked myself if I were behaving wisely. What would Cassie have done? Pearl? Frankie? Would they have walked on by that dealer's room, or knocked and entered? I marvelled that I was even considering the situation from their point of view. Yet as the sole other occupant of the hotel, I felt a moral duty to check on the man. He might need assistance. An ambulance maybe.

I thought I'd head downstairs and phone Cassie, seek her advice, then another part of me reared up. I was not a child. Since when had I ever solicited the advice of the staff? I'd held a managerial position in local government. I took orders from no one other than my superiors and they were few and rarely interfered with my decisions. I did not require Cassie's permission, or her endorsement of the action I chose to take.

Still, it was with stealth that I trod the paces to the dealer's door. Incredibly, it was ajar. I knew he was in there. He had to be. There'd been no movement down the hall since that last thud.

I leaned against the door jamb, most of my body pressed against the wall, and with my free hand I gently pushed open the door. The smell of stale sweat, of that unique odour of men, hit me as I peered into the gloom.

My eyes adjusted and what I saw confirmed my opinion. The drug dealer was an outright wastrel. His rump was pointing at me. He was bent over a body whose limbs lay splayed haphazardly on the floor.

I recognised that body by its mullet haircut. It was that murdering rapist, Wayne. What was he doing here?

I stood in the doorway, struggling to take in the scene. The dealer seemed intent on leaning in closer to the body. I thought he might have been trying to attend to him in some fashion, as though he were consumed by remorse for his previous act, having rendered the intruder prostrate. Really, I had no idea what was happening. I was making a raft of suppositions as I tried to make sense of the goings on.

I had no idea even if Wayne had been an invited guest. They were of a type, those two, and if I hadn't fallen asleep, I wouldn't have missed some of the action. I could have kicked myself over that. I had little choice but to step closer, curious as I was to discover what the dealer was up to.

He was unaware of my presence. They both were. I caught sight of Wayne's hand flinching. The dealer opened his mouth as wide as it would reach and bore down on Wayne's neck. I watched on in puzzlement. Then blood pooled on the floor. The dealer groaned with satisfaction. I realised then that he was drinking Wayne's blood.

I wasted no time backing away and tiptoeing downstairs. I rummaged about in my bag for the note Pearl had given me and dialled Cassie's phone number. She'd have to be interrupted on her nice evening off, there was no other option. Besides, I felt abandoned by her, considering this critical situation. It wasn't my place to have to deal with the dramas of another occupant. It was hers.

By the time she answered, I was filled with indignation. Yet my words met with a dopey and vague response.

I explained as best I could. I had to repeat the story three times before she took in the full weight of my words.

'I don't believe in vampires, Cassie, let me tell you that. But what I saw just now bore great resemblance. What sort of human being drinks another man's blood?'

'A drug addict,' she said. 'I'll be right over.'

CHAPTER TWENTY-NINE

FRANKIE

I received Cassie's message around seven that night. I was on my second beer and I'd been wondering how long it would take Wayne to track down Dan's stash. Dan. Cassie had let the name slip when she told me what was happening. Drug dealer Dan, the phrase had a ring to it and at least he wasn't a Dave.

Despite the urgency in Cassie's voice, I wasn't in a rush to get down there. I wanted to enjoy a few moments of satisfaction before I dealt with the aftermath of my ruse. All afternoon I'd been listless. I'd sluiced the butchering shed, polished the rifle, sharpened my boning knife, and stitched another pair of moccasins for Cassie's stall. Time had ticked by with that slow pace it always had when it's observed.

The outcome of my sly scheme was unexpected. I figured once Wayne found Dan's stash he'd binge. I thought perhaps he'd overdose and release me from the burden I'd taken on. Sometimes fate did humanity a favour. I'd carried that faith inside ever since my father Howard Potter fell foul of a magpie and a sheet of roofing iron.

Dan's desperation to retrieve his drugs in whatever manner

presented itself to his crazed brain may yet have the desired result. A man drained of his blood is a dead man. I hoped Cassie and Miriam were leaving them to it.

I put a log on the fire, slugged the rest of my beer and made for the ute. A fifteen-minute drive and I found the women in the bar. By then a good hour had gone by.

'We have to call the police,' Miriam was saying as I pushed open the door. She looked frantic.

'Settle down, Miriam,' Cassie said. 'Frankie will handle it.' She looked up. 'I've tried telling her.'

'She's distraught. She's had a shock.'

I could to see the situation from Miriam's perspective. She'd plainly led a sheltered life. Yet her incessant complaining that the police should be involved was wearing my patience. She sat there, all tense and round shouldered in her blue slacks and cream blouse, and I felt no sympathy for her.

'Another brandy wouldn't go amiss.' She laughed. It was a lacklustre laugh.

'You having one?' Cassie said, addressing me.

'Maybe later.'

Cassie went to the bar and poured herself and Miriam a large glass. I joined her, keeping my back to Miriam and lowering my voice.

'Cassie, I'll be honest with you. I knew Wayne would turn up here. I told him about your drug dealer's stash.'

'You did what?' she hissed.

'It seemed a good idea at the time.'

'So, you set a trap.'

'In a manner of speaking.'

I filled her in on the real trap I'd set, and how I'd sent Wayne on his way, omitting the spot mill episode to avert the wrong impression. I wasn't evil or macabre and I didn't want Cassie thinking I was.

'He's got quite a sore ankle. Not broken but badly bruised. Ironic that he can't deal with the pain after all he's caused.'

'I reckon.'

'He can't have consumed all of that stash. I thought being a dealer on the run meant he'd have kilos of the stuff.'

'He does.'

She took Miriam her drink and returned to the bar. We both leaned with our elbows on the counter, our backs pointed at the room.

'Wayne must have snuck in while Dan was sleeping and stolen the bag,' Cassie said.

'I wonder what he's done with it.'

'Good question. Obviously, Dan has no idea.' She paused and gulped her brandy. 'Trouble is, Dan can't handle cold turkey.'

'Clearly not.'

'All this was happening while I'd dozed off,' Miriam said, loudly, clearly not enjoying finding herself left out of the conversation.

We both turned.

'You were tired, Miriam,' I said. 'You said you hadn't been sleeping.'

'Weird that I did when I needed to be awake.'

'Maybe not. Maybe it's better you had no idea what was going on.'

'We should go up and see how they're faring,' Cassie said.

'What about the police?'

'Will you stop going on about the fucking cops, Miriam! Go take a Bex!'

I was glad it was Cassie who'd said that.

'I just well might,' Miriam said, taking the Bex comment literally.

'But you can't go up there by yourselves.' She looked up at us both. 'Anything might happen.'

Cassie and I exchanged glances.

'Frankie will take care of it.'

We left Miriam sitting in the bar, nursing her drink and eyeing off the Bex powders behind the counter.

'Do you think she'll call the cops?' I said when we were out of earshot.

'Doubt it. I unplugged the phone.'

We found Dan with his chin smeared with blood. He was pacing the room. Wayne was still on the floor, out cold by the look of him, but still breathing.

'You bloody idiot,' Cassie said, addressing Dan.

'He took my stash. What was I supposed to do?'

'Calm yourself.'

He stopped pacing. The blood on his cheeks and his chin had smudged in a symmetrical Rorschach fashion, a blood blot, and it was as though he wore a devil's mask over his acne-festooned face. I could scarcely take my eyes of him, the caved shape of his body, all bony and weak. He had no strength in him, no force. I thought I could snap him in half, and he'd be gone.

'It can't be far, Cassie,' I said without averting my gaze. 'Check around.'

She left the room.

Dan shifted, awkward in the absence of his guardian, for that was what I presumed she was. Some sort of protector. Otherwise, why hadn't she kicked him out and sent him on his way? He slumped down on the edge of the bed. Careful not to turn my back, I knelt beside Wayne.

I slapped his face. He stirred. Part of me was disappointed. Another felt a curious satisfaction. Compassion didn't enter the frame.

Footsteps on the stairs and I turned to see a figure dash past. I thought it might have been Cassie, but seconds later, the figure dashed past again, this time carrying a plate of food. It was Miriam.

I was about to haul Wayne up when Cassie returned with the bag. Beneath the caked-on blood, Dan's face lit when he saw it. He reached out, trembling, the anticipation too much.

'Put it somewhere less visible,' she said, shoving it at him.

'Where was it?' I said.

'Under the bath.'

Cassie and I looked on as he fumbled inside it for his gear, injecting the liquid heaven into his arm and laying back with blessed relief.

'I need to get better locks on these doors,' Cassie said.

'Don't tell Miriam that.'

I pictured the outrage on her face were she to discover that little truth. She'd call the cops for sure.

I gave Wayne a nudge then grabbed him by the shoulders. He moaned.

'He won't be causing you any more trouble,' I said to Cassie.

'You got plans?'

'You betcha.'

I heaved him to his feet. He felt like a dead weight in my arms. His legs barely held him up. He seemed almost grateful until he recognised me. Yet he had no fight left in him. He came with me, willingly, down the stairs and out the back to my ute. He was weak, traumatised, blood deficient and disoriented, which made it all the easier to return him to my butchering shed. He had no clear idea what was going on until I shoved him against the wall and locked the door. Only then did he holler.

Pearl

. . .

It was a tough afternoon. After delivering the fish pie to that so-called Brent, I kept watching for signs of activity. Time seemed to stretch on and on. I kept busy on tasks that allowed a view of Fred's shack, pottering in the side sections of my garden. There wasn't much to do out there. One side was given over to the rain water tank, and the other the wood shed and a few shrubs.

I weeded around the base of the shrubs and gave them a haircut. It felt ludicrous, as though I was some anal gardener tending her neat suburban patch. I even went out the front where the land sloped down to the track and pulled out the weeds that skirted the edge of the house.

As I weeded, I pictured various versions of Brent, ranging in intensity from Brent belching to Brent in abdominal discomfort, Brent throwing up, and Brent clutching his belly and groaning. In a moment of defeat, I saw my pie in the bin, discarded in its entirety. I replaced the image with Brent taking a large mouthful and screwing up his face. Then I saw him devour the whole pie.

I was vigilant, on my haunches anticipating activity, but my idle speculations had the better of me. When one of those little girls came pounding across the track in a panic, a pulse of shock took me, and I almost lost my balance.

Despite my wishful thoughts, I really hadn't expected it to work. I hadn't tasted the pie and presumed the flavour of the hemlock would be off-putting. The best I could have hoped for was an irate Brent complaining I'd tried to poison him.

'Daddy's sick! Daddy's sick!' the little girl cried, her pretty face all blotchy, tears running freely down her cheeks.

The least I could do was respond straight away. I took her hand and ran with her back to the shack. The front door was wide open. I went in to find Brent spread eagled on the living room floor, convulsing. Beside him, a puddle of vomit. It was putrid. There was a damp patch on his trouser front where he'd wet himself. The combination of odours made me heave.

I looked up at the girl. 'Go get your sister and wait in the kitchen.'

'She's right there.'

The girl pointed at the far corner of the room where the other girl was huddled beside the television. I got up and reached for her hand.

'Come on, you two. Go into the kitchen and wait there so I can help your daddy. You shouldn't be seeing this. Come on.'

They offered up no resistance. I told them to sit together at the table and fetched them each a glass of water. Poor little mites. I opened my cookie tin still on the table where I'd left it and placed it between them. The cookies had hardly been touched.

Back in the living room, Brent's convulsions worsened. His breath rasped in his throat. His eyes were wide in terror.

He reached out to me.

I stepped back.

All I could do was watch.

I had no antidote because there was no antidote.

In a moment of confused pity, I moved forward, picked my way around the vomit and stood over him and tried to haul him up, grabbing him by the shoulders thinking I'd load him in my car and drive for help. I gave up when I felt the weight of him and realised he was in no state to even crawl.

A different course of action was needed.

In the kitchen, the girls hadn't moved from their chairs. I knelt down beside them and told them we needed to fetch help. They eyed me with suspicion, reluctant to leave their father. A natural reaction but I couldn't leave them there.

'Daddy needs a doctor,' I said. 'Come and help me find the doctor.'

The redhead slid off the chair. The blonde followed and I soon had them bundled on the backseat of my car and we were off in a whorl of dust, heading up Fisherman's Track.

The sun was bedding down for the night. Heading for Cann River, I took a left at Point Hicks Track. In my frenzied state of mind, I missed the next turn and ended up on Old Everard Road. Seeing my mistake, I turned into Dinner Creek Track. It was another mistake. I came out on the Thurra Road.

It was surreal. All that bush bright in my headlights, all those twists and turns. I drove for what felt like hours, coming to the end of a track and making a guess at a turn, the girls whimpering on the back seat and my head spinning with the magnitude of the situation, triumph vying with horror in my mind.

I knew, dimly, I needed to find my way onto the Tamboon Road. I chucked a U-turn and went back, determined to get my bearings. When I got to the end of Dinner Creek Track, I did a loop down Old Everard Road and ended up back at Fisherman's Track.

I pulled up outside my place, told the girls to stay put, and locked them in the car to make sure.

Things inside Fred's had quietened down. The Brent creature hadn't shifted from where he'd been before, although he must have done a fair amount of thrashing about, judging by the coating of vomit congealing on his shirt and matting his hair. He was a sorry sight, eyes rolled back in their sockets, mouth hanging open, chin coated in drool, face shiny with sweat. He was scarcely breathing. It seemed the merciful thing to do to put him out of his misery. He was going to die anyway, and I was impatient to get on. Besides, Fred wanted him gone and I thought I'd expedite the matter.

I fetched a knife from the drawer beside the kitchen sink. Serrated, but it didn't matter. I stood over him and pressed a foot down on his shoulder. He turned, willingly, onto his back. I ripped open his shirt, took aim and plunged the blade between his ribs, straight into his heart, or so I hoped.

The gurgle that came with the spasm indicated success, as did the pulse of blood spurting from his chest. I stood well back, enjoying a brief moment of triumph, before realising I'd added to the awful mess on the floor.

I had to act quickly. Those girls wouldn't stay in the car forever and I needed to clean up before the stains set in. I dropped the knife and hurried outside and across the road, unlocking the car and flinging open the rear passenger side door. I hadn't thought to wash my hands. Those kiddies took one look at my bloodied state and started screaming.

Their wails were unrelenting. I herded them into the house and on through to my bedroom. They were only crying one word. Daddy. It was all too plaintive, too anguished and I had nothing to comfort them. The cookies were back at Fred's. Sam looked up at me and sniffed the air. I told her to lie down while I riffled through the bottom kitchen drawer where I was sure I'd left the bedroom door key. I'd never had recourse to use it before. I found it, right at the bottom at the back.

Sorry, girls, I said to myself, turning the key in the lock. Their screams faded, the further I walked away.

By then, my thoughts had switched to practicalities. I couldn't leave the body at Fred's. Somehow, Brent had to be disposed of or once they had a whiff of him the goannas would be queuing at the door. Besides, it only took one blow fly to turn him into a bloated, maggot infested carcass. Fred would be livid if he turned up to face that. But I lacked the strength to shift him. There was only one way to deal with the situation; Frankie's way. I'd have to butcher the beast.

She'd use a knife.

Gutting fish was one thing, jointing a man another.

The chainsaw was on the front deck. I'd been sharpening the teeth in readiness for winter.

After many weeks of use, I had an impressive wood pile that year, the result of a full-grown stringy bark falling across Fisherman's Track and blocking my exit back in February. It had been hollowed out by termites but there was a lot of dry wood in it. Took me days to clear a path through and I'd spent a good few weeks sawing and ferrying the whole lot of it back to mine.

I put the chainsaw in the boot of my car. I grabbed two large black plastic bags from the shed. I kept a tarp spread out in the boot which I thought would suit my purposes as well.

By the time I returned to Fred's, blood had pooled on the living room floor on the left side of Brent and mingled with his vomit. I went to the kitchen for a cloth to clean it up before turning back, realising I'd have quite a clean-up on my hands soon enough.

I pushed the soft furniture back against the wall and covered it with the sheets off Brent's bed.

I fetched the tarp and laid it out on the right side of the body. I paused. Deciding it would be easier to roll the body away from me, left me little choice but to kneel in that blood and vomit and roll Brent onto the tarp. Once there, I went out and fetched the chainsaw.

Dismembering a human body is not a skill I'd acquired. It occurred to me to radio Frankie, who would have handled the task with finesse, but she'd take at least an hour and a half to get down there and I didn't want to leave those kids locked up longer than I had to. Besides, I valued my independence.

I found I had a surprising amount of energy. It didn't prove onerous removing all the clothing.

I tossed his shirt, his pants, his underpants, even his socks over by the door, where it made a sodden pile.

Firing up the chainsaw, feeling its violence reverberate through my arms put me in a focused, resolute mood and I viewed those arms and legs as though they were limbs on a tree.

The goanna must have smelled the blood. It was half way across Fred's front yard when I went out and hurled a leg its way. I was glad I thought to feed it first or I might have been stuck with it for company. I bagged up the second leg for Sam, jointing it at the knee and foot. I didn't like to give Sam the foot, so I put it in the other bag. Two hands soon joined it.

I had to look away when I brought the saw down on Brent's neck, going by feel and resistance to indicate I'd sliced it through. His stricken visage was impossible to look at. I lifted the head by the hair and, ignoring the gushing blood, I deposited it in the bag with the foot and the hands.

A couple of neat cuts at the shoulders and the elbows and only the torso remained. I added the limb joints to the bag with the head. I could have done with a third bag. I had to remove Sam's leg joints and slide in the torso.

Blood. So much blood.

My hands were sticking to the chainsaw. I was soaked. The room was infused with a metallic smell. I took umbrage over all the trouble Brent had put me through. A child abductor hiding out there thinking he was beyond the law. Resulting in me kneeling there sodden.

He'd become an outright inconvenience.

I picked up the chainsaw and ran over to my place, dumping it out of sight behind the rain water tank before heading to the shed for a bag of rags. Back at Fred's I snatched all the cleaning products I could find.

I was rushing. Brent was all bagged up. I told myself to slow down. Breathe. I didn't want blood in my car boot. I found some bin liners in Fred's laundry. Problem solved. I put Sam's limbs in one and lined the boot with the others. I had Brent in the boot in no time.

I folded the tarp in on itself and took it outside. The goanna had disappeared. I suspected all the hungry wildlife in the vicinity would be twitching at the smell. Cats, dogs, foxes, dingoes, goannas. I went around to Fred's garden tap, situated beneath the kitchen window, and was relieved to see the hose still attached.

I turned on the tap. Nothing. Not even a hiss. Then I remembered the lack of water in the rainwater tank Fred used for the garden and bundled the tarp in the boot with the bags. I'd have to deal with the bloodied boot later.

The living room was in an awful state. As was I. It was difficult to choose the best course of action. Should I clean up the room first, and then myself, or the other way around? I chose the former.

Thinking to avoid making more of a mess as cleaned up, I stripped off my blood wet clothes and dumped them in the bath. Naked, I fished out some rags, filled a bucket with water, and set to. I must have looked a right old sight, me with my drooping breasts and sagging belly, down on my hands and knees rubbing and scrubbing Fred's place clean. Back and forth I went, emptying down the laundry trough one bloodied water bucket after another.

I didn't stop until I was satisfied I'd attended to every smear and splash on walls and floor, taking special care with the coffee table, the television and the mantelshelf. I removed the sheets from the couches, relieved to see the spatters had not soaked through. There was not much I could do about the speckles on the curtains but decided the drapes were old and ratty and it was about time Fred replaced them. I made a mental note to charge Fred double for cleaning up after his uninvited guests.

That metallic smell still hung in the room, but I thought it would wear off once the place had dried out. Besides, I was still bloodied from head to toe.

I'd never been one for cold showers, but I was feeling hot and bothered and I found the water liberating. I was tentative at first, standing in the bath beneath the shower rose with my clothes at my feet. Once my body adjusted to the chill of it, I opened the tap some more and let the water do its job. After a thorough rinse, I set to work rubbing bubble bath and soap and shampoo, all the soapy contents of that washroom into my clothes, my hair, my skin. I didn't care that I was using up Fred's tank water. I didn't turn off the tap until I was shivering.

I wrung out my clothes and hung them from the taps to drip. Then I took a pink towel and rubbed my body dry. It was only then I realised I had no clothes to put on. I'd used all the rags to clean up the blood. Which left me no choice, unless I felt game enough to streak across to mine. I did not. My virtue wouldn't let me. Instead, I went into the room Brent had been using and rummaged through his things, extracting a plain blue T-shirt and a pair of casual pants. I was surprised to find the items fitted me quite well with the cuffs rolled up.

It wasn't a pleasant thought, leaving those kiddies locked in my bedroom, but little could they know they were far better off there than witnessing all this.

I bundled the towel and my wet clothes and took them out to the car where I put them on the back seat. I went in for the sheets and used them to stow Brent's clothes. I put the vile mess of blood and vomit on the front passenger side floor. Next, I retrieved my cookie tin and dumped it on the passenger seat.

My mind had gone into automatic. I drove down to the boat ramp, backing the car up as close to the water's edge as I could manage. All the light had gone and the moon was yet to make an appearance. I opened the boot and heaved the body bags, one at a time, to the little jetty, where I deposited them into my boat. I took the tarp as well, and opened it out at the water's edge, immersing the bloodiest patch at one end, leaving enough of it on the riverbank so the current wouldn't take it. I secured the tarp in place with a few rocks. Satisfied, I scrabbled about in my boat, untied the mooring and rowed downstream.

What a chore it proved to be, disposing of the parts. I was hungry and tired, and areas of my body ached with the effort of all the heavy lifting. I rowed downstream until I thought I'd covered a decent distance, keeping the boat centred in the river as it flowed into the lagoon, where a channel deepened the bottom to around eight metres. I drew in my oars and, keeping the boat steady with my own weight, I slopped the contents of first one, then the other bin bag into the river. The head, the feet, the hands, the arms and the torso all hit the water with satisfying plops and disappeared.

I was careful not to lose hold of the bags.

They were brand new and after a bit of a wash I could re-use them.

I'd never liked waste.

I sat there hoping the tailor would have a good pick, or that a goanna might snaffle a limb on its way by. Or a dingo maybe. It only came to me when I was rowing back upstream that the various bits of Brent might float.

I dragged the tarp—still stained with blood—out of the river and folded it over several times. It was too heavy to lift. I left it on the boat ramp. I still had the chainsaw to wipe down, but fatigue was winning me over. The process of Brent disposal had begun to feel never-ending. I decided to leave the chainsaw until the morning. I'd never thought murder would be so labour intensive.

Murder.

Murderer.

No, that wasn't me.

That term applied to others.

My act fell into the category of community service.

Back at the shack, I retrieved the leg joints from the boot and tossed them on the front yard. Opening the front door, I called Sam.

She came bounding out as I went in. I could hear the whimpering from the kitchen. I didn't know what to do about the clothes I was wearing. Maybe they wouldn't realise.

I opened the bedroom door and greeted the girls with a broad grin on my face.

'Cookies and milk are on the table.'

Later, Sam had a full belly, and no doubt the goanna was making a meal of Brent's other leg. The kiddies were finally asleep in my bed, all snug like a pair of cuddly bunnies. I'd changed out of Brent's clothes and tossed them in the fire box. My towel and bloodied clothes were in the wash. The sheets and Brent's vomit-strewn apparel I'd dumped in the shed. Satisfied I'd dealt with everything, I kicked back in my rocking chair with a large glass of whisky. Feeling around in my mouth I found the ulcer well and truly gone. I raised my glass to Gran Parks. I'd done her proud.

I sat in the darkness, watching the flames curl around the log in the wood stove. I had my feet up on a foot stool, my legs draped in the crocheted rug of patterned squares I'd found in a charity shop and paid the inflated price of fifty cents as it reminded me of my gran; a woman my age needed all the comfort she could get.

The thought followed me deep inside and created a softness about my eyes and a kind smile on my mouth as I unlocked the bedroom door.

CHAPTER THIRTY

EMILY

I stood in the centre of my sky-blue, windowless cell, surveying my things scattered around. I wanted to snatch them all up and quit the roadhouse job sooner than I could. I wanted to walk out there and then. It was a shame Pete was heading to Sydney, the wrong direction for me. But I could stay with him and then take the coach to Melbourne. I needn't ever return to Cann River, except to get on the midday coach.

I counted my money. I was still shy of the bus fare. I couldn't travel by bus unless I scrounged the cash off Pete, and I didn't feel comfortable taking money from a dying man.

I felt desperate. My small taste of freedom out at Point Hicks had entered my being and taken root.

Which brought me back to hitching as my only other option. The moment I pictured myself, loaded with my backpack, standing by the roadside with my thumb out, determination to bolt gave way to immobilising fear. I wouldn't hitch. I'd heard too many stories of vulnerable backpackers. There'd been a case recently involving two girls who were abducted, raped and murdered not far from the border.

Besides, Miriam and her friends insisted a murdering rapist was on the loose in the area. It was too risky.

A stubborn sense of wanting what I was owed stopped me as well. All those days and weeks working for Pat and I had almost nothing to show for it. She owed me about a whole month's pay. I knew after she extracted rent and board there would be little left, but it would meet my shortfall and provide enough for me to get by on until I found another job. It was worth the wait.

At least, that was what I hoped. I could hardly believe she was planning to extract two day's pay for an afternoon off. In all likelihood that amount would trap me in Cann River for another month.

I stuffed in my shoulder bag what I needed for an overnight stay at Point Hicks, along with Pete's copy of The Cockatoos. I had a vague sense I should forego the trip to the lighthouse. Not take the pecuniary risk. It was a short-lived idea. I wanted to go with Pete. Even as I realised he could die at any moment. That I could be stuck out there, alone with a corpse, unable to drive any of the vehicles to Cann River because I didn't know how. That I'd be forced to follow the route Pearl had described, a lonely walk on an exposed beach and on through the bush, a whole ten, fifteen kilometres not knowing if I'd make it or get lost and having no alternative. I shoved the thought aside. I reminded myself I was on holiday. I should be having adventures. Isn't that what the whole year in Australia was meant to be about? Exploration and discovery? If I didn't explore then I wouldn't discover, and I'd return home to Oxford with nothing learned and no experiences under my belt to reflect back on in my old age. Tell the grandkids. I didn't want to be stuck with the roadhouse vignette as my only tale. It had the air of a The String of Pearls penny dreadful without the barber and the human flesh in the meat pies.

Those weeks in Cann River felt more like I'd entered a parallel version of Wake in Fright, a film my tutor had shown his students on campus, by way of offering an alternative history of Australia to that provided by D.H. Lawrence. The vast, flat, bone dry interior of Australia depicted in the film, all beer swilling debauchery, licentiousness and wanton killing, replaced in Cann River by the eerie atmosphere of coastal wilderness stripped of its best trees.

I left my room and went down the corridor to the café. The lunchtime rush had passed, the café and forecourt both empty. Outside the hotel, Pete was parked in Simon's car, waiting. I avoided Pat's gaze as I passed the counter on my way out.

I didn't recognise the music Pete had playing on the car stereo. It had a grinding, insistent, menacing drive, industrial in feel. The music lacked melody, and the vocalist spoke his lyrics in a raised voice infused with brittle sarcasm. He was telling the story of Yorkshire Moors murderers Ian Brady and Myra Hindley. It was macabre. I'd never been one for punk. When I asked Pete, raising my voice above the racket, he told me the name of the band was Throbbing Gristle, which I supposed summed up their vibe in two words. The best that could be said was it was not Joan Baez.

We snaked our way through the bush on first one road, then another. The route was as confusing by daylight as it was by night. Without the effect of headlights spotlighting the wizened forms we passed, the wilderness looked less menacing. Yet round every bend there was more of the same and never any sort of view, and the drive felt monotonous, almost boring, evoking feelings of estrangement. It would be a nightmare of a place to get lost in.

Throbbing Gristle went on forever as well. Pete didn't seem inclined to change the cassette and I wasn't game to ask, despite the ache forming in my head. I supposed the grim music suited his situation, yet the heavy, industrial tone was incongruous with the wilderness setting and the two together felt like a sensory assault.

When the road opened out to reveal the ocean between a thin screen of trees, I let out a sigh. Things began to look familiar. To our right, the tangle of coastal bush ascended up a large and steep hill, enclosing the road, forcing the attention on the rocky, wild, seaweed-strewn beach. The tide was out. In places, the sand was wet right to the verge of the road, and I felt relieved when the track, so narrow Simon's car brushed the low growth, wound up the promontory to the lighthouse. I recognised the lay of the land, or I thought I did. When we crested a rise and the lighthouse appeared through a gap in the trees, a chunky white shaft, I found it rudely intrusive, unexpected—though I knew it would appear—and entirely out of place in the wilderness.

The track descended to the three outbuildings set in an area of mown grass overlooking the ocean.

Pete parked Simon's car in the larger of the outbuildings, which served as Simon's garage, pulling up beside Simon's reliable, diesel-fuelled spare vehicle. I opened the car door, relieved to have the natural sounds of Point Hicks greeting my ears after enduring Throbbing Gristle for the last hour.

Pete had said nothing the whole journey. I followed him past the back of the first cottage and down the narrow drive to the bungalow. He was still being quiet. We stood together on the narrow walkway; the lighthouse, standing proud on its concrete concourse a few steps below, bearing down on us. Beyond, the rock-strewn land fell away. In the near distance the ocean, a deep sapphire in the sunshine, rose and fell. Pete leaned on the railing, the wind in his face.

'Will you miss it here?' I said.

'Probably. The isolation is a bit much.'

'I'd be terrified here alone. It's so far from anywhere.'

'Many would agree. But not because of the isolation.'

'I don't follow.'

He didn't speak.

'What is it?' I said, suddenly concerned.

'Nothing.'

'Tell me.'

He sighed. 'The lighthouse is haunted, they say.'

'Haunted? Surely you don't believe that?'

'I don't know what to believe.'

He told me the story. Robert Christofferson, an assistant keeper, lost his life back in April 1947 while tending his crayfish pots. It was assumed he slipped and fell in the ocean and was swept away. Another version of the tale had it his wife, who was unhappy with the way he behaved towards her, pushed him in.

'Whatever happened, many a visitor has reported hearing hobnail boots clumping up the lighthouse stairs or walking in the pantry of one of the cottages.'

'People have vivid imaginations.'

'That's probably true. But lighthouse keepers have described occasions when they turned off the lighthouse lights, only to find them on again some time later. Or the reverse. Then there are those who've seen a lone adult figure wandering around on the rocks.'

He seemed to relish the telling, a typical boy enjoying scaring the girl in his company.

'I don't believe in ghosts,' I said, as a chill went through me and the flesh on my arms tingled.

'Neither do I. Come on.'

I followed him into the bungalow and claimed the couch with my bag. He put the kettle on a gas ring.

'Tea?'

I sat at the table and watched. His hands trembled a little and he seemed unsteady on his feet.

'I can do it, if you'd rather.'

'I wouldn't hear of it. You're my guest.'

While we waited for the kettle to boil, he leaned his back against the sink and stared at me. Beneath his beanie, his face looked paler than ever. His eyes, sunken with dark rings beneath, appeared filled with something like longing, but I couldn't identify what was behind that gaze. I was disconcerted by it.

'What will you do in Sydney?' I said, making conversation.

'Hunt for a cure.' He emitted a short laugh yet there was no mirth in it.

He told me he'd been searching for a cure ever since he was diagnosed. He'd hoped for some clinical trial, but nothing eventuated. He'd experimented with alternative treatments, but they'd come to nothing. The despondence in his face was heart breaking.

'I suppose you'd try anything. I know I would.'

'I'm glad you decided to come here today,' he said, changing the subject. His eyes searched my face. I looked away. The kettle hissed and he turned to make the tea.

I didn't know what to make of his last comment. Although a dying man wanting to share his last experiences with someone likeminded seemed reasonable. I remembered I had *The Cockatoos* in my bag and went to the couch to fetch it.

'I brought your book with me.'

I put it on the table.

'Did you like it?' he said, passing me a mug.

'It gave me a new window on Australia.'

'Patrick White is a little mocking.'

'Better that than ignorance. Have you seen *Wake in Fright*?'

'Who hasn't? I have the book somewhere, if you want it.'

'I'd love it, but how will I return it?'

'I don't think that matters, considering. You can keep that as well.' He gestured at *The Cockatoos*.

He left the room, returning with his copy of Kenneth Cook's classic.

'You are giving me quite an education on Australia,' I said, trying to sound light and breezy.

'Am I?' He seemed to drift off, losing focus and I suggested he sat down.

'I think I might lie down instead, Emily. I'm sorry to be such poor company, but the drive has taken it out of me. Will you be all right on your own? You can climb the lighthouse stairs again if you wish. The keys are there,' he said, pointing at the hook screwed into the side of the cupboard by the sink. 'Don't go outside while you're up there. It's too dangerous.'

'It isn't that windy.'

'No, but it can be. I expect it will be. You won't be able to tell the signs. So, promise me.'

I put a hand on my chest. 'I promise,' I said with mock obedience, charmed by his care.

'Mind that you do.'

I drank my tea, pocketed the keys and left him to rest.

Out at the edge of the promontory, where the rocks flattened and the boulders tumbled down to meet the ocean, there on the rough granite, I stood with my arms spread wide, feeling the wind pressing my dress to my thighs, billowing the fabric behind me. Cloud hung in long threads. A short distance from the shore, waves surged over barely submerged rocks, hitting the high spots, shooting columns of spume. I imagined the Christofferson figure, crouching down over his crayfish pots, reaching too far, falling in. And as if in unison with my imagination, the weather changed. It changed as I watched, the wind strengthening, low cloud scudding towards the shore as though from nowhere. In accord, the ocean heaved, sending forth wave after wave, each to boom as it broke on the rocks nearby.

I ventured closer, daring myself to the edge, ignoring Pete's cautionary voice in my ear. Fascination drew me, the power of the ocean, and I couldn't recall ever feeling more exhilarated. I waited, making myself stay there, until the water drew away and I knew a big wave was coming, much larger than the others. Then I edged back, not taking my eyes off the water, taking it slow, careful not to trip. I underestimated the spray, caught on the wind, and received a good hosing. I screamed; my voice lost amidst the chaos of the moment.

My legs were quaking when I turned and veered away to higher ground. I'd never been given to recklessness. I wandered about the promontory caught in the grip of a nervous thrill.

First, I headed over to where the rocks were orange, and then I followed a narrow path cut into the steep slope of the hillside, a safe distance from the waterline. The path ended before I gained a complete view of the beach Pearl had mentioned, and I realised it wasn't the path she'd meant when she'd issued her directions.

I saw a section of the long beach in the distance, a thin sliver of sand below a line of thickly wooded hills. There was no indication of human habitation anywhere. No boats out on the water. No lonely figure wandering about. I was in the company of the birds and the

fish and whatever lurked in the undergrowth, the lizards and the snakes, and the little furry critters that hid from them.

It must have been getting on for five o'clock when I opened the lighthouse door.

The smell of the ocean was stronger inside, as though it were trapped in there, splashes soaked into the concrete over decades and decades, outgassing an odour of seaweed and fish.

For ventilation, I propped open the door with a hunk of timber I found lying around outside. Not that it made much difference.

The light in the tall shaft with its central void was dim, much dimmer than outside, the small windows providing patches of thin light here and there. I gazed up, sent dizzy by the spiral, and hoped I had enough day left to make it up and down.

The dampness of my clothes and the cool lighthouse air persuaded me I needed to work up some heat. I mounted the first turn of the spiral with energy and enthusiasm, determined to get to the top without a pause.

By the time I'd reached the fifth turn I'd given up that idea. I was panting and my thighs burned. I'd underestimated the arduousness of the ascent. I hadn't taken into account all the walking I'd already done. And I'd overestimated the unfurling dusk.

As I neared the top I was sweating. I forced myself to climb the last round of stairs so I could tell myself later that I'd done it, before heading back down to the large window to watch the last of the sunset. I stood, letting my heart beat steady, enjoying the few streaks of orange cloud slowly darken. It was still light outside, but when I shifted my gaze to the interior, I was shocked at how dark it was. I thought I would just about manage to reach the bottom of the lighthouse before it became impossible to see, my faith buoyed by the open door at the bottom which let in all the exterior light there was.

Making my gloomy descent, I wondered when the beacon light would come on, warning passing ships. It was Pete's responsibility. Surely, he had to flick a switch? I suddenly wondered if he was okay.

I hadn't made it down one spiral turn when I heard a distant clunk. I looked down into the void. The bottom of the lighthouse had darkened, the patch of light filtering through the open door was gone. My body stiffened. The sound was the closing of the door. How could that have happened? Maybe the wind had caught it. But the wind was coming up from the south and the lighthouse door faced north. Besides, that lump of timber would have stopped it closing properly by itself, surely?

It had to be Pete. I called out his name, my voice echoing round the walls. There was no answer.

Maybe he was playing a practical joke.

I doubted it.

My senses sharpened. There was no sound other than the distant call of birds. My hand gripped the cold metal of the handrail. Each step made a bonk that gave forth a soft echo. I couldn't avoid it, no matter how light footed I tried to be. I leaned against the wall and removed my plimsolls, deciding bare feet would make less noise and I'd be able to feel the purchase of my toes on the metal.

I forewent the handrail and used the wall to steady my descent. Every step took me deeper into darkness.

I made another turn of the spiral and had begun to gain confidence when I heard footsteps other than my own. They were heavy, slow and regular. My pulse raced. My throat constricted. At first, I thought the footsteps were coming from below, but when I stopped and concentrated on the sound, I realised they were coming from above me. Yet that was impossible. There was no one up there, or at least as far as I knew. Could Pete have made the ascent while I was on the rocks getting doused by spray and been up there hiding outside all that time? Or inside with the giant light itself? Could he be playing a trick on me, trying to scare me? If so, then how did he close the entrance door and be above me all at once?

I hurried on down, taking the treads as fast as I dare, as fast as the near darkness and my trembling legs would allow. I'd reached about halfway when the lights went on. I froze. It was just as Pete had said. The footsteps and now the light. It seemed too predictable, too obvious. He had to be setting me up. I was about to yell out for him to stop it when I heard the footsteps again, descending behind me, much closer this time, and with the same regular clunk.

I couldn't look up. I wanted to run down the stairs, but my legs were stiff and wobbly, my feet cold on the treads, and I trembled so much I was convinced I'd fall. I still had a couple more turns of the spiral to make when the lights went out again. I was rendered blind. And still, those clunking footsteps followed me down.

It was all too much. I no longer cared if I fell. I stumbled down the remaining stairs and once I'd reached solid ground, I scrambled for the door handle. The keys were still in my pocket. I shut and locked that door as fast as I could manage, hoping to trap inside whatever was determined to scare me.

Can you lock in a ghost?

Unlikely, but if it was Pete, then, cancer or no, he could damn well stay in there as punishment for scaring me out of my wits.

By then, I was shaking so hard I could hardly walk. My mind fogged. My legs found a will of their own and ferried me to the bungalow.

Inside the bungalow, I was greeted by darkness. I dropped my plimsolls by the door and inched my way around the table and found where Pete kept the candles and matches. I lit one. The room was empty and cold. I took the candle with me and knocked on his bedroom door. There was no reply. I opened it to find him sprawled on his bed, sleeping soundly.

'Pete?'

He didn't stir. I thought he might have been play acting.

'Pete.'

I said his name sharply that time, hoping for a reaction. There was none.

I left him to sleep. In the main room, I saw he hadn't lit the woodstove. I went around lighting the candles, and then I set about laying a fire, finding some old newspaper, kindling and a few cut logs on the floor nearby. It took a few attempts, but I got the wood alight and the room took on a semblance of cosiness. I found some chocolate in my shoulder bag and devoured it in a few mouthfuls. The comfort it gave me was not sufficient to steel my nerves. Then I sat down at the table and opened *Wake in Fright*. I wasn't sure it made for ideal reading after what I'd just been through, but there was nothing else to do. I started to feel hungry, and a gnawing loneliness and vulnerability set in. I needed Pete to be awake. I needed the company of another human. For what had just taken place was nightmarish and I needed it explained to me, rationalised, shunted away so I could feel calm again.

Another hour passed. I'd managed to read the first chapter and was pitying that teacher bonded to the outback, when Pete emerged, bleary eyed and disoriented. Before long there was the kettle's hiss, the radio playing softly, and the smell of frying onions and bacon.

'You look like you could do with a stiff drink,' he said, eyeing me huddled on the couch with my legs folded under me.

I thanked him as he handed me a large glass of red wine. It was my opportunity, but I chose not to tell him. Why load up a dying man with a story of supernatural terror? Although I could have done with his reassurances. Part of me kept wanting to go over what had happened, re-living every tread of that spiral staircase. Yet the larger portion of my nerve-shot being was numb.

We spent the evening chatting about books and movies and

happy memories. Pete re-filled my glass again and again, and when I settled down to sleep, I felt mellow and fine. It was as though that terrifying experience in the lighthouse hadn't happened. But it had, and later in the night, I awoke in a cold sweat, thinking if Pete hadn't told me of the haunting, I wouldn't have heard those footsteps and the light wouldn't have switched itself on and off, and the door would have stayed open.

CHAPTER THIRTY-ONE

MIRIAM

The room was bright when I awoke. I hadn't expected to sleep for long or deeply. It must have been the Bex. After the accumulated exhaustion, the strain of the previous days, the waiting, the apprehension I'd felt listening to drug dealer Dan through the wall, those powders sure hit the mark coupled with all the brandy I'd knocked back in the bar, waiting for Cassie and Frankie to reappear with news of the goings on upstairs. They were up there a fair while. Alone in the bar I was suddenly famished, and I nipped up for my chicken dinner to find, as I glanced in Dan's room, Frankie had matters in hand.

Later, when I heard a commotion in the stairwell—I didn't dare look to see who was coming down the stairs, never mind how—I anticipated a bit of a scene, but it was only Cassie who returned to the bar.

She poured herself a stiff drink and downed it in one before joining me. Frankie had taken Wayne away with her, she said. Dan was resting. Resting? Cassie told me she'd given him a strong sedative and he'd be out for the night. Apparently, he was very weak and traumatised.

He was traumatised?

'He was the one doing the blood drinking,' I said, eyeing the bones of my chicken on an otherwise empty plate.

'Desperation,' she said. 'Panic.'

The way she described the situation, he sounded like a naughty child, not a hardened criminal.

In the cool light of the morning, I felt justice had not been adequately served on either man. Nor would it ever be, not in that fashion. Having your blood drunk away was no punishment for the crimes that hoon had committed. Allegedly committed. For no one knew whether even if Wayne were arrested, he would be charged for rape and murder, let alone found guilty and sentenced. Still, I didn't care. It was none of my business. What I did know and care about was that it was Tuesday. Only two more days and I'd be on my way.

I threw off the bed covers.

To celebrate my imminent release, I enjoyed a long soak in the bath. Back in my room, I dressed in my preferred outfit of plain blouse and slacks, donning a cardigan as well, to ward off the autumn chill. Feeling a touch fuzzy-headed after the brandy, I took a second pouch of Bex powders I'd snaffled from behind the bar with me to the dining room.

Cassie had set my place for breakfast.

I sat down and observed the goings on outside. The café lights were on in the roadhouse. A car pulled up for petrol. Con appeared. A logging truck thundered by. It was an ordinary day in Cann River.

I was halfway through my Bex-laced orange juice when Cassie appeared with my plate of eggs, poached this time, with two plump sausages and a grilled tomato. She seemed chirpy. I meant to quiz her about the town's attitude to the police, but I couldn't think of a way to broach the topic without appearing obsessive.

'Looks set to be a lovely sunny day,' I said instead.

'Sure is. My bees are going mental.'

She hovered, tea towel in hand. I felt compelled to offer a reply. 'How long have you been keeping bees?'

It was all the encouragement she needed.

'I took over from my mum about ten years ago,' she said. 'This time of year, they have a big clear out.'

I wasn't that interested. I picked up my fork, keen to tuck in before my eggs grew cold, but Cassie went on. 'The female worker bees are kicking the males out of the hive.'

'Poor drones,' I said, indifferently, knocking back my juice. I glanced up. Her face was alight with enthusiasm; bees were her pet topic.

'It's a death sentence,' she said. 'They can't feed themselves, so they end up starving.'

I put down my fork and sat back in my seat. 'Nature can be cruel.'

'Not really. I think nature is fair. Those drones don't collect nectar or pollen or build wax. All they do is roger the queen while the girls do all the work.'

'Not much fun being a drone then.'

'Oh, I dunno. Their whole life is given over to sex so it can't be all bad. It's a lazy life. Self-indulgent. A bit like men, when you come to think of it, and I don't have any sympathy for them either.'

We both laughed.

'I better let you eat.'

She strode off back to the kitchen.

I was reminded of an old folk tale, The Little Red Hen. It was Russian, as far as I knew, and my mother used to read it to me. I supposed all those lazy farmyard animals would have starved to death too, under the tyranny of that ethical hen.

Tucking into my eggs, I smiled inwardly at the justice, my mind turning to the day ahead.

CHAPTER THIRTY-TWO

FRANKIE

I threw off the heavy grey blanket that kept me warm when the chill bit on autumn nights and faced the day with grim resolve. Wayne was interfering with my routine. I had deer to hunt. Cash to earn. Food to put on my own table. I needed to keep up supply with those city restaurants or they'd source the venison elsewhere and Pat always needed more meat for her pies.

Thankfully she wasn't that discerning. I always sold her the rough.

Pearl's dog Sam enjoyed a bit of the offal which I traded for fish, and then there were the skins to transform into wares for Cassie's stall. In all, I had a good business happening and I couldn't afford interruptions.

Embers glowed in the firebox. I inserted some kindling, thin and dry, and the fire soon caught. I watched the flames travel down the sticks before adding some more, and then the larger cuts, feeding the blaze.

Outside, the birds were welcoming the day with their usual enthusiasm. Dew moistened the scraps of grass in the clearing outside the shack. A currawong sat on a tree stump, eyeing the ground with interest.

I put enough water in the kettle for a single cup of tea and spooned enough crushed oats into a saucepan for a single bowl of porridge, adding the right amount of milk. I bought ultra-heat-treated milk in small cartons. There was enough for my porridge and my tea. It was a perfect system. No waste. The lighted gas on both rings of the little stove produced a comforting hiss. I stirred the milk and oats, round and round and round, slipping into reverie, taken back to when I was a little girl, stirring soup in my mother's kitchen.

It was she who taught me about waste. She never threw out a drop or a crumb of anything. She always found a way to make use of whatever was left over. It was her greatest skill. Not that Howard Potter saw any merit in her ways. He had the opposite attitude, which I supposed was to be expected. He liked to offend her sensibilities by throwing his dinner up the wall. Poor old mum never could hold back her anguished cry. That was all the cause he needed to lay into her. I'd be forced to watch. I tried to get up from the table one time and I was told, by both of them for their various and contradictory reasons, to stay put and finish my tea.

The kettle boiled. I made a brew. Then the porridge thickened, and my stirring grew vigorous. The mixture heaved in the pan as large bubbles forced their way up. Satisfied, I scraped the contents in a bowl and drizzled on the molasses.

I always found hard work easier on a full belly and I had a big day ahead. I ate slowly, savouring every mouthful, licking the spoon clean and washing down the sugary coating in my mouth with my tea.

I left the saucepan and bowl to soak in the sink and I took out my cleaver and whetstone. The long, slow scrapes of the blade soothed me, and I sunk into the deeper parts of myself, to that place that had its own unquestionable wisdom.

I doubted the drugs were out of his system. I didn't think it mattered. The world needed rid of the man.

It occurred to me a single bullet would have saved me a lot of trouble, but a rifle shot would scare off the deer.

It was with an aura of almost managerial efficiency that I took myself off to the shed, cleaver in hand, as though I had absorbed something of Miriam's officious manner in my attitude, my stride. I found it strengthening, adding another dimension to the process, a sense of authority, of expertise.

My eyes narrowed to slits. Somewhere high on the ridge I heard a long sonorous howl. A dingo. I didn't answer.

As I neared the shed, I slowed my pace and crept along, hoping to surprise my captive.

There was nothing I could do about the jangle of the key in the lock. Not even the old Kelvinator would drown out the sound. I eased open the door.

He was on the other side of it, ready to barge past me. When he saw the cleaver, he backed away and pressed himself against the far wall.

'You're having a lend of me again, right?' he said with an uncertain laugh.

I stepped forward.

'What do you think?'

I stepped forward again, a pace to the left, herding him away from the fridge and into the opposite corner.

I swear he giggled.

My body went rigid. My heart drummed a steady beat in my chest. I grinned to put him at ease.

I came to about two feet away, holding the cleaver behind me.

'Stop it, will you. You're scaring me.'

He made to step aside to his right. I blocked his path with my left arm. He'd moved the wrong way. The cleaver always worked better in my right.

I brought the blade down on his shoulder. It sliced through the T-shirt he had on and sheared through to the collar bone.

He doubled over, clutching his arm, moaning.

'Shut up!' I screamed.

His racket made me go straight for the neck. It was a reflex. I could have made him suffer longer. I could have hacked at other parts of him. But when he fell on his knees it looked like surrender and I raised the cleaver. I hacked again, once, twice, until I'd severed the artery, the vertebrae cracking, the head separating, rolling forward, coming to rest on its side. I watched the life drain out. The look of alarm on his face was comical. Wayne had fused with Howard Potter in my mind and from that moment, it was my stepfather I was butchering.

I didn't stop. I didn't want to have to think.

I heaved the torso onto the bench and stripped the clothes. From then, it was a question of going through the motions, skinning and butchering, just as I would a deer. The principles were the same. Only the shape was different.

I started with the manhood. A single swipe and the entire appendage sat limp on the end of the bench. Then I paused and decided not to bother with the torso, other than the rump. Save the gutting.

As it was, the bloody smell of him made me recoil. The meat was fatty and sinewy all at once. I cut the flesh from the limb bones and tossed the cuts in a bucket for the roadhouse.

Sweeney Todd sprang to mind.

The goannas and the dingoes and the currawongs could tackle the rest. I hurled the various parts of Wayne, the head, the torso, the hands and feet, the flaccid penis and ball sack, all of it, I hurled into the forest.

I took greater care with the clean-up. Scrubbing out the butchering shed occupied the whole of the rest of the morning. I even skimmed the bloody dust with a spade and bucketed the congealed muck outside, depositing it around the base of a tree. I scrubbed the bench, the walls, the back of the door, the fridge, everywhere to erase the presence of Wayne. Then I sprinkled a generous layer of sawdust on the floor. By the time I'd finished, my composure was restored.

I put the remnants of Wayne in the fridge and headed up to my shack for a cuppa.

Job done.

When I opened the door and saw the fire glowing in the stove, I knew from then on it would be a good day.

CHAPTER THIRTY-THREE

PEARL

The kiddies wanted their daddy. Of course, they did. They were teary and terrified and I could tell it was going to be a very long day. I told them my name was Pearl and they could think of me as a grandma. I told them I had twin granddaughters about their age. For breakfast, I made them pancakes with wild berry jam. I even made mock cream with some fresh butter, sugar and what I had left of a carton of milk. All that sugar and fat settled them down and I realised they were probably half starved. Even so, they eyed me suspiciously. I knew that with full bellies would come questions, and I had no answers I could give them.

I had quite a labour ahead of me holding the whole situation together. Little mites they were, and I had nothing to keep them entertained. Then I recalled a gift I'd bought for my grand twinnies for last Christmas and never got to give them as that wretch of a daughter refused to visit and I was buggered if I was travelling to the city loaded up with it on the coach. I'd bought the gift as a lure and it hadn't worked, so I'd stuffed it somewhere.

I had to ferret about throughout the house before I found it at the bottom of my wardrobe, all wrapped up in festive paper beneath a couple of old coats.

'Sally! Kim!' I cried, for those were their names. 'I have something for you. I real treat.'

'What is it, Grandma Pearl?'

My heart did a little squeeze, hearing that.

'A very special present for two very special girls,' I said, carrying it into the living room and setting it down on a rug near the fire.

They were both instantly on their feet. Sally, the blonde, came closer.

'Aren't you going to tear off the wrapping paper?' I said, reaching out for Kim.

She came forward, and when Sally started ripping, she joined in as well and pretty soon it was all squeals of cautious delight.

It was a doll's house I'd bought second hand at the market and fixed up until it was good as new. The girls admired the rooms, the furniture, the windows and doors that opened, the staircase at the back, the pretty wallpaper and fireplaces. A family of four came with it: mum dad, boy and girl. The ideal.

I stood up, hovering.

'Now girls,' I said authoritatively.

They looked up at me.

'Promise me you'll be good and sit here for a bit while I go and fetch some things from across the road.'

'We'll be good,' they said in unison.

'No fighting, now.'

'We never fight,' Kim said. Somehow, I believed her.

I grabbed Fred's door key off the table in the hall and nearly tripped over Sam on my way outside. She'd put her thigh bone on the front-door mat and was gnawing a knuckle end.

I took my wheelbarrow down to the jetty and heaved in the bloodied tarp to hose down in the back garden.

Over at Fred's, I ignored the living room and went on through to the girl's bedroom. There, I gathered up their things and stuffed them into the suitcase, open on the floor. Deciding not to strip the sheets, I straightened the bed. Then I went and gathered up all that remained in the bathroom, and ferried the lot out onto the front porch, thinking I'd better tell Fred about the broken window in the spare room.

Next, I went to the kitchen and removed all the groceries, stuffing them in a large plastic bag I found squashed at the back of a cupboard. I didn't think much of the quality of all that food. It was all processed muck. I collected my pie dish and went out the back and tossed the remainder over Fred's fence. I doubted anything would go near it. Animals are not stupid.

Back inside, I washed up a couple of stray glasses, gave the table a wipe and pushed in the chairs, and had a quick scan around to ensure all was in order. From there I tackled Brent's bedroom, forcing myself across the threshold. I could smell him on his clothes. Shit happens, I told myself; shit happens and sometimes you have to deal with other people's shit.

I tossed his clothes into the holdall and zipped it shut. I didn't want any of Brent back at mine, so I shoved the holdall under the bed. I'd deal with it later. Burn it or take it to a charity shop.

I found clean sheets in the linen cupboard in the hall and made the bed.

I attended to the living room last. The floor had dried out. I admired my cleaning efforts of the night before, but I couldn't help seeing Brent on the floor, thrashing. A wave of contempt rose up in me in the remembering. I dragged the sofas back the way Fred liked them, resenting Brent for forcing me to deal with all his mess.

Thinking I didn't want Fred to find his door key missing from its hiding place, I went around the back and tucked it under the upended flower pot. Then, I strode back across the road laden with the suitcase and bags of toys, bits of food and my pie dish, knowing I'd rescued those girls.

I found them playing on the floor, good as gold. I felt much better with all their things at mine. Much better after confirming that Fred's was clean as a pin with not a spot of blood anywhere to be seen other than on his tatty old curtains. I thought the place smelled fresher than it had before too, and decided I'd done Fred a favour. A sort of post-slaughter spring clean.

I tidied things up in my kitchen, skirted round the girls on the living room floor and straightened things out in my bedroom. It was my way of dealing with difficulties. A bit of domestic calm never went amiss. Never a thing out of place at my grandma's and I wanted to set the same example to my new little girls.

Cleaning out the pie dish got me thinking that I didn't have much in to tempt the littlies, so I whipped up a batch of chocolate cookies, keeping an eye on their play, smiling at their absorbed faces, the way they spoke softly to each other. When the smell of freshly baked cookies filled the living space, the girls began to lose interest in their doll's house. I decided Sally and Kim might enjoy some fresh air, so I suggested an outing.

'Have you ever been in a boat?'

'We don't like boats.'

'Why ever not?'

'They sink.' Sally was emphatic about it.

'I have a boat and it doesn't sink.'

'It doesn't?'

'That's right. Because I won't let it.'

'What if it gets a hole in it?'

'It won't get a hole in it.'

'But what if it does?'

'Then we'll put a plug in it.'

'Sally can't swim,' Kim said.

'Neither can you.' Sally shot her sister a dark look. It was the first time I'd witnessed any discord between them.

'I know. You can both wear life jackets,' I said, infusing my voice with enthusiasm. 'That way, if you fall in the water, you'll float.'

'But we'll get swept away by a big wave.' Sally's eyes were round with fear.

I laughed. 'There are no big waves. No waves at all. I'm taking you to a shallow lake. It's very pretty.'

'Will there be fish?'

'We don't like fish.'

'You don't like fish?'

'Mummy says they taste yucky.'

I began to lose patience.

'You don't have to eat them. And I won't take my fishing rod so we won't catch any either. But we can see if we can spot some. Won't that be fun?'

I left them and went and retrieved the life jackets from a chest in the sleep out. I hadn't anticipated the girls would be such hard work. What sort of mother instils so much fear in her children? I didn't have to search far in my imagination to know the answer to that.

My own mother had been full of little apprehensions she passed on to her progeny, hammering them into us like staples in an effort to clothe us in a protective suit of her making.

She didn't factor in the spirit of rebellion in every child's heart, even the feeblest.

When I was planning to move to Melbourne with Mal, she did everything she could to dissuade me. Which only increased my determination. Had she not smothered me with her warnings, I might have seen Mal for who he really was. Then again, I was that keen to leave Tasmania I'd have taken off with anyone.

Sally and Kim needed to be set free from the shackles of their mother's fears. I jollied them along with promises of a big fire and some homity pie when we got back. They had no idea what homity pie was, but it sounded homey and they warmed to the idea. I bundled them into the life jackets I'd been saving for my own grandchildren and rushed them out the door before either of them could change her mind.

We passed Sam on the front deck, still busy with her thigh bone. She didn't even glance up. She had it gripped between her front paws and was licking at it lazily, her belly, flat on the wooden slats, bloated.

Getting the girls in the boat proved a challenge. I made the mistake of getting in first and reaching out my arms. They were standing on the little wooden jetty and both backed away from me. My patience was waning.

'Come on,' I urged, reaching further. 'It's completely safe.'

Neither of them would budge. I thought if they took another step backwards, they'd fall in the water on the other side. Then I heard a series of low hissing puffs, like small bellows, and my eyes drifted to a goanna hugging a nearby tree behind them.

My face expressed the shock and fear I did not feel.

'Girls! I said as the lizard emitted a closed mouth roar. 'Quickly!' They both screamed and hurried forward.

'One at a time,' I said, hauling Kim in first.

Sally did a little jig on the jetty and whimpered.

'It's all right. I've got you.'

They both sat together facing me, their little faces all pinched and nervous. I told them to sit still.

'You mustn't wriggle about or you'll tip over the boat.'

'Yes, Grandma Pearl.'

'And you mustn't shout, or you'll scare away the fish.'

'Yes, Grandma Pearl.'

Their obedience was born of terror. I could see it in their eyes.

Sometimes it is better to flow with the messages of resistance that life gives you and choose a different path.

We were out in the middle of the inlet, and Sally and Kim had grown in confidence and gone all wide eyed, leaning tentatively over the sides of the boat looking for fish, and we were chatting in low tones about their life back in the city and how their mum had run off with another man, and how their daddy had told them he was going to take them on a big adventure. But then they said that mummy was dead, and I was confused and had to ask some delicate questions to try to get to the bottom of what really happened. I ended up no wiser. They couldn't tell me if daddy had killed mummy.

Of course, he had.

I knew he had.

He must have, surely.

They were telling me about the games they liked to play at home in the city and how daddy had said he was taking them back there soon, when I felt a thud right beside me and when I looked down there he was, his face, somewhat bloated, staring up at me.

I averted my gaze, lest I drew his daughters' attention to what I'd seen.

I had to think quickly. I pointed at the sky up ahead of me and pretended I'd seen a bird.

'Where! Where!' they cried, turning, and I kept them engaged in the skyward search as I tried to shunt their father's head away from the side of the boat.

He seemed determined to stay put, so I grabbed the oars and rowed. Seeing the head was about to pass by, I cried out to the girls to look over the other way, where fluffy clouds wafted in the sky. 'A pelican. Look! There it is!' I cried, and the girls strained to see what wasn't there.

I had no idea how long I'd be able to keep up the distraction. When Brent had drifted on downstream, I told them to sit back around in their seat. With their faces pinned to mine, I rowed hard and fast, steering the boat back to the river and on upstream, hoping we wouldn't pass any more body parts on our way back to the jetty.

Trust him to be a floater.

I tied the boat to its mooring and scanned around for the goanna, but it had gone. I helped the girls alight, admonishing myself for bringing them out on the water. What had I been thinking? I hadn't been thinking. Bits of their father were scattered about and had I stopped to ponder I would have known a portion of him might emerge at any moment.

As we walked back to my shack the girls, sensing my anxiety, became agitated and started to blubber for their daddy. The ungrateful wretches. I supposed they weren't to know I'd just saved them from a sight that might have stayed with them for life, but part of me wanted to march them back to the boat, telling them I'd take them to him if they wanted him so much.

Instead, I found myself saying, 'I'm sorry, darlings. But your daddy got sick, remember, and he's no longer with us. But now you've got me. He must have wanted you to be with me because this is where he came. He brought you to me so that I could look after you. I'll make sure nothing bad happens to you ever again.'

I'd forgotten how hard childrearing was. How tedious and fundamentally unsatisfying. Still, I was resigned to it. I'd never renege on a commitment.

We were on the front porch when I heard a vehicle in the distance. I waited, poised. It drew closer. Unease stirred. I wondered who it could be. Then the sound faded and was gone. I cautioned myself against paranoia, stepped over Sam nursing her thigh bone and shunted the girls inside.

CHAPTER THIRTY-FOUR

EMILY

Nothing settled me. Not the wine or Pete's pleasant chatter. After he retired, I lay awake for hours trying to reassure myself that there were no such things as ghosts, running the whole terrifying ordeal over and again in my mind, trying to come up with alternative explanations.

Pete had been asleep when I'd entered his bedroom and he hadn't awoken for hours, but that didn't mean he hadn't carried out an elaborate practical joke. What if he'd had some kind of hidden tape recorder that played a sound track of footsteps? In the dark, I'd have imagined those footsteps were coming down the stairs and getting closer all the time. It must have been Pete who closed the door, too, and flicked the light on and off. He'd only told me the ghost story—which probably wasn't even true —to add to the impact, and then scurried back to bed to feign sleep to complete the ruse. But I wasn't convinced. Lying on the couch in the small hours of the night, I was petrified.

Pat wanted me back at the roadhouse by eight, mostly because she wanted me to clean up Con's mess. She'd issued that pecuniary threat typical of her, too. The combination of laziness and meanness in her methods made my blood simmer. As dawn made its appearance, I was in no mood to satisfy her demands. I was tired, and angry and overwrought and the last thing I wanted was to go back to that roadhouse to be her skivvy.

I could hear Pete breathing his slumber through the wall. I had no idea what time it was, but I decided not to wake him. I threw off the blanket and tossed it on the armchair. Then, I yanked at the cushion that had wedged itself between the arm of the couch and the seat pad under the weight of my head. The cushion came free and a magazine, also stuffed in the crack, slid to the floor. I took it outside to read.

I strolled down to the water's edge, found a smooth and flat rock and sat watching the ocean rise and fall. The tide was high but the water calm, small waves smacking. Gulls glided in the air, chirping and cawing. I felt calmer in the beholding, more centred out in the air.

When I tired of the view, I leafed through Pete's magazine, idly, as though I were seated at the doctor's awaiting my turn.

He'd dog-eared a page. I straightened the fold and pressed it back, feeling mildly irritated. I never liked to see a dog-eared page. My eyes settled on the article. It was a feature piece on experiments conducted on mice who had somehow developed brain cancer. Some maverick scientist had set about feeding them the live brains of healthy mice to see if it would affect a cure. Astonishingly, or at least according to the scientist's results, or rather his testimony, the tumours had disappeared, and the mice were cured.

I put the magazine down, revolted by the experiment. I couldn't believe the scientist had even secured funding. The journalist didn't seem all that enamoured with it either, judging by the tone. She raised the issue of ethics in her last paragraph and questioned how anything comparable could ever be achieved for humans, given the need for living brain tissue. Although, I could understand Pete taking an interest. After all, he had brain cancer; he'd be searching for any way imaginable to cure himself. Poor guy.

The sun was making its way up over the hills to the east. I took the magazine back to the bungalow and returned it to its hidden home down the side of the couch. Pete was still asleep. I was hungry and thirsty. I found bread and cheese, and wandered about the room, eating. Then I poured myself a mug of water and downed it in seven large gulps. Still thirsty, I poured another, wiping my mouth when I was done.

Listless, I went back outside. This time I decided to explore the cottages. I wandered around the walled gardens, onto verandas where I peered in windows at interiors filled with drop sheets, ladders, paint tins, and sundry tools. The view from out those front windows couldn't have failed to elevate whoever happened to find themselves inside. With the lighthouse, a dominant feature, out of the sight line the panorama of ocean and rocky coast opened out. I imagined guests enjoying the solitude, the intensity of the pristine wilderness.

In the second cottage, the one to the east, I located the annex room with the short-wave radio. The door was unlocked, just as Pearl said it would be. I tried to remember how to use the device. I looked around for instructions but there were none. In a moment of regret, I recalled binning the detailed note Pearl had me write. She'd given me a frequency. I strained but couldn't recollect it. Maybe the radio was pre-set. I found the on/off switch and picked up the handset. The radio crackled and I heard a distant voice. I pressed the handset button and both the crackle and the voice cut out. I supposed that had to be all there was to it. A sudden caw close by, and I put down the handset and switched off the radio.

My ambling over, I headed back to the bungalow, resolved to wake up Pete. If I was to get back to the roadhouse before eight, I needed to leave straight away. I didn't want to, I especially didn't want to return to the hardened mess of pie detritus in the kitchen, but the thought of losing all that pay was beginning to make me feel ill to my core.

As I entered the small, walled driveway between the cottages, I noticed the lighthouse door was ajar. I went down the short flight of steps and stood on the concourse that encircled the monolith, coming to a halt a few feet from the door, not wanting a repeat of last night.

'Pete?'

Only the gulls answered, squawking in the distance.

'Pete!' Much louder that time.

Still no answer.

What compelled me to go inside? Defiance? I was determined to prove to myself without equivocation that no ghost by the name of Christofferson haunted that lighthouse. I knew it was Pete. I thought of checking to see if he was still in bed, but I knew he couldn't be, not with that door sitting open, a door I had been at pains to lock. Besides, I only planned to step inside, shout up the stairwell. I wasn't going to ascend those steps again. Not on my own.

I pushed open the door and walked in.

My eyes hadn't adjusted to the dim light when I felt a blow land on the back of my head with such force, I fell forwards.

That was the last I remembered for heaven knew how long.

When I came to, I was greeted by a pounding pain at the back of my skull.

I raised my head, tried to sit up, disoriented. My eyes watered and a wave of nausea swept through me. I slumped down again, dizzy. It took three more attempts before I could get myself upright. The pain radiating through my skull overrode the lesser bruises I'd incurred through my fall, bruises that vied for a place in my awareness.

It took a few moments for my location to sink in. I was still in the lighthouse. The smell of the ocean, of fish and seaweed, were strong. Sunlight filtered down through the windows. I guessed the time to be around midday.

I sat, leaning against the wall, recovering, taking in the awful truth that someone had whacked me on the head and knocked me unconscious. Who? Who would do such a thing? Did they even know who they were hitting? It was dim, and they'd hit me straight away. They might have been intending to hit someone else? Pete?

Eager for fresh air, I crawled to the door, and hauled myself to my feet. I turned the handle. I pulled on the door. Confused, I turned the handle again. It was locked.

I took a lung full of air, ready to holler, but thought better of it. Whoever was out there had locked me in and therefore didn't want me to get out. Drawing attention to myself was not a good idea. For all I knew, Pete had gone for help. Or whoever had done this to me had found him and hurt him as well. The perpetrator could be outside, right there on the concourse.

A chill passed through me. I'd already alerted them to my awake presence by trying to open the door.

The next thing I noticed was my full bladder. Those two mugs of water I'd downed with my bread and cheese had worked their way through me and were demanding an exit, but I wasn't about to down my pants and pee in a corner. I decided I could hold on.

I waited, listening, trying to decide what to do next. Stay where I was, ready to defend myself from further attack? What with? I had no weapon, only my bare hands. I felt defenceless. I had no strategy and I needed one.

The only other option was up.

I took hold of the banister, felt the cold iron seep into my gripping hand. I placed my foot on the first tread. My other foot on the second. Tread by tread I ascended, my legs still sore from the day before, each footfall a labour.

At the first window, I peered out, tentatively at first, in case I was seen, before realising the depth of the window and the height made visibility impossible. The window afforded a view of the cottage on the western side of the lighthouse, and the garages beyond. There was no one about, no stranger's car parked on the grassy patches. The second window looked out to the east, over at the other cottage. Again, there was no sign of anyone. The ocean was calm, the sky clear and the wind light. It looked like a perfect day. Although it wasn't. It was anything but perfect.

With my head pounding and my legs complaining, I kept climbing, tread by tread, snaking my way up as silently as I could. No heavy footsteps joined me. I was thankful for that, but their absence did nothing to reassure me.

It took a long time to reach the large window at the top. I scanned the promontory for signs of human life, but again, nothing.

I climbed the last steps to the final platform, where the door led outside, and another into the light room. I tried both doors, but they were locked.

It was there that I huddled with my head in my hands, trying to still my nerves. The effort of holding my bladder was almost as challenging as enduring the pain radiating through my skull. I should have peed at the bottom. If I did it now, I'd leave a trail of wee dripping down off the treads.

Time dragged. Hours went by. It was almost dark inside the lighthouse when the door at the bottom of the stairs opened and clunked shut.

Footsteps up the treads were soon to follow, a slow, steady rhythm of ascent.

I huddled on the platform, pressed myself in against the wall, and hugged my knees to my chest.

I counted the steps I heard.

Twenty.

I repressed my compulsion to scream for help. What would have been the point?

Thirty.

The footsteps kept coming.

Forty.

The pace slowed.

At eighty, even slower. Whoever it was lacked stamina. Either that, or they were adding to the menace.

At ninety the pace was so slow I wondered if they'd make it the rest of the way.

Suddenly there was hope.

It didn't last. At one hundred I heard his breathing.

Pete's.

I held my own light and shallow. Was he coming to rescue me?

Shouldn't I call out to him? Tell him not to bother with the climb and I'd be right down?

I couldn't.

Another ten treads. He had about fifty-five to go. There were long gaps of silence as he regained his strength.

Clomp, clomp, clomp.

One hundred and twenty, thirty. I knew that soon I'd see him, and he'd see me.

And there he was, hunched, panting, using the wall to keep himself upright. He stood at the multi-paned window, swaying. Then he turned and clasped the railing with both hands, raising his head and locking his gaze with mine. Without his beanie, he looked unnatural, almost inhuman. With that scar encircling half his face, he scarcely looked like the Pete I'd come to know at all.

'Pete?'

He didn't answer.

'What do you want?'

He continued his climb.

There were ten steps of separation between us when he stopped and said, 'I need to pick your brains.'

It was then I saw the tool belt tied around his waist.

The realisation that he wasn't being metaphorical surged through me like a dark electric current.

'The article in the magazine,' I said slowly. 'The one you dog-eared.'

'You saw it?'

'But you can't think that was true. Or if it would work on humans.'

'I have to try. Surely you can understand that.'

No, I couldn't. I couldn't understand how he could think to place a higher value on his own life over mine. Over anyone's in fact, anyone who happened to chance along.

What I could understand was simple. It was my life, or his.

Neither of us was in a good physical state. Looking at him, I thought I might be the stronger. He had me trapped at the top of the stairs, but I had the advantage of being above him. I walked to the end of the platform to meet him as he climbed to the last tread. He was taking his time over it. I waited, poised, not knowing what I was capable of.

He had a foot on the penultimate tread, the other behind him. His hands trembled on the railing. His torso rocked back and forth, his head lolling. Then he clung to the rail and leaned over, groaning. A seizure had him in its grip. He seemed unaware of the precariousness of his position. He tried to correct his posture, but he couldn't. If he'd made it to the platform, he might have gained some balance. As it was, the slope of the banister confused him. He slumped further over the railing, his left arm and shoulder hanging in the air.

He seemed to have found some stability, for he hung there at a point of balance, with half his body poised to succumb to the dictates of gravity, the other providing the counterbalance. It was as though he'd lost consciousness.

I did the only thing available to me. I made to ease by on my way down the stairs. My intention was to get past him and bolt to the bottom, but as I tried to get by, he shifted his weight and I sensed he was about to fall on me.

I wasn't having that.

I pushed him the other way.

It was a reflex.

I pushed and hurried on down the stairs.

I didn't get far before I saw him fall down the void. I waited. The thud came in an instant. It was a much faster way of making the descent.

My bladder reacted. I could do nothing but feel the warm flow spreading down my legs and into my plimsolls, splashing onto the stairs, a great yellow puddle.

Then the warmth of my urine went cold, and my feet squelched inside my shoes. I wanted to take them off but then I'd need to carry them and I didn't feel able. I was weak. The ache in my head was sharp and pulsing. My legs wobbled as though they didn't know how to support my weight. I couldn't descend quickly yet I was desperate to get out of there. I half expected the lights to flash on. Or the clunk of boots to start. But there was only me, my heartbeat, and Pete, dead at the bottom.

With every turn of the spiral, the interior darkened as dusk shaded into night. I had to feel my way, keep hold of the wall and take it tread by tread as there was less chance of my feet getting in a tangle, less chance of overstepping and losing my footing, tumbling to my own demise.

I greeted the cold concrete of the floor with relief and edged around Pete's body that was crumpled in a heap in the centre.

The door was locked. I had to search through his pockets for the key. As I approached the body, my plimsolls landed in something slippery and I knew it was his blood.

The shaking started.

With trembling hands, I fumbled and rummaged. I found the keys in his left trouser pocket.

I had to use both hands to insert the key in the lock. The sound of the shaft releasing and I was outside, closing the door, locking it behind me. It took all the strength I had.

It was dark, too dark to see. I couldn't leave Point Hicks. I didn't have the strength. I couldn't take Pearl's advice and follow the coastal path to the beach and then trek along until I somehow found her cottage. Not in the dark. Not in my state.

I entered the bungalow and made straight for the candles, the matches. With one alight I searched around and took an unopened bottle of whisky from under the sink. It occurred to me that I should find some food, but I felt too nauseous to eat. I had no intention of staying there. The vibe of the space with all of Pete's things scattered about was unbearable. Besides, he might be dead, but his corpse was too close.

My instinct was to hide. There was only one place I could think to go. The annex with the unlocked door and the short-wave radio. It was small and dry and safe. I could try and radio for help.

Inside, I relit the candle and rammed a chair against the door, just in case.

CHAPTER THIRTY-FIVE

MIRIAM

I greeted Wednesday morning in low spirits. I should have slept well after spending a relaxing Tuesday strolling about and sitting in the churchyard in dappled shade, enjoying the end of My Brilliant Career, along with my usual sausage roll and vanilla slice.

For much of my time tucked away in those hallowed grounds, whenever I turned my gaze to my surroundings, I searched for a bee and when I spied one, I wondered if it were a drone or a worker. All the bees I saw seemed active and very much alive. I decided they were all workers, all female, none of them males with a death sentence.

Back at the hotel, I partook of the pork chop and braised vegetables Cassie had made, thinking she deserved an award for her cooking. In my room, I spent the evening watching television.

It was when I switched off the entertainment and readied for bed that I knew Dan had resumed his nocturnal habits. All that banging about and moaning. What was he doing in there? What was there he could be doing other than injecting drugs, drugs I'd have thought would render him comatose? Instead, he seemed to spend his nights colliding with the furniture.

I supposed he was fed up being confined to that room, although he might just as well have gone out for a long walk since there was no one about. Cann River didn't stir once the hotel had closed its doors.

With daylight, all had gone quiet. In anticipation of a long drive the next day, I rose, had my bath, and went down to the dining room. Cassie was nowhere about. She'd set my place. I sat down before my orange juice and a plate of eggs—hard boiled and cold—a slice of ham, a quartered tomato and a hunk of thickly buttered white bread. No coffee. It wasn't very imaginative, and I wondered if something was wrong with Cassie.

After breakfast, I returned to my room to tidy up my things, repacking my suitcase and sundry bags. In the process, I discovered I was short of underwear. I didn't fancy washing out my smalls in the bathroom, leaving them to drip dry on the back of a chair as I imagined other women doing. Besides, I doubted my smalls would dry in time for me to put them on the following morning. I decided to fetch what I needed from my car and have a leisurely coffee in the roadhouse while I was about it.

I thought I'd start on A Kindness Cup upon the recommendation of a work colleague who'd said I'd like the writing of Thea Astley, as she more or less wrote as I thought. I had no idea what Megan was referring to. I supposed I was about to find out. The novel had won an award, apparently, which was how Megan had heard of it. I popped my copy in my handbag.

I hadn't opened the roadhouse door when I sensed something was wrong. Pat was at the counter, ranting to Con.

Her arms were waving in the air. I pushed open the door on his wheedling defence.

'I searched everywhere, Ma.'

'You can't have done.'

'I drove down all the roads around there, from the inlet all the way to Mallacoota, just about.' 'Liar.'

'There was no sign of her.'

'You can't have checked the lighthouse properly.'

'It was locked. Everywhere was dark, Ma. I called out, Ma, I really did.'

My gaze slid from son to mother. I hadn't a clue what or who they were talking about. I cast an eye around for Emily.

'Get yourself back out there!'

'But Ma, what about the pies?'

'The pies can wait. They have to wait. First, she has to come back and clean the kitchen.'

Realising they were talking about Emily, I broke into their altercation with certain impatience. 'You should call the police,' I said, anticipating the reaction.

A look of incredulity appeared in Pat's face.

'The police? What will they do?'

Nothing, it would seem. Besides, if the girl had any sense, she was already halfway to Melbourne.

'Sorry to interrupt,' I said my gaze sliding from Pat to Con, 'but I need to fetch some things from my car.'

They both turned to me at once. I felt an attack was imminent. I was saved when some customers entered and in my side vision I saw a car had pulled up at the bowsers. Con lumbered off. I followed him outside.

The sun warmed the air, which felt damp. Touches of dew glistened on the mown grass of the nature strip. A logging truck juddered into town on its compression brakes. A sedan and a station wagon both pulled up at the bowsers, forming a short queue. With no purpose, I felt instantly self-conscious. I stood with my back to the café windows and extracted the Astley and commenced reading, holding the book up prominently in both hands. Straight away I enjoyed the premise of the book and the prose, and I was particularly drawn by the implication that a town of past misdeeds was about to get its comeuppance.

I had never been one for reading standing up, but I determined not to move from my post, for fear Con would disappear and I'd remain short of fresh smalls.

I was accompanied by petrol fumes wafting my way on the lightest of breezes. Another car pulled up. Not being fast off the mark, Con was dealing with fuel and dollars for the following fifteen minutes.

At last he came out to give the remaining driver his change and the car drove off leaving an empty forecourt. I seized the moment and confronted him with my request.

He obliged, albeit reluctantly, and I followed him to the garage, where he handed me my keys that seemed to have taken up residence in his trouser pocket.

He had the audacity, or rather the stupidity to stand and watch me scrambling through my second suitcase which I'd left in the car since it was packed with winter clothes I hadn't thought I'd need, rendering it impossible to extract my undergarments without him noticing.

I stuffed the items in my handbag and removed myself from the car, knocking the top of my head on the car door frame as I straightened. A sharp pain radiated through my skull. I winced.

The day was not unfolding well.

Con reached out his hand for my car keys. I didn't want to hand them back but there was no choice.

Despite craving a coffee, I had misgivings about going back inside the café. The seat in the churchyard would have been a much better option, were it not for the early time of day. The cold night air pooled in shady places and my seat would be damp. I found myself standing around on the forecourt in the sun, making up my mind, when I saw a dusty old car drive up from the south, execute a U-turn and park across the street outside the general store. It was Pearl.

As she got out, I waved, but she hadn't seen me.

I never considered myself nosy and it was with an inexplicable curiosity that I went over to her car. Although I did know her, casually, and felt I had every right to mosey over for a chat. After all, I had nothing else to do.

I decided to wait on the corner, but first I glanced in the car. I had no idea what I thought I'd see inside but to my astonishment, there were two small children seated in the back. I wondered how Pearl had managed to get them away from that man.

They stared up at me, two pretty little girls in short dresses, one blonde, the other ginger. Their hair was not brushed and no doubt their teeth were not as well.

I gave them a little wave and went inside the store where I found Pearl carrying a wire basket loaded with packets of Iced VoVos and Coco Pops and all manner of children's foodstuffs. She'd even tossed in two packets of frozen chicken croquettes and another of hamburgers. Next it would be frozen chips.

She started when she saw me, and then she forced a grin. She was standing at one end of the centre aisle. I was at the other. It felt suddenly like a stand-off.

'Fancy meeting you in here,' I said lightly.

'Stocking up.'

'So I see.'

The man behind the counter didn't take an interest. He was dull-witted and more interested in looking down at the magazine he had half tucked on his lap out of sight. When

Pearl dumped the basket in front of him, he grunted, shifted, and proceeded to ring up each item.

Pearl extracted a twenty-dollar bill from her back pocket and waited for her change. No one spoke throughout the entire transaction.

I followed her outside to her car.

'Hey, Pearl,' I said as she opened the boot. 'I saw the girls on the back seat. How come they are in your care?'

She wouldn't look at me. 'He's no longer with us, since you ask,' she said between her teeth.

I didn't know how to respond to that. I had no desire to find out what she meant.

'Was he...?' I said, not finishing my question. 'The father? Yes.'

'What will you do?'

'Do you really think that is any of your business.'

Her tone was snappy.

I was taken aback.

I had no intention of uttering another word.

Coffee beckoned, and I was about to walk away when I glanced across the intersection and saw, heading down from the north, an old white ute. As it came closer, I saw the driver was Frankie.

Pearl followed my gaze.

CHAPTER THIRTY-SIX

FRANKIE

With a mug of tea in hand, I squinted into the sun already threatening to crest the tree line. I'd slept in and it was nine before I'd loaded the ute.

Tuesday had been arduous. I'd given the butchering shed another scrub down. I spent the afternoon hand-washing clothes, a rare event but I was keen to get every bit of me and my apparel clean and fresh smelling. At dusk, I went out on the hunt. I hadn't expected to get lucky, but I came back with two small deer, probably because Con hadn't gone out on his usual road-kill expedition. What with the field dressing, and then the skinning, I was exhausted by the end of it all. Needing to keep my fridge going overnight, I had to drag myself to the generator to top up the diesel. Then I radioed Rick to arrange collection and fell into bed and into a deep sleep.

I drained my cup and set off for town. Despite the clear-felled patches where the loggers had made merry on the ash, and the otherwise scarred forest stripped of its best trees, it was always a pleasant drive down through the foothills, following the twists and turns of the road. Arriving in Cann River I approached the intersection in good spirits, anticipating cash in my pocket, the final eradication of Wayne, and an afternoon stitching leather for Cassie's stall.

When I saw Miriam and Pearl talking beside Pearl's old bomb, I sensed the day was not going to unfold as I'd hoped.

I waited at the crossroads for a cattle truck to pass by, then steered the crooked path of the crossroads, pulling up in the road alongside Pearl's dusty old Holden. My passenger-side window was wound down. I leaned across and called out, 'You girls want a coffee?'

'Nah, I gotta get home,' Pearl said, tilting her head behind her at the back seat where two kids were seated.

'Hang about a bit, would you, Pearl?'

Miriam made to cross the road with me.

'You too, Miriam. You'll want to hear this, I reckon.'

She stopped in her tracks and returned to the pavement.

'I'll not be long.'

Leaving two puzzled looking women, I parked round the side of the roadhouse and entered the kitchen through the backdoor. The place was filthy. Pat shot me a look from behind the counter. There was no sign of Con or any pie making.

'I've got some fresh meat for you, Pat.'

'Bring it in, then.'

Wayne didn't weigh much without his bones and his guts. I placed the plastic bucket on the draining board. Pat came in and peered into the bloody cuts. 'That looks too pink for venison,' she said.

'It's bush meat,' I said. 'A bit on the tough side.' 'Bush meat?'

'Bush meat.'

'Hamburger back on then. I tell Con to get mincer. How much you want?'

We struck a deal at twenty dollars which was fine by me for ten kilos of Wayne.

She disappeared, returning with the note which she shoved at me. She seemed troubled, distracted, the café oddly silent. No Joan Baez.

I asked her what was wrong.

'Stupid girl gone missing.'

'The backpacker?'

'She went to lighthouse and not come back.'

'When was this?'

'Monday night. I told her be back by eight.' She stabbed her wrist watch.

'This morning?'

'No. Yesterday morning. Eight at the latest.'

'And you waited this long to tell someone?'

'Con been out looking everywhere for her.'

'He's been to the lighthouse?'

'Of course he's been to the lighthouse.'

The sneer in her voice made me back away.

I pocketed her money and returned to the kitchen, where I grabbed from under the bench by the door the bucket I'd brought the deer cuts in, and headed outside.

I slung the bucket in the back tray and moved the ute, parking in the road opposite the general store. I joined Pearl and Miriam on the pavement where Pearl was keeping an eye on her car. Judging by their body language, it didn't seem they'd been having much of a banter. They both looked at me expectantly.

'I gotta get a wriggle on, Frankie,' Pearl said the moment my feet touched the kerb.

'I was only going to tell you that Wayne won't be giving us any more trouble.'

Miriam looked at me strangely.

'Two down then.' Pearl said it in that matter-of-fact tone she put on.

I laughed, if only to lighten the mood but it didn't have the desired effect.

Miriam froze. The colour drained from her face. 'You mean...?' she said, her voice faltering. 'I, I can't bring myself to even say it. How can you both stand there all proud? How, when two men are...are...'

'Dead.'

'They got what was coming to them, Miriam,' I said with something like sincerity in my voice.

'You can't go around killing people. That's not justice. It's murder.'

'Don't be ridiculous. I can't help it if their father gorged himself on my fish pie.' Pearl didn't bother to lower her voice. I hoped the car revving its engine as it cornered the intersection had drowned out her voice. That, or in the minds of those kids, incomprehension prevailed.

'And I can't help it if Wayne...' I said.

'Err, yes, actually, you could have, Frankie,' Pearl said. 'But never mind.'

I caught the look of mild amusement on Pearl's face. She knew the vengeance building up in me all those years after my mother's demise had been waiting for another outlet. She often said I was acting out a script deep inside, and that I'd stepped into the unknown and experienced what life was like after, after I'd taken a life with my own hands. Did she really think I would ever feel regret?

'So, hamburger's back on the menu, then,' Pearl said.

I turned to Miriam. 'I wanted to tell you not to eat the hamburger. It'll give you bellyache, just like the hunter pie.'

I could see her imagination filling in the gaps.

'You heading back to Peachtree?' I said to Pearl.

'I got to see to these kids.' She pointed her thumb behind her. I sensed she wasn't all that pleased.

'Only, something's come up,' I said. 'I'm worried about that backpacker, Emily. Pat's been sending Con out on the search. No sign of her since Monday night.'

Pearl leaned back against a side panel of her car.

'So, it was him driving around last night.'

I looked at her quizzically.

'I heard a car in the bush. Driving all over the place he was.'

'Would have been. I certainly didn't hear him up my way.'

'Where did she go?' Miriam asked.

'The lighthouse,' Pearl said. 'Where else?'

'There's something not right about that guy,' I said. 'Who has a scar running around the rim of his face like that?'

'It was a surgeon's knife,' Miriam said.

'Looks like it took the face right off him.' I paused. 'I've got a bad feeling, Pearl.'

'I can't do anything. I've got those kiddies to look out for.'

'Why don't you leave them with Miriam? She'll take care of them.'

Miriam looked none too pleased.

Before she had a chance to respond, Pearl shot her a cool look and said, 'Why don't you come back with me?' I caught her private smile. 'All their stuff is at mine.'

'Makes sense.'

'But my car,' Miriam said, taking a step back. 'I need to head off tomorrow. Or at least, that's when the spare part arrives.'

'That part won't get here until lunchtime,' Pearl said. 'Don't worry, we'll have all this sorted out by then.'

'I'd do it,' I said, hoping to quash Miriam's doubt. 'But I

have a couple of deer to shift this afternoon. Rick is coming by to collect.'

'Hop in,' Pearl said, opening the passenger side door.

Miriam obeyed. She didn't look happy but at least she did what she was told.

CHAPTER THIRTY-SEVEN

PEARL

Miriam wasn't in a talkative mood. Other than her few stiff comments to the kids on the back seat, she sat in silence. I was relieved, as I couldn't help seeing Kylie there in the passenger seat in her stead and it put me in an ill temper. Not that they were anything alike in appearance or manner. Maybe flashbacks didn't work like that. All I knew was I couldn't shunt away the memory of that day I left Mal.

I'd packed up the car to its roof with my things and Kylie's, and then I had to endure her sitting in the front seat blubbing for her dad. She must have been two at the time, and she screamed her little heart out, and there was me struggling to get the car into third gear as I headed up the street in Moonee Ponds. Back then I scarcely knew how to drive.

The months and years slipped by, and Mal would visit every Sunday and little by little he bought my daughter's heart with his gifts. She thought the sun only shone when he was around. All week from Monday to Saturday I put up with her moods and her tantrums. As the years dragged on, I had to endure her blame and resentment as well.

Nothing I did was ever good enough for Kylie.

I had no idea if Mal lived in Daintree, but I knew he'd gone to Queensland and I saw him there in her house, how I imagined her house would be—all happy families.

I'd had a thing about men who stole the kids ever since.

I'd had a thing about that passenger seat too, and I liked to keep it empty. The moment anyone sat there, all I could picture was Kylie. Thankfully Miriam seemed absorbed by the landscape and had settled in for the drive.

We arrived at Peachtree a bit before lunch. I showed Miriam around, told her where to find things. Once they were all gathered on the rug before the doll's house, Miriam all coos of false wonder, I threw together a cheese salad and fried some chicken nuggets for the kids.

Sally and Kim warmed to Miriam and she warmed to them. Seated at the kitchen table listening to their chatter I was grateful and resentful all at once. When the table was cleared, I brought out the dominoes I'd bought at the market and saved in case Kylie ever visited with my grandkids. It turned out Miriam knew how to play. She taught Sally and Kim, step by step, and pretty soon it was all Auntie Miriam this and Auntie Miriam that and I felt thoroughly squeezed out.

Which suited me.

After telling Miriam I'd be back late, I left the three of them playing Snap with a pack of cards I tossed on the table on my way by. I'd managed to interject in their cosy happy families for long enough to explain to Miriam how to use the short wave. She'd never seen one before, and asked questions and took notes. I felt a sudden if brief respect for her. At least she was reliable.

As I readied for my ordeal, I cursed myself for telling Emily about the beach walk. I'd wanted to help, give her an exit knowing she couldn't drive. In retrospect it seemed thoughtless, almost reckless and I half expected to find her on route to mine, collapsed in some awful state of terror and dehydration.

I packed a torch, water bottle, my sunnies and a few leftover nuggets in a canvas bag and drove slowly to the beach, all up about a six-kilometre stretch of dirt road that threaded its way through the undulating terrain of forest and coastal scrub, keeping my eye out for evidence of human life, a piece of clothing, a bag, a shoe. It was then I decided I'd been half mad to advise such a walk. Then again, she'd only have done it out of desperation.

I arrived at Clinton Rocks at about one o'clock. The tide was low, but the ocean was wild. Emily wouldn't have walked further along the beach than the rocky headland as I'd told her not to, and I had a clear view of the beach to those giant granite boulders smeared in orange lichen and of the low cliff behind, and there was no sign of anyone, no footsteps in the sand. I figured with the tide out, one way or another her footsteps would have been visible in the width of beach, even with the wind obliterating the evidence. She wouldn't have walked at the shoreline, for even at low tide a king wave would wash and slosh up the beach, surprising the unsuspecting. By the time she'd reached Clinton Rocks, Emily would have been fully acquainted with that.

Walking the full length of that inhospitable beach was not for the likes of young Emily.

I didn't like it either.

It was a long hike to Point Hicks. The wind was angled behind me, cold and blustery, pushing me along in fits and starts, whipping my hair into my eyes. Bracing didn't cover it. I wished I'd brought a hat, not that it would have stayed on my head. The swell was up too, the ocean slapping its load, wave upon wave at the shore. The roar of all that thrashing water was deafening. About half a kilometre later I remembered I had my sunnies in my bag and put them on.

The going was tough. My legs felt the strain. I kept eyeing the harder sand by the shoreline, but even though it made for easier walking, even though the tide was low, I didn't dare walk there.

Two kilometres further and my feet were complaining. Darts of pain shot through my ankles on every footfall. I kept the ocean in my side vision, not trusting it. The wind gathered its forces, and to some extent I was grateful for it, but that swell was on the rise. Before long I saw the bulges, up and up they went, twice my height and more, the crests of white spilling as the swell neared the shore. I edged to the left, further from the shoreline, watching the waves as they crashed, the spume flying on the wind, the ocean surging, sending water almost to my feet. The spray wetted the jacket on my back.

I scanned the undergrowth in the bush to my left for any signs of Emily and pressed on.

A healthy two-hour hike on a pleasant day for someone young and agile was proving to be the ordeal I'd anticipated, not that I slowed my speed. If anything, I walked faster, pushed by the wind, egged on by my unease, adrenalin on the march through me, matching the zeal of that bad-tempered ocean. Shit happens, I told myself, and right then it felt like God himself was readying for another dump.

Rising up on my left were steep-sided hills of scraggy forest and heathland, and in amongst it all were vast sand dunes formed out of the beach sand blown by the wind and plastered to the rising land in smears that had thickened and broadened over time. Evidence of what sort of place Tamboon was.

It was well after three o'clock when I came to the end of the beach. There, I had to scramble over a cluster of rocks with the ocean roiling by my side. Emily would never have made it at high tide. As it was, I lost my nerve and scrambled up to the bush that coated the low cliff. I waited for the wash of another king wave to subside before entering the small beach, which was divided in two by another pile of boulders that were exposed at low tide.

The beach soon tapered into a line of rocks before disappearing into the cliffs of Point Hicks promontory. I took the track that wended up the hillside, the sun casting sharp rays from the west. I trudged on up and before long the track dipped behind the rise where the wind couldn't pass through the thicket of bush.

I was suddenly violently hot.

I stopped and breathed and slugged my water and waited for my heart to slow and the heat to fade, and then I went on. Before long, the track opened onto the road that led to Point Hicks.

By the time I reached the compound, I was done in. I found Simon's cars parked in the garage. There were fresh tyre tracks gouged into the grass, as though someone had made an about turn and hightailed it out of there. Con.

I figured I had about two more hours of daylight. I went straight to the lighthouse, cornering the narrow strip of driveway and meeting the full blast of the wind. At the lighthouse door, I was buffeted on both sides as the wind curled round its great white trunk. The door was locked. I went back up the steps to the porch of the bungalow, where a wheelbarrow half full of firewood was parked by the door. I went inside.

The place looked recently occupied. There were candles everywhere, all unlit, a loaf of bread on the kitchen bench—half gone—along with a knife, a block of cheese hacked in two and a half-drunk cup of coffee. Some empty glasses were piled in the sink and I noticed a wine bottle on the floor. It, too, was empty.

They'd been enjoying themselves, that much was clear. Two books lay side-by-side on the table. I glanced at the titles. *The Cockatoos* and *Wake In Fright*, neither took my fancy. In the only bedroom, the bed was crumpled but I guessed from the blanket on the couch that one of them had slept there.

Something must have happened the following morning. A lover's tiff? I hardly thought so, not judging by the sleeping arrangements. Besides, the idea revolted me. The man was half dead.

Where were they?

While there was still good light I strode over to the skirt of rocky cliff and, battling the wind, I tracked along the edge, looking down into the churning, heaving ocean for a body or two.

I found nothing.

By then the sun had begun to dip below the western horizon of wooded hills, and it was in the subdued light that I went back to inspect the cottages, praising myself for having the presence of mind to pack a torch. I poked around the cottage on the left, peering in windows, noting the renovations. It looked like nothing had been moved in a while. No sign of any recent drama.

The second cottage was the same. No sign of recent activity.

I went around to the annex where Simon kept the short wave. The door was shut. I tried to open it but it wouldn't budge. Simon kept that door open on principle. In an emergency, there was no time to fuss about searching for the key. I tried the door again. Something seemed wedged behind it.

'Emily?' I hissed, although I could just as well have yelled. 'Are you in there?'

Silence.

'Emily!' I rattled the door handle. 'It's Pearl. Come on love. Open up.'

No one spoke but I heard a whimper.

'Emily, it's going to be all right. Just open the door.'

The scrape of furniture and the door fell open. The smell of stale sweat, booze and piss hit me like a punch.

Emily was a mess, crouched on her knees on the floor, rocking.

I'd never seen such a wretch of a human, cowering like a chicken. I thought she must have been attacked. It seemed unfathomable that a man in Pete's condition could manage such a thing, but then she was the supine type, feeble.

Why hadn't she radioed for help? After all, I'd told her how it worked. Educated girl like her should have been able to figure it out. And why the cowering? Why not head down the beach like I'd told her to and save me the hassle of finding her? She'd had a whole day or maybe two to do it. All those thoughts ran through my mind as I stared at her teary, blotchy face. I was ropeable.

CHAPTER THIRTY-EIGHT

EMILY

Pearl blocked the doorway. The cold air forging its way in made me reel. She wouldn't stop interrogating me. The same questions, over and again. I don't know why I hadn't moved. Or why I couldn't get any response from the radio. I did know I'd drunk an entire bottle of whisky on an empty stomach, then sat in a stupor for the whole of the rest of the night, too scared to get up and fetch myself some water or food.

I'd heard a car pull up late, a man's voice hollering, but in my comatose state I couldn't make out who it was. The sound of heavy boots on the veranda decking did nothing to ease my harried state of mind. I was convinced it was that ghost, or worse, Pete had come back to life, a Zombie.

I'd fallen asleep at some point and awoken in daylight with a mouth like sandpaper and an insufferable hangover, worsened by the head blow I'd received in the lighthouse. All I could do was huddle and try to summon the will to go outside. I was so dehydrated after all that time I still didn't need to pee, although by then hunger was beginning to gnaw. For hours, I'd sat there in that annex, lacking courage. I was thinking I'd better get a grip when Pearl called out my name.

My head felt like it had a cleaver through it. I felt so ill I could scarcely lift myself from the floor.

'For heaven's sake, get up,' Pearl said. 'I've got aching hips and aching feet and all you can do is sit there.'

I wasn't sure why she was saying those things. I stood up slowly and she moved aside for me to leave the annex.

I didn't say much. Not at first. I waited until she'd finished her rant about having to walk the beach to make sure I hadn't taken her advice. When at last she stopped talking about the wind and the waves and the endless soft sand we were back at the bungalow.

She stood in the doorway and watched as I downed a whole litre of water and ate a slice of bread. Slowly, I started to feel human again and recounted the events of the previous two days.

She had little patience for the early part of my story, the evening I'd climbed the lighthouse steps only to be haunted by a ghost on the way down. It was a necessary preamble; she needed to understand the context, the implication that Pete had staged a sort of terror, one that would shed light on what was to follow. I pulled out Pete's magazine from the side of the couch and handed it to her, open at the dogeared page, but all she did was rifle through that pages, somehow failing to land back on the page that was dog-eared. I felt like snatching it from her and showing her the article about that crazy researcher and the mouse brains.

I fast forwarded to the next day. The blow on the back of head piqued her interest. I related the rest, how I'd climbed to the top of the stairs, how Pete had followed, how I saw from his tool belt that he planned to do to me what that whacky researcher had done his mice—eat my living brain—how before he had a chance to execute his plan he had a seizure and how I used that moment to push pass him on my way down the stairs.

Her eyes hadn't left my face.

'I only gave him a nudge.'

At which she broke into a fit of laughter.

'Served him right,' she said, wiping her eyes.

'You think so?' I said, scarcely able to believe her reaction. It wasn't funny. None of what had happened warranted laughter. 'Where is he now?' she said.

Where did she think he was?

'Where he fell,' I said flatly. Did she think—no, surely not—that I'd somehow managed to dispose of his body?

I still had the lighthouse keys in my trouser pocket. I extracted

them and she led the way.

Outside, the wind whorled around the lighthouse, buffeting us as we went down to the concourse. She shone the torch on the keyhole. My hand trembled as I inserted the key. She didn't say a word.

Her torchlight found him in an instant. He lay there exactly as I'd left him. The blood had congealed around the edges of the pool that had formed at one side of his head. His eyes had that blank stare of the dead.

The first thing Pearl did was try to close them, but they wouldn't. Rigor mortis had set in.

The second thing she did was flick on the light. It was then that I noticed the light switch just inside the door.

I stood, numb. She told me to fetch the wheelbarrow. I went outside, relieved to be out in the wind. I fumbled my way up the steps. My eyes adjusted and I saw the wheelbarrow filled with firewood. I tipped out the wood and took the barrow to the lighthouse, forcing myself back through the door.

She lined up the wheelbarrow against the wall.

'Grab his legs.'

I didn't argue. She had him by the shoulders. His head, turned to one side, pressed against her thighs, his eyes gazing absently down at the floor.

I grabbed his calves. His knees didn't bend. He was surprisingly light. Then again, he hardly had any flesh left on him. The cancer had taken it all. Even so, I hadn't expected to find the strength to lift him.

I had him by his knees. Pearl took most of the weight. Heaving his torso higher than the rim of the wheelbarrow proved strenuous but not impossible. He landed with a thud, releasing an echo, an echo that bounced somewhere up the lighthouse chamber walls.

It was then Pearl revealed what sort of woman she was.

First, she rummaged through his clothes, extracting his wallet and keys which she pocketed. Then she went out and returned with a log. She stood over the wheelbarrow, raised her battering ram up above her head and brought it down on Pete's diaphragm with astonishing force. Once, twice, and again until I heard a crack and his body caved in.

She tossed the log outside and followed with the wheelbarrow.

'Tide's up,' she said, wheeling the barrow down the narrow path to the water's edge. Stiff with rigor, his legs sticking straight out, his arms bent as they'd been when he fell, Pete bumped and bounced as the barrow bumped and bounced, Pearl taking no care as she trudged along. I followed, not knowing what else to do. The wind thrashed about and even in the dark I saw the spume of the waves hitting the rocks.

It seemed she'd already had a tipping point in mind. She went to where the edge fell away sharply, where the waves made glancing blows at the low cliff. She came to a stop and without a pause she tilted up the barrow. Presumably, she'd hoped he would slide out, but Pete didn't cooperate. She set the barrow down and yelled at me to help.

I had to pull on his legs as she made the barrow tilt, making him tumble.

I didn't hear the splash.

'Good riddance to bad rubbish,' she said, walking away and leaving me with the barrow smeared with blood.

Back at the lighthouse she had me on my knees scrubbing the floor, the barrow, anywhere there was evidence. She left me there and went to straighten things out in the bungalow and the annex.

'Come on, you,' she said when we were done, and I followed her to the garage and Simon's cars.

'Get in this one,' Pearl said, pointing at the car Pete had used.

Sitting in the passenger seat, I picked up the empty tape case of Throbbing Gristle and put it on my lap. Pearl ran through the gears, reversing out and heading down the track to the gate.

I felt like an accessory to a crime I hadn't committed. The way Pearl had taken charge, the way she'd known exactly what to do without pausing to think or discuss it with me was more disturbing than the acts themselves. She'd done it before. No one could step into a situation and follow through like that, step by step, without some sort of experience.

We drove out of Point Hicks in grim silence. She didn't even ask me to get out and open the boundary gate. Instead she did it herself. Knowing what sort of music waited to be played in the cassette player, I had half a mind to press play. Then I thought better of it. I was no Myra Hindley. I sat there, subdued, keeping my gaze fixed on the side window, replaying the scene over and again in my mind.

CHAPTER THIRTY-NINE

MIRIAM

P earl returned around nine. By then, I'd fed and bathed the girls—who'd been in dire need of a wash judging by their smell—and settled them down in the only bed in the shack, Pearl's, with a story. I'd helped myself to her whisky, too, and sat dozing by the fire with the dog at my feet. Despite the haphazardly arranged, dubiously clean state of the place and overall shabbiness of the furniture—dog hair whorls in the corners of the floor, stained patches on the couch—it felt pleasant out there in the bush, far enough away from the hotel, the roadhouse, the town altogether to forget they existed, and without the presence of Pearl I relaxed, almost contented. She then pulled up outside and ruined it all.

Her heavy steps on the deck, the door opening and closing with a slam, and I was convinced the girls would wake up. I didn't move even though I knew she'd react when she saw me.

I was right. She eyed me sitting there all cosy by her fire, drink in hand, and said, 'I see you've been having a fine time.'

I offered her a drink and some food and relinquished my

chair. She accepted all three, and when she was settled in her seat, her belly full of the leftovers I found in the fridge—and several whiskies—she filled me in on the events of her afternoon.

After hearing all she'd been through, I didn't dare ask her to run me back into town. Instead, I sat perched on the edge of the couch, holding out my glass for a refill as she topped up her own. I had no idea if she was telling me the truth, except for the part where she described her trek along the beach, and her journey back to Cann River with Emily. The rest sounded made up.

Eventually, she tossed a set of car keys at me and said, 'You can drive yourself into town in Simon's car. It's parked out the front.'

By then I'd had too much to drink to manage a drive in the dark, especially as I hadn't a clue of the route.

'Can I stay the night here?'

It occurred to me she might offer me a bed at Fred's, but she said, 'I had you down for a city pussy,' she said. 'Guess I was right.' She finished her drink and heaved herself up. 'Good luck on the couch.'

She stared down at me for a moment, then went into her bedroom. I didn't like to think of her sleeping in the same bed as those girls but there was nothing I could do about it.

I had never before enjoyed the privilege of spending a whole night trying to sleep on a small, two-seater couch. I failed. Judging by the pre-dawn chorus, I guessed what the time was and took my chances, gathering my things and heading off with Simon's car keys and a splitting headache.

Fortunately, I had a good sense of direction and my efforts the night before to memorise the route paid off. I parked Simon's car on the roadhouse forecourt near the air-pressure hose and crossed the highway, arriving at the hotel in time for breakfast.

I walked past the dining room window to see Cassie lay my table setting. I waved and she came and opened the front door. In all, the day felt like it was off to a good start.

'I had no idea you were out,' she said with a reproachful look in her eye.

'I'm famished,' I said, placating her with a friendly smile and barging through to the dining room despite the fact that I always had a bath before breakfast.

She remained doubtful. I thought better of telling her where I'd been.

'He's really no harm,' she said, with a tilt of her head. 'More desperate than anything. Besides, he'll be leaving later. Got wind those bikie mates of his have found out where he's hiding. Personally, I think he'd be safer staying put but he won't be told.'

'You know him, then.'

She paused. 'He's connected to the town, yes.'

It was all she said. As she made to return to the kitchen, I pulled out my chair and sat down heavily, slaking my thirst with the orange juice and pondering fetching myself another Bex.

When she returned with my food, I told her I would be checking out as the spare part was due to arrive.

'It won't get here until lunchtime,' she said, as if to say my car would not get fixed that day, no matter what.

'I'm sure it's only a five-minute job,' I said. I hadn't meant to sound clipped.

'If you say so.'

I held her gaze, refusing to let go of my earlier inquiry. 'I don't understand why you people won't get the police involved. Dan's a criminal. That Wayne character was even worse.'

'Was?'

'I meant, he isn't staying in this hotel,' I said quickly, as a wave of unease coursed through me. I had no idea how much Cassie knew, and I didn't want to be the one revealing Frankie's awful deed.

'Miriam, this isn't your town,' Cassie said, folding her arms across her chest. 'You don't know its history.'

'Then tell me.'

She remained tight-lipped.

'Look, I'm leaving tonight. I've had an awful week. Your hospitality has been the only thing keeping me going.' I gave her an ingratiating smile. 'I really would like to know.'

'It's ancient history,' she said, at last giving way. 'Back in the day when the highway was a dirt road, Old Gran Parks ran the hotel.'

'You mentioned her before.'

'Gran Parks was a much-loved woman, and everyone called her "Gran" because she went grey in her forties, long before she was one.'

'She murdered her husband, if I recall.'

'With a meat cleaver.'

'Here in this hotel?'

'In the kitchen. She was so stricken by what she'd done she stepped out onto the highway one night in the path of an oncoming logging truck. Just out there.' She pointed at the crossroads.

'That's tragic.'

'It was. It also meant there was never much of a police investigation into her motive. No trial, obviously. And no need for the cops to admit that one of their own was a total bastard.'

'One of their own?'

'Her husband was the local copper.'

Things started to make sense.

'He was violent towards her?'

'And then some. He controlled her in every way you can think of. He was brutal.'

'Probably what sent her grey.'

'That's what Frankie reckons.'

'I don't understand what this has to do with your collective ambivalence towards the police.'

'The current cop is a relation of Parks. Distant, but the town won't have anything to do with him regardless. I'll fetch your bill.'

I watched her walk away. It made sense on some level, but her story was born of a fishbowl. The profound lack of trust was understandable among the locals, but what of Frankie and Pearl? They weren't from Cann River. Yet they were thick with Cassie and she was the loyal type. What knitted those women together? Gran Parks?

She returned to take away my breakfast and handed me my bill. I wrote a cheque and thanked her for her hospitality, privately wondering if she even knew what life was like outside Cann River or even if it existed.

It took a couple of trips across the highway laden with my things and I was done with the hotel. Leaving the room one last time, passing by Dan's door, the only thought in my mind was good riddance.

I left my suitcase and bags by the garage door and went inside the café.

Con was standing behind the counter, his torso wrapped in an apron. I had to badger him for my keys.

'Whad'ya wanna load up now for?' That same doubtful tone, as if he knew, just as Cassie knew, that the chances of me leaving Cann River before nightfall were nil.

'I'm leaving, obviously,' I said, refusing to surrender to the inertia.

Pat, who'd been standing in the kitchen doorway, bustled over, telling me not to get Con stressed.

'He's no good under pressure.'

With the two of them side by side, I was momentarily defeated. I could see it was to be a long and tedious day. I ordered a cup of coffee to while away some time and went and ferried in my things and plonked them down at the end of my preferred table by the window.

Pat brought over my coffee then went to the jukebox. In seconds, I was graced with the company of Joan Baez. The song wasn't unlikeable in my view, but there was no harm in variety, and it was all she seemed to play. My headache worsened in the listening.

I'd taken the seat facing the general store and the road heading south. I had my back to the café entrance and felt a draught whenever someone entered.

A rush of air and I turned to see Emily trudging in carrying a mop and bucket. She looked dazed and overwrought. She disappeared out the back, reappearing a short while later with a dish cloth and proceeding to wipe down tables. From my purview, I could watch her wander back and forth. She clearly didn't want to be there. I wasn't surprised, after her ordeal. What did surprise me was Pat's insistence that Emily work at all. For she must have insisted. Emily looked in no fit state to string together a single thought and without Pat's badgering she would no doubt have remained in bed or sipped sweet tea by a fire.

I was keen to talk to her, but she was hard to get on her own. Pat's eyes and ears were everywhere and even from the kitchen she could see the table where I sat.

A short burst of custom that constituted the breakfast rush, was followed by the entry of the man I recognised from the general store as the cashier with the magazine on his lap. He ordered the single Kitchener bun on display in the sandwich cabinet and sat down at a table two over from mine, thankfully with his back to me.

The coffee eased my headache. Joan Baez stopped lamenting Dixie, and the roadhouse slipped into a lull. I guessed what was to come. When a strong smell of stewing meat had filled the air, I decided to leave Con to finish baking his pies. I relocated my bags to a discrete area behind the jukebox and asked Emily to keep an eye on them, and then I went up the street to while away the hours at my favoured spot in the churchyard, calling in at the bakery on my way by.

I'd finished the Thea Astley at Pearl's and was enjoying *Tirra Lirra by the River* by Jessica Anderson, a novel gifted me by my mother as my leaving present. It was quite good. At the end of a chapter, I put the book down and I reflected on the novels I'd already consumed in Cann River: the Barbara Hanrahan set in Adelaide, the Miles Franklin in an idyllic setting near Goulburn, and the Thea Astley in Queensland. I seemed to be roaming around Australia with those authors but nothing I'd read resembled where I was. With its suburban Sydney setting, *Tirra Lirra by the River* was no different from the others, even if I could relate to Nora wanting to escape a small country town. The context couldn't compare to mine. In fact, the sentiment was so distinct, and the concerns of all those carefully crafted characters so unlike my own experience, I wondered whether I was stuck inside some false reality, living out an altogether distinct narrative. Or if there were multiple Australias, like parallel universes, and I had entered the darkest of all. Yet there were similarities between me and all those protagonists. I was an independent woman.

Despite having a rapport with those Brent children, I never wanted the responsibility of my own. I'd chosen the solitary life, the hardworking life, a career of sorts, only to have it all brought down to a pitiful end by a fire. One not of my making, I noted.

Although, my story didn't end there. My life was set to end happily. My bright new future was ahead of me. Cann River was nothing but an interlude. Setting aside all the goings on what with Dan, and between Frankie and Pearl and their despatching of wayward men, I decided my time in that town had been markedly uneventful. After all, most of it had been spent immersed in books.

Seated in the dappled shade of the churchyard I ran over in my mind the key events of the week and reflected on various conversations. I realised that even as I recoiled hearing their words, part of me had doubted the veracity of Frankie and Pearl's accounts. As if that old fisherwoman would poison a stranger who happened to take possession of a shack across the track. As if a feral bushie who hunted deer would do away with an interloper even if he was wanted on suspicion of murder and rape. I even doubted Emily had pushed that terminally ill man over the banister. After all, I hadn't heard it from her own lips. I only had Pearl's version and it was second hand and no doubt embellished. The previous days had unfolded like a farce and I, the innocent bystander, wanted no part in any of it.

Shortly before twelve, I dined on my sausage roll and vanilla slice. I returned to the roadhouse immediately after. The midday Sydney to Melbourne coach had pulled up in my absence and inside the café I was confronted by a party of four out-of-towners, ordering hamburgers with the lot. The smell of frying hamburger was enough to make me want to march back outside.

Instead, I waited for a quiet moment, acclimatising to the smell. When at last Pat was free, I asked her if the spare part had arrived and she answered with a cursory nod.

To my mounting frustration, Con was still in the kitchen, baking.

'Surely it doesn't take him that long to bake a ruddy pie,' I said.

'He's doing a double batch,' Emily said, coming up behind me. 'And the hamburger is back on, so he gets distracted.'

I wanted to suggest someone else made the burgers but decided not to push it. Surveying the café, there was nothing to be done other than summon more patience.

The lunchtime rush that day was exceptional. All the passengers exiting the one o'clock Melbourne to Sydney coach headed straight into the roadhouse. Just as Emily said, they were all in for the burgers. Someone had put out the sandwich board while I was at the church. I'd almost walked into it on my way in. "Burgers with the Lot Hungarian-stile" which must have been what drew the customers, in spite of the misspelling.

I waited and waited, enduring the smell of frying meat that mingled with the smell of the pies. It was rich, overwhelming. Whatever was in those hamburgers, the customers loved them. At half past one, as the coach from Melbourne pulled away on its journey to Sydney, Pat had to send Emily across to the general store for more lettuce and tomatoes.

I ordered a coffee and waited some more. The tedium and my frustration could scarcely be assuaged by my book. I considered returning to the churchyard but felt compelled to monitor the situation.

After two o'clock, the café emptied. There was still activity in the kitchen, and it was almost three before Con appeared in his overalls. He went outside carrying my spare part under his arm.

With the knowledge that he was at last under my bonnet, I fetched my bags and arranged them beside my table and set my mind to talking to Emily. I had to wait again, this time until she was done with cleaning up the mess Con had left in the kitchen. I must have heard Joan Baez's lamentations another four times, Pat dashing out and opening the jukebox, fiddling about inside to get a free play before darting back to the kitchen. I could have throttled that Joan on the last listening.

At about four, Emily went around with a broom, sweeping up under tables. When she approached mine, I managed, without Pat's eavesdropping, to ask if she was okay.

She wasn't.

Hearing her strained tone, something in me reared up and I urged her to get out of town on the next coach.

'I can't.'

'Why ever not?'

When she told me about her pay and Pat's shenanigans, I fished out my wallet and extracted a twenty-dollar bill.

'That's too much. I couldn't.'

'Take it.' I shoved it into her hand.

She shot a look behind her. There was no sign of Pat.

'When will the coach come in?'

'It's Thursday, so there's a second coach at six.'

'Be on it.'

I told her I'd hang around to make sure. I told her I was leaving as well, and I didn't like to think of her there all alone. The place smacked of evil.

She resisted.

She avoided my gaze.

She didn't seem to like me much.

I couldn't explain to her the source of my concern. I couldn't understand why she'd even resist leaving. I had to curb an impulse to snatch my money back in the face of her ingratitude. Then I reminded myself that the poor girl was traumatised and not capable of knowing her own mind.

A blast of a car horn followed closely by another and we

both looked over at once. Two vehicles pulled up across the road from each other. Frankie got out of one and Pearl the other.

'Emily!' Pat yelled. Emily rushed away.

CHAPTER FORTY

FRANKIE

The forest was quiet. The sun, low to the east, warm on my skin.

I paused outside the butchering shed, enjoying the light, the stillness. The generator was off and the fridge door ajar to air the interior. A healthy smell of bleach infused the shed.

My knives were sharp. I was ready for my next kill. Peace descended, laced with satisfaction. The Howard Potters of the world would do well to drive straight on through Cann River. Pat could live without her hamburger meat.

I headed up to the shack. The only matter spoiling an otherwise perfect day was Pearl. She was losing perspective. Bringing those kids into town displayed poor judgement. Any number of passers-by could have seen her, seen them in her car, seen her with them.

I figured by nine she'd be up. No matter how much whisky she'd drunk last night, those kids would make sure of it.

Two attempts and she answered, her voice gravelly.

I spoke on the pretext of finding out about Emily. We had a veiled exchange in case anyone was listening. Then I tried to reason with her. She was evasive, distracted, didn't want to hear me, but I managed to persuade her to bring herself and the kids into town.

We both arrived at the same time. I went over as she got out of her vehicle. We were standing at the crossroads, her with her hands in her pockets, me leaning against her Holden, tracing clean tracks through the dirt on the roof with a fingertip, watching the odd station wagon drive by, waving at Cassie as she left the hotel on her way back to her bees. I listened. Pearl kept her voice low, any spill drowned by the logging truck that had pulled up at the roadhouse, the driver leaving the engine on while he went inside, no doubt lured by 'hamburgers with the lot' on the sandwich board.

Sounded like both her and Emily had had a challenging time. I had to marvel at Pearl for taking the beach route. Showed determination. I'm not sure I would have done it, at least, not before I'd driven to Point Hicks and checked the scene. Although that would have taken a good few hours in itself, and there'd have been no daylight left for the beach dash.

Hearing Pearl's re-telling of the demise of Pete, I felt strangely proud of Emily. I'd never have thought her capable of dispatching. It was an initiation, and I was transported back to my own in the listening.

Of the day I'd rid myself of a guy called Swan, who'd tried to take possession of my shack, making out like it was his. Said he had some claim on it based on a distant uncle. I hadn't believed a word of it, especially after his strategy shifted and he thought he'd lay claim to me as well.

I learned a lot about death that day. I learned to hold myself steady as the life drained out and something living was no longer. Stood me well in the deer hunting business, for until then, I'd struggled with the killing side.

It occurred to me to invite Emily up to mine. I could teach her how to handle a rifle, how to hunt.

Then Pearl went on about the body in the barrow and I steered the conversation back to her current situation with those kids, eyeing them sitting like dolls on the backseat. Pretty things, they were.

Eradicating vermin was one thing, holding onto life that didn't belong to you another. Besides, she'd never get away with it. Social services would swarm in and there was no telling what they'd dredge up.

The best solution was to find a way to persuade Miriam to take them with her. She could do whatever she wanted once she was across the border. It was a risk, but even if she went to the cops, what would they find? It was a rescue story, nothing more, and the real perpetrator, Brent, was in bits. I even offered to help Pearl deal with those body parts floating in the lagoon. Said I'd drive down to Peachtree and make sure everything was cleaned up.

'What about Simon's car?' she said. 'Miriam came into town in it.'

'I'll drive it back to Point Hicks. You can follow me in this,' I said, giving her rust bucket a pat. 'And I'll get rid of Brent's for you.'

'You will?'

'Not a problem.'

She wavered, as if coming to the realisation that she had to let go. Before she changed her mind, I made the whole situation public by opening the car door and ushering the girls onto the pavement. With one in each hand we all crossed over to the roadhouse.

CHAPTER FORTY-ONE

PEARL

K im and Sally woke up in a fractious mood. 'Where's Aunty Miriam?' they cried in unison upon finding the couch empty and no sign of her in the house. They looked around. I looked around. But I knew she'd gone. Simon's car was no longer parked outside. We all felt abandoned by her. Me most of all, as I was stuck having to appease two whining brats.

They refused to eat their breakfast because the milk was too warm and tasted funny. As did the tank water I gave them. The red cordial I'd brought over from Fred's and poured into their glasses to obliterate the twang did nothing for their state of mind. They glared at me and screamed at each other. The situation spiralled into mayhem. Bits of doll's house were being thrown about by the time Frankie called me on the short wave.

Frankie went on a long monologue in an attempt to persuade me to bring the kids into town. I needed no persuading. Sally and Kim were going crazy in the background, screaming and carrying on, and I had to keep interrupting

Frankie with 'buts' and 'hang on a minute', and in the end, I said I'd be there, and she told me to come at four.

In a sudden rush, I packed up their things and loaded them in the boot. Then I went back inside and the five hours ahead of me stretched out like infinity. Kim and Sally, who apparently never fought, started hitting each other and yelling. Then it was, 'Where's Daddy?' and 'We want Aunty Miriam?' I told them if they didn't shut up, I'd take them out on the boat. They quieted after that, but it didn't last. Unable to endure the bickering, I grabbed hold of them by their hair and dragged them screaming into my bedroom, closing and locking the door. Then I spent the morning in the garden, weeding and harvesting and chopping wood and ignoring their cries.

For lunch, I cooked up the kid's food I'd bought at great expense at the general store. They wouldn't eat it. Sally said it tasted like muck and Kim started to cry for her mother. It was as much as I could do not to set my dog on them. I tried playing dominoes, but Sally swiped the tiles on the floor in a hissy fit when I told her she couldn't put a blank on a three. The doll's house didn't satisfy them either. I felt like radioing Frankie to make the arrangement earlier in the day, but I knew she'd be out and about up there in the forest. By the time three o'clock came around I had to raise my hand as if to smack their behinds to get them in the car.

All the way into town they yabbered, and Kim kept kicking the back of my seat.

I drove in silence, thinking children, all children were a liability. If they'd been my own kids... but I'd never really hit Kylie. I'd slapped her bare thighs once or twice when she was playing up in the car, but that was it. She was a belligerent child too, always up to something, always nagging, always demanding. Nothing I did would ever satisfy her.

I'd always considered myself good intentioned. I was the

sort of woman who strove to do the right thing by those around her, even if they showed no gratitude. That was what I'd done with Kylie for all those years and I was repaid with cruelty, forced to be estranged from my own flesh. Shit happened, but it didn't stop it feeling like shit.

I pulled up as Frankie did. Leaving the girls squabbling on the back seat, I got out and stood on the pavement, watching her cross the street, her stride purposeful.

I paid attention to Frankie's lecture, heard her go on about social services, but I'd already made up my mind to go along with her suggestion. Miriam could have them. It wasn't anything she said that swayed me. It was the knowledge that Miriam would make a good mother, that she had developed a rapport with those girls straight away. They trusted her. They'd do anything she asked without playing up.

With me, the wretches were stubborn, petulant and uncooperative. Where was their gratitude?

Frankie swung open the back door and told the girls to get out, tugging on Kim's arm. They both went all meek in the face of her, towering over them with her skunk mullet hair. We headed to the roadhouse, where I saw Miriam seated at the window surrounded by her luggage, no doubt waiting for her car to get fixed and suddenly, there we were, playing happy families, me, Frankie, Miriam and those brats.

We were the only customers.

Emily wandered about, pretending to clean. She avoided catching my gaze. I kept my eye on her, my expression hard, conveying on my face the ire I felt inside should she look my way. My mood soured at the sight of her busying about doing nothing and doing everything to keep away from me. The unappreciative wretch, after all I'd done for her. She ought to be thanking me. After all, I was the only witness, the only one who could testify to the location of Pete's body on the lighthouse floor. She was behaving as though nothing had passed between us. Shit happens, girlie, make no mistake. I glanced out the window at Simon's car parked where Miriam had left it over by the air pressure hose and wondered if he'd notice anything different about Point Hicks when he got back.

It was then that an image of Pete, washed up on the rocks, flashed into my mind, and I hoped the ocean had done its job of carrying him off.

Miriam had ordered hot chips and Pat brought out a bowl piled high and doused with her tomato sauce.

Those two ratbags tucked in as though they hadn't seen food in a week. In seconds their faces were smeared with sauce.

I couldn't wait to see the back of them.

After all, they weren't my kin. Kylie's were my kin. Kylie, in Daintree, up there with Mal.

Some situations would never resolve. You were doomed to spend your days wading in whatever shit life had dumped you in, and I was ankle deep in mine.

I felt suddenly, overwhelmingly grim.

I didn't wait for Frankie to put the proposal to Miriam. While they sat around chatting about Emily, Frankie musing on how she wanted to invite her up to hers and teach her to hunt and Miriam looking askance, I slipped out to my car and unloaded the boot.

It was starting to get dark. Soon the street lights would come on. A gust of cold wind hit me as I walked across the forecourt. I managed to get the suitcase and bags into the café before Miriam and Frankie appeared to notice.

'I'll just leave this lot with you,' I said to an astonished Frankie, dumping the bags beside Miriam's before taking off without looking back. I knew they were all staring at me as I headed out the door. 'Fish to catch,' I called out, making my exit with a backward wave.

CHAPTER FORTY-TWO

EMILY

A t the sight of the two hags talking in the street, I left Miriam and went back behind the counter. Searching for something to do, I wiped down the sandwich cabinet. Before long, Frankie and Pearl walked in with the two little girls. My stomach clenched.

Pearl hadn't saved my life. I would have come out of the annex on my own. I was about to, before she turned up. I'd have got something to eat, figured out how to use the radio, or Con would have come back and found me. Pat said he'd been looking for me, and she was going to send him out again, only I turned up before he needed to.

I'm not sure what would have happened to Pete. I suppose someone would have come and taken away the body. A doctor maybe, or a police officer. There would have been an inquiry. Accidental death would have been the outcome. He'd had a seizure. They would have seen how traumatised I was. That I didn't have it in me to commit murder.

Only, I had.

What Pearl had done, what Pearl had me do, was irrational

and unnecessary. It was as though she hadn't been trying to help me dispose of evidence that could be held against me, more that she wanted to cause me further distress, rub my nose in the ghastly situation. She'd been so splenetic about it, so aggrieved. It felt as though she'd wanted to punish me.

Pat had treated me little better. When Pearl had dropped me off and left me stranded on the forecourt, I'd had to hammer on the café door and then the kitchen door around the back, before Pat had come out all cross and arms folded.

'Where the hell have you been?' she said. 'Get inside.'

I flinched as I hurried by her, convinced she would hit me.

I slept poorly, still shaken from my ordeal. In the morning, knowing Pat would never give me a day off, I dragged myself out of bed and into my black t-shirt. It was a horrible morning. First, Pat made me rid the kitchen of the two-day old pie spillage. Then she'd put the hamburgers with the lot on the menu and it caused a lunchtime rush. I was in and out, serving petrol and serving burgers. When Miriam had thrust a twenty-dollar bill at me, I saw hope, but I knew I wouldn't leave on the next coach as she insisted. I wanted my pay. I wasn't going to leave Cann River without the money Pat owed me.

Exhausted, hollowed out and destitute, I watched from my sanctuary behind the counter, secure with my rag-cloth in hand, and there they all sat, the three women and the two small girls, like a family. Only there was no sense of conviviality at that table. Frankie and Miriam talked furtively, glancing my way. The kids ate the chips and Pearl sat there, arms folded, a scowl fixed on her face.

Almost an hour passed and then Pearl marched out. I saw her ferry in the girls' baggage. Then Frankie and Miriam pulled together in a conversation that morphed rapidly into an argument, each of them pulling back in her seat, the girls in their charge looking up, nervous.

Miriam folded her arms across her chest. Frankie had hers on her hips, elbows out.

'What's the matter with you?' Frankie yelled.

'I can't take them with me.'

'Of course, you can.'

'There's no room in my car.' Miriam sounded indignant.

'What am I supposed to do with them, then?'

'Ask Cassie. She'll think of something.'

'I don't have time for this,' Frankie said. 'I've got deer to hunt.'

'You're the expert,' Miriam said to Frankie's back as she stormed off.

Pat must have heard the commotion. She came out and ordered me to clean the toilets.

I hurried off, startled by her tone, slowing once I was on the forecourt, mop and bucket in hand.

Frankie must have seen me. She glanced back, and came straight over, her manner, now that she was beyond the reach of Miriam, relaxed, almost friendly.

'Hey, Emily, glad I've caught you.' She grinned.

It was all too forced. She might as well have said 'trapped'.

'I'll be heading down to Pearl's later. Fancy a ride?'

'Pearl's?'

'You need to get away from here for a bit. Am I right? Kick back and get to know some real women in the area. This roadhouse isn't healthy for your head.'

'That sounds lovely,' I said. 'About what time?'

'Seven-thirty, I reckon.'

'Sounds good,' I said, trying to match her gaze.

Satisfied, she strode off, and I attended to the toilets.

I had to remain out there for the appropriate length of time or Pat would send me back to do it properly. I emptied the bins, wiped down the basins, and scrubbed and mopped just as I always did. But I did it all with half attention. My mind was elsewhere. Frankie's invitation had given me focus.

The toilets cleaned, I stood outside, taking in the crossroads, the neon sign outside the roadhouse, the hotel across the highway, the general store on the other side, it all looked normal, like an uneventful kind of place. Only, it was far from it.

I wasn't about to enter whatever hell lurked down at Peachtree. Instead, Miriam's earlier attempts at persuading me to leave town shone with virtue and salvation.

I emptied the bucket down the drain outside the toilet block and made to go back inside the café hoping Miriam and the kids were gone, my mind on the time, on the dollars in my pocket, on my bags in my room.

CHAPTER FORTY-THREE

MIRIAM

A little before five, Con at last came in holding my car keys. I snatched them from him and followed him to the counter. He took an age writing out the invoice. I expected him to charge an exorbitant amount, but the price seemed fair and I was in no mood to haggle. I paid and went back to my table.

Seeing Emily emerge from the toilet block, I left the children to finish the last of the chips and dashed outside, accosting her on the forecourt. She put down her mop and bucket with reluctance when she saw I wasn't about to let her go by.

I'd never negotiated a matter so fast. It was as though I was back at my desk, issuing directives to inexperienced staff. I told her she was not only to get on the next coach out of town, but she would be taking those two girls with her.

'I can't,' she said.

'Why ever not?'

'What will I do with them in the city?'

'Here,' I said, and handed her a piece of paper with my parents' address on it. 'They take in strays,' I said, thinking they'd adopted me all those years ago so they must be predisposed to others' children. Besides, I didn't much care what they thought when Emily turned up with her charges. I looked at her appealingly. 'Tell them I sent you. I'll phone ahead and warn them.'

'But...'

'No buts. I'll pay the fares and some extra for your trouble.'

Judging by her reticence, I thought Emily would be resistant to the last, but she soon grew compliant. Eager, in fact. She went and packed her things, told Pat where she could stick her job and waited with me at the crossroads.

Nothing much was happening in the town. The general store had closed. No cars went by. The street lights came on. Before long, I spotted a figure in black scuttling across the northbound arm of the crossroads. He was carrying a holdall. Looked as though he'd exited the hotel. Not Dan, surely? He must have been petrified of those bikie friends of his to be leaving the hotel in the gloaming. I averted my gaze and continued waiting.

The bus pulled up at six and Emily got on the moment the doors opened, leaving me to coax the girls up the steep bus steps and on down the aisle to where Emily was seated, all eyes on me as I went by, the supposed harried mother, laden with their little suitcase and bags.

Once the girls were settled with the bars of chocolate, potato chips and apple juice I'd purchased at the roadhouse before it closed, I shoved another twenty-dollar bill into Emily's hand and returned to the nonplussed driver seated behind the wheel to pay all their fares.

It wasn't until I saw the back end of the bus disappear down the highway that I made my own way out of town.

It was twenty minutes past six by the time I'd loaded up my

boot. The sun had already set and the night sky beyond the street lights was fast edging towards black.

I eyed the stagger of the crossroads one last time. I pictured Frankie in the forest in the north and Pearl in her shack in the south. I pictured Emily arriving from the east and me from the west and it occurred to me that we four women had been momentarily bound by fate as though Gran Parks herself had stood at the centre of those four directions and beckoned us, doomed us to meet. I looked up at my hotel room and its unlit window. I stared and stared but no ghost appeared. No ghost appeared because ghosts didn't exist. Gran Parks was a symbol, that was all, a dark talisman, an energy it was best not to invoke. I imagined her there in the centre of the crossroads, flattened by a truck, her body testament to the evil deeds of men.

I went over to my car and opened the driver's side door. The seat had been pushed right back. I adjusted it to my comfort, straightened the rear vision mirror, put the key in the ignition and let out a sigh when I heard the purr. Without a backwards glance, I pulled out of the roadhouse and took off up the highway heading east.

I had always been a careful driver. I prided myself on my cautious manner. Behind the wheel I never took risks. I was the sort of driver who left a safe distance between me and the next vehicle, who slowed in anticipation at traffic lights on green, who waited, patiently, for a safe place to overtake, who kept an eye out for the unexpected. I knew the bush at night was filled with wildlife, awake, hungry, on the prowl. I knew I needed to be vigilant.

That night my patience had run dry. My desire to put distance between me and Cann River narrowed my vision. All I saw was the road ahead, opening into the wilderness, a high curtain of trees parting as the road carved its way.

Eager to get to my brand-new home in the open

countryside, I put my foot down. My car bulleted out of town. At the last road sign, I was triumphant. Without my usual easing off the accelerator, I cornered into the next bend, assured of my own safety, following the curve.

As I exited the bend, I felt the impact, the dull thud of a glancing blow. A figure hurtled in the air and came down hard on what looked like a lone star picket. My car veered towards the roadside. I corrected my steering, slowed, squinted in the rear vision mirror as the scene receded, the lights of a logging truck approaching behind me lighting the carnage. The figure hung, impaled.

I wavered.

I expected the truck driver to pull over.

Instead, the truck was fast closing the gap between us.

It seemed to leave me no choice.

I looked again at the truck in the rear vision mirror, trying to make out the driver, but I couldn't. I thought I glimpsed a woman on the passenger seat. When I looked again, she was gone.

I kept driving, on into the dark, maintaining a good speed, my rear lit by the headlights of my companions.

END

NOTES

The Parts of this Story that are True:

The Ash Wednesday bush fire really happened on that day in February. I used to live in Cockatoo and based my description on first-hand accounts of that day.

Point Hicks lighthouse, the history and its ghost.

The logging that occurred throughout the region.

Incidental facts such as the end of the Vietnam War and the opening of the first Women's Refuge.

Tamboon Inlet and the wild beaches of Croajingolong.

As for Cann River itself, my version is nothing like the real Cann River. I used to stop off at the petrol station at the crossroads on my way down to Melbourne and every time I stood waiting to get back on the coach, I thought the area would make the perfect setting for a dark comedy thriller. So, I wrote one.

Dear reader,

We hope you enjoyed reading *The Legacy of Old Gran Parks*. Please take a moment to leave a review, even if it's a short one. Your opinion is important to us.

Discover more books by Isobel Blackthorn at

https://www.nextchapter.pub/authors/isobel-blackthorn-mystery-thriller-author

Want to know when one of our books is free or discounted? Join the newsletter at

http://eepurl.com/bqqB3H

Best regards,

Isobel Blackthorn and the Next Chapter Team

You might also like:

The Cabin Sessions by Isobel Blackthorn
To read the first chapter for free, head to:
https://www.nextchapter.pub/books/the-cabin-sessions

ABOUT THE AUTHOR

Isobel Blackthorn is an award-winning author of unique and engaging fiction. She writes gripping mysteries, dark psychological thrillers and historical fiction. She is the author of *The Unlikely Occultist: A biographical novel of Alice A. Bailey.*

Other Works

The Drago Tree
Nine Months of Summer
All Because of You
A Perfect Square
The Cabin Sessions
A Matter of Latitude
Clarissa's Warning
A Prison in the Sun
The Unlikely Occultist
Voltaire's Garden

The Legacy Of Old Gran Parks
ISBN: 978-4-86752-828-0

Published by
Next Chapter
1-60-20 Minami-Otsuka
170-0005 Toshima-Ku, Tokyo
+818035793528

6th August 2021